DUKE OF MY DREAMS

By Grace Burrowes

(originally published in the novella duet
Once Upon a Dream)

Dedicated to the odd ducks

CHAPTER ONE

"I do not ask this boon of you lightly, Sedgemere, but you *are* my oldest and dearest friend."

Elias, Duke of Sedgemere, strolled along, damned if he'd embarrass Hardcastle with any show of sentiment in the face of Hardcastle's wheedling. His Grace of Hardcastle was, after all, Sedgemere's oldest and dearest friend too.

Also Sedgemere's only friend.

They took the air beside Hyde Park's Serpentine, ignoring the stares and whispers they attracted. While Sedgemere was a blond so pale as to draw the eye, Hardcastle was dark. They were both above average in height and brawn, though Mayfair boasted any number of large, well-dressed men, particularly as the fashionable hour approached.

They were dukes, however, and to be a duke was to be afflicted with public interest on every hand. To be an *unmarried* duke was to be cursed, for in every ballroom, at the reins of every cabriolet, holding every parasol, was a duchess-in-waiting.

Thus Sedgemere endured Hardcastle's importuning.

"You do not ask a boon," Sedgemere said, nodding to a fellow walking an enormous brindle mastiff. "You demand half my summer, when summer is the best time of year to bide at Sedgemere House."

They had known each other since the casual brutality and near starvation that passed for a boy's indoctrination at Eton, and through the wenching and wagering that masqueraded as an Oxford education. Hardcastle, however, had never married, and thus knew not what horrors awaited him on the way to the altar.

Sedgemere knew, and he further knew that Hardcastle's days as a bachelor were numbered, if Hardcastle's estimable grandmama was dispatching him to summer house parties.

"If you do not come with me, Sedgemere, I will become a bad influence on my godson. I will teach the boy about cigars, brandy, fast women, and profligate gambling."

"The child is seven years old, Hardcastle, but feel free to corrupt him at your leisure, assuming he does not prove to be the worse influence on—good God, not these two again."

The Cheshire twins, blond, blue-eyed, smiling, and as relentless as an unmentionable disease, came twittering down the path, twirling matching parasols.

"Miss Cheshire, Miss Sharon," Hardcastle said, tipping his hat.

Sedgemere discreetly yanked on his friend's arm, though nothing would do but Hardcastle must exchange pleasantries as if these women weren't the social equivalent of Scylla and Charybdis.

"Ladies." Sedgemere bowed as well, for he was in public and the murder of a best friend was better undertaken in private.

"Your Graces! How fortunate that we should meet!" Miss Cheshire gushed. The elder by four minutes, as Sedgemere had been informed on at least a hundred occasions, she generally led the conversational charges. "I told Sharon this very morning that you could not possibly have left Town without calling upon us, and I see I was right, for here you both are!"

Exactly where Sedgemere did not want to be.

"We'll take our leave of—" Sedgemere began, just as Hardcastle winged an arm.

"A pleasant day for pleasant company," Hardcastle said.

Miss Cheshire latched on to Hardcastle like a Haymarket street-walker clutched her last penny's worth of gin, and Miss Sharon appropriated Sedgemere's arm without him even offering.

"You weren't planning to call on us, were you?"

Miss Sharon posed exactly the sort of query a man who'd endured five years of matrimonial purgatory knew better than to answer. If Sedgemere admitted that he'd no intention of calling on anybody before departing London, the Cheshire chit would pout, tear up, and try to shame him into an apology-call. If he lied and protested that, of course he'd been planning on calling, she'd assign him a time and date, and be sure to have her bosom bows lying in ambush with her in her mama's parlor.

Abruptly, three weeks trudging about the hills of the Lake District loomed not as a penance owed a dear friend, but as a reprieve, even if it meant uprooting the boys.

"My plans are not yet entirely made," Sedgemere said. "Though Hardcastle and I will both be leaving Town shortly."

Miss Sharon was desolated to hear this, though everybody left the pestilential heat of a London summer if they could. She cooed and twittered and clung from one end of the Serpentine to the other, until Sedgemere was tempted to push her into the water simply to silence her.

"We bid you *adieu*," Hardcastle said, tipping his hat once more, fifty interminable, cooing, clutching yards later. "And we bid you farewell, for as Sedgemere says, the time has come for ruralizing. I'm sure we'll see both of you when we return to London."

Hardcastle was up to something, Sedgemere knew not what. Hardcastle was a civil fellow, though not even the Cheshire twins would accuse him of charm. Sedgemere liked that about him, liked that one man could be relied upon to be honest at all times, about all matters. Unfortunately, such guilelessness would make Hardcastle a lamb to slaughter among the house-party set.

Amid much simpering and parasol twirling, the Cheshire ladies minced back to Park Lane, there to lurk like trolls under a bridge until the next titled bachelor came along to enjoy the fresh air.

"Turn around now," Sedgemere said, taking Hardcastle by the arm and walking him back the way they'd come. "Before they start fluttering handkerchiefs as if the Navy were departing for Egypt. I suppose you leave me no choice but to accompany you on this infernal frolic to the Lakes."

"Because you are turning into a bore and a disgrace and must hide up north?" Hardcastle inquired pleasantly.

"Because there's safety in numbers, you dolt. Because if Miss Cheshire had sprung that question on you, about whether you intended to call, you would have answered her, and spent half of Tuesday in her mama's parlor, dodging debutante décolletages and tea trays."

Marriage imbued a man with instincts, or perhaps fatherhood did. Hardcastle was merely an uncle, but that privileged status meant he had his heir without having stuck the ducal foot in parson's mousetrap.

"I say, that is a handsome woman," Hardcastle muttered. Hardcastle did not notice women, but an octogenarian Puritan would have taken a closer look at the vision approaching on the path.

"Miss Anne Faraday," Sedgemere said, a comely specimen indeed. Tall, unfashionably curvaceous, unfashionably dark-haired, she was also one of few women whose company did not send Sedgemere into a foul humor. In fact, her approach occasioned something like relief.

"You're not dodging off into the rhododendrons," Hardcastle said, "and yet you seem to know her."

Would Miss Faraday acknowledge Sedgemere? She was well beyond her come out, and no respecter of dukes, single or otherwise.

"I don't know her well, but I like her very much," Sedgemere said. "She hates me, you see. Has no marital aspirations in my direction whatsoever. For that alone, she enjoys my most sincere esteem."

EFFIE WAS CHATTERING about the great burden of having to pack up Anne's dresses in this heat, and about the dust of the road, and all the ghastly impositions on a lady's maid resulting from travel to the countryside at the end of the Season.

Anne half-listened, but mostly she was absorbed with the effort of *not* noticing. She did not notice the Cheshire twins, for example, all but cutting her in public. They literally could not afford to cut her. Neither could the Henderson heir, who merely touched his hat brim to her as if he couldn't recall that he'd seen her in Papa's formal parlor not three days ago. Mr. Willow Dorning, an earl's spare who was rumored to enjoy the company of dogs more than people, offered her a genuine, if shy, smile.

If Anne wanted freedom from Papa's sad eyes and long-suffering sighs, the price she paid was not noticing that, even in the genteel confines of Hyde Park, most of polite society was not very polite at all —to her.

"It's that dook," Effie muttered, "the ice dook, they call him."

"He's not icy, Effie. Sedgemere is simply full of his own consequence."

And why shouldn't he be? He was handsome in a rigid, frigid way, with white-gold hair that no breeze would dare ruffle. His features were an assemblage of patrician attributes—a nose well suited to being looked down, a mouth more full than expected, but no matter, for Anne had never seen that mouth smile. Sedgemere's eyes were a disturbingly pale blue, as if some Viking ancestor looked out of them, one having a grand sulk to be stranded so far from his frozen landscapes and turbulent seas.

"Your papa could buy and sell the consequence of any three dooks, miss, and well they know it."

"The problem in a nutshell," Anne murmured as Sedgemere's gaze lit on her.

He was in company with the Duke of Hardcastle, whom Anne

had heard described as semi-eligible. Hardcastle had an heir, twelve estates, and a dragon for a grandmother. He was notably reserved, though Anne liked what she knew of him. He wasn't prone to staring at bosoms, for example.

Always a fine quality in a man.

Sedgemere was even wealthier than Hardcastle, had neither mama nor extant duchess, but was father to three boys. To Anne's dismay, His Grace of Sedgemere did not merely touch a gloved finger to his hat brim, he instead doffed his hat and bowed.

"Miss Faraday, hello."

She was so surprised, her curtseys lacked the proper deferential depth. "Your Graces, good day."

Then came the moment Anne dreaded most, when instead of not-noticing her, a scion of polite society *did* notice her, simply for the pleasure of brushing her aside. Sedgemere had yet to indulge in that particular sport with her, but he too, had visited in Papa's parlor more than once.

"Shall you walk with us for a moment?" Sedgemere asked. "I believe you know Hardcastle, or I'd perform the introductions."

A large ducal elbow aimed itself in Anne's direction. Such an elbow never came her way unless the duke in question owed Papa at least ten thousand pounds.

"Sedgemere's on his best behavior," Hardcastle said, taking Anne's other arm, "because if you tolerate his escort, then he'll not find other ladies plaguing him. The debutantes fancy Sedgemere violently this time of year."

The social Season was wrapping up, and too many families with daughters had endured the expense of a London Season without a marriage proposal to show for their efforts. Papa made fortunes off the social aspirations of the *beau monde*, while Anne—with no effort whatsoever—made enemies.

"The young ladies fancy unmarried dukes any time of year," Anne replied. Nonetheless, when Sedgemere tucked her hand onto his arm, she allowed it. This time tomorrow, she'd be well away from

London, and the awful accusations resulting from a chance meeting in the park would never reach her ears.

The gossips would say that the presuming, unfortunate Anne Faraday was after a duke. No, that she was after two dukes.

Or perhaps, wicked creature that she was, she would pursue a royal duke next, for her father could afford even a royal husband for her.

"Will you spend the summer in Town, miss?" Hardcastle asked.

"Likely not, Your Grace. Papa's business means he will remain here, but he prefers that I spend some time in the shires, if possible."

"You always mention your father's business as early in a conversation as possible," Sedgemere said.

Anne could not decipher Sedgemere. His expression was as unreadable as a winter sky. If he'd been insulting her, the angle of his attack was subtle.

"I merely answered His Grace of Hardcastle's question. What of Your Graces? Will you soon leave for the country?"

Miss Helen Trimble and Lady Evette Hartley strolled past, and the consternation on their faces was almost worth the beating Anne's reputation would take once they were out of earshot. The gentlemen tipped their hats, the ladies dipped quick curtseys. Hardcastle was inveigled into accompanying the ladies to the gates of the park, and then—

Like a proud debutante poised in her newest finery at the top of the ballroom stairs, Sedgemere had come to a full stop.

"Your Grace?" Anne prompted, tugging on Sedgemere's arm.

"They did not acknowledge you. Those *women* did not so much as greet you. You might have been one of Mr. Dorning's mongrel dogs."

Well, no, because Mr. Dorning's canines were famously well-mannered, and thus endured much cooing and fawning from the ladies. Abruptly, Anne wished she could scurry off across the grass, and bedamned to manners, dukes, and young women who were terrified of growing old without a husband.

"The ladies often don't acknowledge me, Your Grace. I wish you would not remark it. The agreement we have is that they don't notice me, and I don't notice their rudeness. You will please neglect to mention this to my father."

As calculating as Papa was in business, he was a tender-hearted innocent when it came to ballroom warfare. In Papa's mind, his little girl—all nearly six feet of her—was simply too intelligent, pretty, sophisticated, and lovely for the friendship of the simpering twits and lisping viscounts.

"An agreement not to notice you?" Sedgemere snapped. "Who made such an agreement? Not that pair of dowdy poseurs. They couldn't agree on how to tie their bonnet ribbons."

The park was at its best as summer advanced, while all the rest of London became malodorous and stifling. The fashionable hour was about to begin, and thus the duke's behavior would soon attract notice.

"Your Grace will please refrain from making a scene," Anne said through gritted teeth. "I am the daughter of a man who holds the vowels of half the papas, uncles, and brothers of polite society. The ladies resent that, even if they aren't privy to the specifics."

Anne wasn't privy to the specifics either, thank heavens.

Sedgemere condescended to resume sauntering, leading Anne away from the Park Lane gates, deeper into the park's quiet greenery. She at first thought he was simply obliging her request, but a muscle leapt along his jaw.

"I'm sorry," Anne said. "If you owe Papa money, I assure you I'm not aware of it. He's most discreet, and I would never pry, and it's of no moment to me whether—"

"Hush," Sedgemere growled. "I'm trying to behave. One mustn't use foul language before a lady. Those women were ridiculous."

"They were polite to you," Anne said.

"Everybody is polite to a duke. It's nauseating."

"Everybody is rude to a banker's daughter. That's not exactly pleasant either, Your Grace."

The rudeness wasn't the worst of it, though. Worse than the cold stares, sneering smiles, and snide innuendos were the men. Certain titled bachelors saw Anne as a source of cash, which her father should be eager to turn over to them in exchange for allowing her to bear their titled heirs.

Which indelicate undertaking might kill her, of course.

Such men appraised her figure and her face as if she were a mare at Tatt's, a little long in the tooth, her bloodlines nondescript, though she was handsome enough for an afternoon ride.

"Everybody is rude to you?" Sedgemere asked.

Sedgemere carried disdain around with him like an expensive cape draped over his arm, visible at twenty paces, unlikely to be mislaid. His curiosity, as if Anne's situation were a social experiment, and she responsible for reporting its results, disappointed her.

She hadn't thought she could be any more disappointed, not in a titled gentleman anyway.

"Must you make sport of my circumstances, Your Grace? Perhaps you'd care to take yourself off now. My maid will see me home."

He came to a leisurely halt and tucked his gloved hand over Anne's knuckles, so she could not free herself of him without drawing notice.

"You are sending me away," he said. "A duke of the realm, fifty-third in line for the throne, and you're sending me packing like a presuming, jug-eared footman who neglected to chew adequate quantities of parsley after overimbibing. Hardcastle will not believe this."

Incredulity was apparently in the air, for Anne could not believe what she beheld either. The Duke of Sedgemere, he of the icy eyes and frosty condescension, was regarding her with something approaching curiosity. Interest, at least, and not the sort of interest that involved her bosom.

"Perhaps you'd better toddle on, then," Anne said. "I'm sure there's a debutante—or twelve—who will expire of despair if she can't flaunt her wares at you before sundown."

"I'm dismissed out of hand, and now I'm to toddle. Dukes do not toddle, madam. Perhaps the heat is affecting your judgment." His tone would have frozen the Serpentine to a thickness of several inches.

Sedgemere, poor man, must owe Papa a very great deal of money.

"*Good day*, Your Grace. Have a pleasant summer."

Anne did not curtsey, because Sedgemere's scolding and sniffing had brought her unaccountably near tears. She was wealthy, a commoner, female, and unmarried. Her transgressions were beyond redemption, but why must Sedgemere blame her for circumstances she'd had no hand in creating?

Why must everybody?

Anne would have made a grand exit toward the Long Water, but some fool duke had trapped her hand in his.

"I must make allowances," he said, his grip on Anne's fingers snug. "You're not used to the undivided attention of so lofty a personage as I, and the day is rather warm. When next we meet, I assure you I will have the toddling well in hand. I enjoy a challenge, you see. You have a pleasant summer too, Miss Faraday, and my kindest regards to your dear papa."

Sedgemere's demeanor remained crushingly correct as he bowed with utmost graciousness over Anne's hand. When he tipped his hat to her, she could have sworn those chilly blue eyes had gained a hint of warmth.

He was laughing at her then, but half the polite world would have seen him bowing over Anne's hand, so she was at least a private joke.

"Thank you, Your Grace. Effie, come along. A lofty personage cannot be unnecessarily detained without serious consequences to the foolish woman who'd linger in his presence."

When Anne swept off at a brisk pace, the duke let her go, which was prudent of him. She was not above using her reticule as a weapon, and not even Sedgemere would have managed loftiness had

Anne's copy of *The Mysteries of Udolpho* connected with the duke's...
knees.

"The Quality is daft," Effie huffed at Anne's side. "Dafter by the
year, miss, though he seemed nice enough, for a dook."

"Effie Carsdale! You were calling him icy not five minutes ago."

Sedgemere was cold, but not... not as easily dismissed as Anne
had wanted him to be. He noticed where others ignored, he ignored
what others dwelled upon—Anne's bosom, for example.

"Nice in an icy way," Effie clarified. "Been an age since anybody
teased you, miss. Perhaps you've lost the habit of teasing back."

Anne's steps slowed. Ducks went paddling by on the mirror-flat
water to the left. In the tall trees, birds flitted, and across the Serpentine, carriages tooled down Rotten Row. Another pretty day in the
park, and yet...

"You think Sedgemere was *teasing* me?"

Effie was probably ten years Anne's senior, by no means old. She
studied the trees overhead, she studied her toes. She was a bright
woman, full of practical wisdom and pragmatism.

"I was teased by a duke and didn't even know it," Anne said,
wishing she could run after Sedgemere and apologize. "I thought he
was ridiculing me, Effie. They all ridicule me, while they take Papa's
money to cover their inane bets."

And they were all polite to Sedgemere, which he apparently
found as trying as insults.

"You'll have the last laugh, Miss Anne," Effie said. "Mark me, that
dook will lead you out, come the Little Season, but thank goodness
we'll soon be away from the wretched city. A few weeks breathing
the fresh air, enjoying the lovely scenery up in the Lake District will
put you to rights, see if it don't."

CHAPTER TWO

Part of the reason Sedgemere had agreed to join Hardcastle at the
Duke of Veramoor's "little gathering" was that Sedgemere House lay
in Nottinghamshire, partway between London and the Lakes, and
thus Sedgemere could dragoon his friend into visiting the Sedgemere
family seat.

Hardcastle was nearly impossible to pry away from his ancestral
pile in Kent, but he was godfather to Sedgemere's eldest, an imp of
the devil named Alasdair.

"I've left instructions the boy's to use the courtesy title, having
turned seven," Sedgemere said as he and Hardcastle moved their
horses to the verge to make way for a passing coach. "The twins insist
on thwarting my orders, of course, because it irritates their older
brother."

A plume of dust hung in the morning air as the coach rattled by.
The sun was so hot every sheep in the nearby pasture was panting,
curled in the grass in the shade of a lone oak.

"Perhaps," Hardcastle replied, "the twins thwart your orders
because they're barely six years old and have always known their

brother by his name. My brother never referred to me by anything save my name when we were private."

Hardcastle was a good traveling companion, offering an argument to nearly every comment, observation, or casual aside Sedgemere tossed out. The miles went faster that way, and when traveling from London to Nottinghamshire, one endured many dusty, weary miles.

"You're nervous of this house party," Sedgemere said. "You needn't be. Simply follow the rules, Hardcastle, and you'll get some rest, catch a few fish, read a few poems. Veramoor is a duke first, a matchmaker second."

Or so Her Grace of Veramoor had assured Sedgemere, though one never entirely trusted a duchess with twelve happily married offspring. Thus Sedgemere had rules for surviving house parties: safety in numbers, never be alone in one's room without a chair wedged beneath the door, never over-imbibe, never show marked favor to any female, always ride out in company.

"You do recall the rules, Gerard?"

"Don't be tedious."

Sedgemere had used Hardcastle's Christian name advisedly, there being no one else left to extend him that kindness when he clearly missed his late brother. Hardcastle acknowledged Sedgemere's consideration by keeping his gaze on the road ahead as they trotted into Hopewell-on-Lyft, the last watering hole before the Sedgemere estate village.

"Shall we have a pint?" Sedgemere asked. "The summer ale at The Duke's Arms is exceptional, and tarrying here will give my staff a few extra moments to flutter about before they must once again deal with me."

Sedgemere wasn't particularly fond of ale, though he felt an obligation to give his custom to the inn when he passed through the area. The innkeeper and his wife were good folk, and the service excellent for so small an establishment.

Though a delay here meant the boys would have to wait longer to see their father, and their lack of patience never boded well for the king's peace—or Sedgemere's breakables.

"A pint and a plate here will do," Hardcastle said. "I'm in no hurry to complete any part of this journey."

"One wonders how will you corrupt my firstborn if you never see the boy. A pint and a plate it is."

"Mustn't forget to corrupt the future duke, the present one having become such a ruddy bore," Hardcastle said, brightening as much as he ever brightened. "I must see to the boy's education, and make a thorough job of it too. Several months should suffice."

"As if you'd winter in the—what the deuce?"

An altercation was in progress in the coaching yard of The Duke's Arms, between a sweating, liveried coachman and the head hostler, an estimable fellow named Helton.

"Gentlemen," Sedgemere said, swinging off his horse. "The day is too hot for incivilities. What is the problem?"

Hardcastle dismounted as well, though he—having only the one nephew in his nursery—knew little about sorting through disputes. The buffoonery of the House of Lords didn't signify compared to small boys in the throes of affronted honor.

"Your Grace." Helton uncrossed beefy arms and tugged a graying forelock. "Welcome to The Duke's Arms, Your Grace. My pardon for speaking too loudly. John Coachman and I was simply having a discussion."

John Coachman was another muscular individual of mature years, though in livery, the heat had turned him red as a Leicestershire squire's hunting pinks.

"Yon fellow refused me a fresh team," John Coachman snapped, "and this a coaching inn. I never heard the like, and my lady having had to make do with as sorry a foursome of mules as I ever cursed in my life for the past seven leagues."

The coach horses were not mules, but they were on the small side, a bay, a chestnut, and two dingy grays, and every one was heaving with exhaustion, their coats matted with dusty sweat.

"John?" came a feminine voice from around the side of the coach. "What seems to be the problem?"

Sedgemere's body comprehended the problem before his brain did, for he knew that voice. Brisk, feminine, and pitched a trifle lower than most women's, that was the voice of a few memorable dreams and one interesting encounter in Hyde Park nearly a week past.

"Miss Faraday," Hardcastle said, bowing and tipping his hat.

"Miss," Sedgemere said, doing likewise. "Your coach appears to be in need of a fresh team."

She wasn't wearing a bonnet, perhaps in deference to the heat, perhaps because she was indifferent to her complexion. Summer sunshine found red highlights in her dark hair, and the midday breeze sent curls dancing away from her face.

Desire paid an unexpected call on Sedgemere, a novel experience in broad daylight. His waking hours were spent avoiding the notice of the ladies, and thus he was usually safe from his own animal spirits. Miss Faraday, fortunately, was more interested in the horses than she was a pair of dukes idling in a rural coach yard.

"These four beasts have gone ten miles past a reasonable distance," she said. "I'll not be responsible for abusing them with the weather so miserable. If the inn hasn't any teams to spare—"

"You'll bide with me and Hardcastle for the space of a meal," Sedgemere said, while in the back of his mind, Alasdair—the Marquess of Ryland, rather—led his brothers on a shrieking nursery revolt. "By the time you've refreshed yourself, I'll have a team on the way from Sedgemere House."

"A fine plan," Hardcastle chorused on cue. "You must agree, Miss Faraday, it's a pretty day for a quiet meal in the shade, and Sedgemere has, in his inimitable style, solved every problem on every hand."

Hardcastle was laying it on a bit thick, but such was his habitual sincerity, or so oppressive was the heat, that Miss Faraday sent a longing glance to the oaks shading the inn.

"You're suggesting we dine *al fresco*?" she asked.

Insects dined *al fresco*. Birds came dodging down from the
boughs to interrupt outdoor meals. Stray bits of pine needle found
their way into the food. A father of three boys had firsthand experience with these and other gustatory delights.

"The breeze is lovely," Sedgemere said, drawing the lady away
from the horses by virtue of tugging on her wrist. "The Duke's Arms
has a pretty garden around to the side, and Hardcastle will be happy
to place our order with the kitchen."

"I shall be ecstatic, of course," Hardcastle muttered, passing the
reins of his horse to a stable boy. "You see before you a duke in
raptures."

Sedgemere saw before him a duke half in love, which would not
do. "Come along, Miss Faraday. Mr. Helton can send to Sedgemere
House, and you'll be on your way in no time."

Helton bustled off, John Coachman bowed his overheated
thanks, and Sedgemere led the only woman with whom he felt
comfortable being private to the seclusion and sweet scents of the
coaching inn's garden.

"My maid," Miss Faraday said, slipping her hand from Sedgemere's. "Carsdale has gone around to the—"

"The inn's goodwife will doubtless inform your maid of your
location," Sedgemere said. "Many patrons avail themselves of the
garden, if you're concerned for the appearances."

Miss Faraday was a beautiful woman, though contrary to current
fashion, her hair was dark, her eyes were green, and her features were
on the bold side. Her brows were particularly expressive, and Sedgemere happened to be studying them—mentally tracing them with his
tongue, in fact—so he noticed when unexpected emotion flitted
across Miss Faraday's features.

"I ought to be concerned for the appearances," she retorted.
"You should know, Your Grace, I'm considering getting myself
ruined."

"Lucky you," Sedgemere said, batting aside his ungentlemanly
imaginings. "You *can* be ruined, while I am hopelessly ensnared in

respectability, even if I wager irresponsibly, waste my days in opium dreams, and neglect my estates and my children."

Sedgemere had no experience with damsels in distress, but he suspected making them smile might be a good step toward slaying their dragons.

Miss Faraday refused to oblige him.

"I am half in earnest, Your Grace. Do not jest when I face days more travel. The last coaching inn gave us the same story. The Quality is off to the house parties, leaving London for the shires, and for me, no fresh team is available. If I didn't know better, I'd think somebody was traveling ahead, warning the inns not to spare me a single decent horse."

Sedgemere led the lady to the shade of the venerable oaks at the side of the inn. His attraction to her was inconvenient, but under-standable. Her testiness around him made her safe. She was comely, and he was in the midst of one of his increasingly frequent periods of sexual inactivity.

Frequent and bothersome.

"You are tired," Sedgemere said. "You are vexed by the heat, your lady's maid has likely been complaining the entire distance from London, and you haven't had a decent meal for three days. Let's find a shady seat, Miss Faraday, and you can curse me, the Great North Road, and the summer heat, not in that order."

The scowl Miss Faraday turned on Sedgemere was magnificent. "Don't patronize me, Your Grace. I much prefer the disdain of my betters to anybody's condescension."

She reminded him of his cat, Sophocles, a temperamental soul who hissed first and apologized never. And yet, Sedgemere was always unaccountably pleased to be reunited with his cat, just as he was pleased to find himself thrown into company with Miss Faraday.

"Oh, very well," he said, opening a tall door in a taller stone wall. "*I* am vexed by the heat, *I* haven't had a decent meal for three days, and Hardcastle's whining and arguing have about driven *me* to Bedlam. Are you happy now, Miss Faraday?"

The daft woman was smiling at him, beaming at him as if he were Alasdair—Ryland, rather—and had just recited the entire royal succession perfectly.

"Effie was right," she said, which made no sense. "Come along, Your Grace. A hungry duke is not a patient creature."

She took him by the wrist and led him into the cooler confines of the shaded garden, where, as fate or a lucky duke would have it, not another soul was to be seen.

~

SEDGEMERE WAS A TEASE.

Anne marveled to reach this conclusion, but what else explained that slight warmth in his eyes, the affection with which he complained about His Grace of Hardcastle, or the way he'd invited her to curse him?

She preceded the duke into a garden redolent of honeysuckle and lush grass, for this was a cottage garden, not the manicured miniature park found behind the town houses in London's wealthy neighborhoods.

"I've never seen heartsease in such abundance," she said, as the duke closed the garden door. "And the lavender is exquisite." The border along the garden's south-facing wall was thick with silvery green leaves and vibrantly purple flowers.

"It's been years since I took a moment to tarry in this garden," Sedgemere said, taking off his hat. "There's as much delight here for the nose as for the eye, and the quiet pleases even the weary traveler's ear."

His pale hair was creased from his hat brim. Anne riffled the duke's hair back into order, as she would have with her papa.

"Better," she said. "Can't have you looking like John Coachman at the end of a hard morning's drive, Your Grace. I must have a whiff of that lavender."

Anne marched across the garden, expecting her escort to follow.

Sedgemere remained in the shade near the gate, his hat in hand, his expression chilly indeed. Perhaps one didn't put a duke to rights, but Sedgemere would probably have expired of excessive dignity before running his hand through his own hair.

Anne plucked several sprigs of lavender, squeezing the flowers gently to release their scent. "Have you a penknife, Your Grace?"

He emerged from the shadows and passed her not a penknife, but a folding knife extracted from his boot.

"Don't you have outriders, lackeys, footmen, and such to carry arms for you?" Anne asked, cutting the lavender stems short.

"A duke is a target, Miss Faraday, and thus the duke himself should be armed at all times. Do you travel to your father's estate in Yorkshire?"

He meant he was a target for more than matchmakers. That the ducal person would be endangered by wealth and status had not occurred to her.

"Yorkshire is my final destination, and I hope Papa will join me there, but he takes his work seriously."

Anne had done it again, brought up her father's work early in a conversation. She must learn to be more careful around Sedgemere, though nobody else had noticed her tendency to mention commerce so readily.

"May I?" Sedgemere took the lavender from her and divided the bundle, passing half back to her. The remaining sprigs he attempted to tuck into the lapel of his riding jacket.

"Let me," Anne said, taking back the lavender and grasping the duke's lapel. "You'll break the stems, and it wants..."

She fell silent, fashioning an informal boutonnière for His Grace. Standing this close to him, she caught the scent of horse, exertion, and something like the garden itself. Private greenery and summer flowers, with the lavender note more prominent.

"There," she said, smoothing the shoulder of his jacket. "You're marginally presentable."

Anne was tall, but Sedgemere had nearly six inches on her. He stood gazing down the ducal proboscis, his expression much like it had been at the garden gate.

"I'm sorry," Anne said, stepping back, as heat rose up her neck that had nothing to do with the oppressive weather. "I don't mean to presume, but my father has long been widowed. I'm more than of age, and thus I'm the lady of his house. He'd go about half-dressed, a laughingstock, unless I took him in hand, and I don't—"

A single bare finger landed gently on Anne's lips.

"My own duchess," Sedgemere said, "who was very mindful of the appearances, never troubled herself over my attire. I am in your debt."

Was he teasing? Scolding? "You are not mocking me," Anne concluded. "Papa is frequently the object of ridicule. The titled gentlemen, and even some of the ladies, will call upon him, all of them in need of money. They do not respect him."

Too late, Anne recalled that Sedgemere had called on Papa too, more than once.

"Let us find a bench in the shade," Sedgemere said, placing Anne's hand on his arm. "I respect your father very much, and I suspect half the sneering, impecunious younger sons who seek his coin not only respect him, they fear him."

"Not only younger sons," Anne said. "Papa has been summoned to call upon more than one royal duke, Your Grace."

The duke found them a worn wooden bench beneath a spreading oak, where the fragrance of honeysuckle was thick in the air. Propriety was appeased by a clear view of the open doors that doubtless led to the inn's common.

"I enjoy puzzles," Sedgemere said, coming down beside her. "Two solutions present themselves to the riddle of why a royal duke would take tea with a lowly, if wealthy, banker. Your father was summoned to Clarence or Cambridge's parlor either to buy a minor title for himself or a lofty title for you."

How easily Sedgemere divined the disrespect that characterized all of Anne's days. "Well, no, actually. In exchange for the privilege of enduring an aging royal duke's intimate company, Papa would be considered for the honors list, for a sum certain."

The intimations had been delicate, but clear: Papa had been invited to *pay* to ensconce Anne as the mistress of a royal duke. She'd laughed when Papa had come home fuming and sputtering, poured Papa a brandy, and calmed him down, then gone to her room and sobbed into her pillow.

Sedgemere took Anne's hand when she would have bolted from the bench. "Your tale confirms what most of the realm has long suspected: With few exceptions, the present royal dukes are parasites and trollops. On their behalf, I apologize, Miss Faraday."

How had she blundered onto this subject, and why did Sedgemere's apology make her throat ache?

"Papa said the entire conversation progressed by innuendo and intimation, and that he might have been mistaken." He'd needed three brandies to concoct that bouncer.

"But he warned you nonetheless," Sedgemere said. "No wonder you have no patience with dukes or debutantes. You must consider the lot of us beneath your notice."

His hand was warm, and while Anne hadn't held hands with a man before, she suspected Sedgemere was good at it. The duke had the knack of a grasp that comforted rather than restrained, a gentle hold that was in no wise tentative.

"It's worse than that, Your Grace. I have no idea what to do with any of you. I can't afford to mistake a false smile for one that's genuine, I can't trust a gentleman to be a gentleman, I can't say the wrong thing, and thus even what I don't say becomes a means of judging me. I have decided that once I get home to Yorkshire, I will remain there. Papa can argue all he pleases, but I'm tired—"

Effie marched through the French doors, two serving maids behind her, the Duke of Hardcastle bringing up the rear. When Anne would have snatched her hand back, Sedgemere held firm, patted her knuckles, and only then allowed her to retrieve her hand.

"You have all the burdens of being a duchess," he said, "but none of the benefits. I know of this weariness you mention, Miss Faraday, and the longing to retire to the country, for it plagues me as well. Don't tell Hardcastle, though, for somebody must keep an eye on him in Town, and that somebody is me."

Sedgemere assisted Anne to her feet, while Hardcastle fussed the maids about where to spread the blanket, and Effie fussed generally. For a progression of astonished minutes, Anne remained arm in arm with the only titled person to ever, ever offer her kindness and understanding rather than judgment and ridicule.

"I THINK SHE LIKES ME," Hardcastle said from his side of the picnic blanket. "I have an instinct about these things, and Miss Faraday likes me."

"She felt sorry for you," Sedgemere replied, brushing his fingers over the lavender scenting his lapel. "Your entire conversation dealt with your prodigy of a nephew, your prodigy of a horse, or your nephew's prodigy of a governess."

Sedgemere had been particularly interested to hear about this governess—Miss Ellen MacHugh—for Hardcastle's rhapsodies on her behalf sparked memories of similar flights from him over the past several years.

No wonder Hardcastle was so devoted to the family seat, poor sod.

"My nephew and my horse are very intelligent," Hardcastle retorted as the serving maids cleared away the detritus of the picnic. "Miss MacHugh is..."

Sedgemere let the silence lengthen. Miss Faraday had followed her maid inside, and the fresh team of horses had yet to arrive. The meal had been delightful, with Miss Faraday gently teasing Hardcastle, and Hardcastle's expression turning as dazed as Sedgemere felt.

"Miss MacHugh is... my nephew's governess," Hardcastle said. "The boy is devoted to her."

"You are a duke," Sedgemere replied as the last of the serving maids left them the privacy of the garden. "If you want to marry a governess, then marry her. Dukes have married serving maids, mistresses, commoners of every stripe. Marry your Miss MacHugh."

"Don't be daft. A duke must marry responsibly, or gossip will plague his duchess all of her days."

Sedgemere got to his feet, for a commotion beyond the garden walls suggested the new team was in the stable yard.

"That is your grandmother talking, Hardcastle. If *you* are plaguing your duchess all of her days and nights, and your duchess returns the compliment, what matters gossip?"

Hardcastle was off the blanket in one lithe movement, dusting at his breeches and tapping his hat onto his head.

"Your circumstances are different," Hardcastle said, pulling his riding gloves from a pocket. "You married quite well, your nursery is full, and the rest of your days *and nights* are your own to do as you see fit."

Where had Miss Faraday got off to, and what was Hardcastle hinting at? "I'm in no mood to repeat the error of my first marriage, Hardcastle. No more need be said on that matter."

Hardcastle had no graces, but he was brave, as all dukes needed to be. "Miss Faraday *likes* you too, Sedgemere. She's an heiress, she's pretty, she's situated not far from your family seat, and you are smitten. I can excuse you from the house party if you'd rather woo the fair maid this summer."

Sedgemere wandered over to the lavender border, cut off a fat bunch of sprigs, and stuffed them in his pocket. He wouldn't know how to woo Miss Faraday if she wrote him instructions. Dukes were excused from the wooing portion of a young man's education, which might explain why duchesses could be a sour-natured lot.

"Miss Faraday is justifiably unimpressed with polite society," Sedgemere said, for Hardcastle had wandered right along beside him. "She longs for a life of peaceful spinsterhood, and has nothing but bad associations with titled men."

"*You* have nothing but bad associations with titled men *and* women," Hardcastle retorted, "present company excepted, I hope. What would it hurt to ride over to Yorkshire and see how she's getting on in a week or two?"

It would hurt, to see Miss Faraday happily ensconced at her father's lovely estate, relieved to be free of dukes, dowagers, and talk of her dowry.

"We have a house party to endure, Hardcastle, and Miss Faraday is intent on a repairing lease at her father's estate, if not a full retreat. I'd have better luck with your governess."

Dark brows drew down fiercely at that suggestion, while Miss Faraday emerged from the inn, her hair somewhat tidier.

Which made Sedgemere want to un-tidy it.

"I'll see to the horses," Hardcastle said, touching a finger to Sedgemere's boutonnière, then taking his leave of the lady.

Miss Faraday smiled at Hardcastle in parting, patted his shoulder, then his hand, and all the while, she didn't seem to know she was taking liberties with a ducal person. She'd spoken honestly, then. She was simply accustomed to life as her papa's companion, which struck Sedgemere as... wrong.

"Your Grace," she said, her smile dimming. "I must thank you for your company and for the loan of your team. I'll send John back with them within the week."

"No hurry. My stables are extensive, and I've plenty for my own needs." He also kept teams of his choosing at various coaching inns, as did Hardcastle. The loan of a team of horses was nothing to him.

"Do you even know how dismissive you sound?" she asked.

They were alone in the garden, and though they were in full view of the common, the midday hour had passed, and thus they had relative privacy for a few more minutes.

"I've cultivated the ability to dismiss with a word, a silence, a lifted eyebrow," Sedgemere said. "You have the same talent, though."

Ah, he'd surprised her. What a treat, to see confusion instead of a wariness in her eyes.

"I am not a duke, sir. I don't cultivate haughtiness."

Sedgemere leaned closer. "You, madam, have glowered at me from across a ballroom so loudly I was certain I had failed to button my falls, at the very least. Had perhaps even dribbled gravy on my cravat."

"I did that?" She was pleased with herself, as well she should be. "Are you certain I was looking at you? If you were standing near a royal duke, for example, or a certain viscount, or possibly—there's nearly a regiment of earls I avoid at all costs."

"So you turn that glower on us all," Sedgemere said, "and here I thought you cherished a special disdain for me. I'm crushed to know I merit not even your particular dislike, Miss Faraday."

Out in the inn yard, Helton called for the team to be backed into the traces. The time to part had arrived, and were Sedgemere another man, he would have admitted to anger. Miss Faraday would depart for Yorkshire, there to hide from polite society. He would travel on to the Lakes to dodge the matchmakers while keeping Hardcastle from their clutches as well.

What a waste of a lovely summer, and of a lovely woman with whom Sedgemere had found an odd commonality of interests.

"We should go," Miss Faraday said. "Where's your hat, Your Grace?"

"You truly have to manage your father, don't you?" Sedgemere said, retrieving his hat from a bench.

Miss Faraday's features arranged themselves into the expression he'd seen from her before. Banked distaste, not a sneer, more like controlled martyrdom.

"Papa is hopeless. People seek his counsel either because they need coin, or because they need to turn two coins into three. He helps as many as he can, but the interest he reaps is disrespect. He doesn't even see most of it, and has no idea why a man's cravat ought to be a basis for judging him."

They ambled into the shade, pausing before the closed garden door.

Sedgemere cast around for some encouraging words, some cheering sentiment he could leave Miss Faraday with. Her course was set: She would retire to the country, nurture her affronted dignity, and grow thorny roses—or something.

"What's the worst part of it?" he asked, settling his hat on his head. "What makes London unbearable?"

For London was the only place he was likely to see her, assuming she ever again ventured south.

"The money," she said, in the same tones somebody else might have referred to the scent downwind from a shambles. "People don't see me, they see the money. They resent it, they covet it, they gossip about it, and all I am is a means to that money. Papa doesn't understand. I didn't understand myself until the marriage proposals started."

From that pack of nasty, presuming earls, no doubt.

"For me, it's the title," Sedgemere said. He and the lady were parting, their paths likely would never cross again, and he could be honest with Anne Faraday as he wasn't honest with even Hardcastle. "I never wanted a damned title, much less a ducal title. I'm not a man, I'm a title, a deep pocket, consequence, estates."

"So," she said, straightening a wrinkle in his coat sleeve over his biceps, "you snarl and sneer, and arch the eyebrow of doom, lest any presume on your good nature. Good for you, sir. You're entitled to your privacy, and to deal with the world on your own terms."

Anne Faraday addressed him not as a duke, who endured toadying and deference without limit, but rather, as a man who'd put up with enough, and had a right to order his affairs as he saw fit. Nobody else had spoken to him thus. Nobody else had dared.

Nobody else had understood.

Sedgemere meant to kiss her cheek, truly he did. Maybe she meant to kiss his too, for when Sedgemere lowered his head, lips at the ready for a chaste—if bold—buss to her cheek, she presented her lips, also at the ready, and a kiss occurred.

Not a kiss to anybody's cheek, but a collision of lips, surprised at first, then curious, then... enthusiastic.

Wonderfully, lustily enthusiastic. Everything external fell away from Sedgemere's notice—the inn yard commotion beyond the garden wall, the clatter and clank of dishes from a kitchen window ten yards off, the lowing of a cow in the pasture behind the inn.

While everything inside Sedgemere, everything that brushed up against the slightest aspect of that kiss, woke up.

And rejoiced.

CHAPTER THREE

Anne had three more days on the king's highway before she reached her destination, three days of jostling, bouncing, and ignoring Effie's prattle.

Three days and two nights of failing to find the right words to describe the Duke of Sedgemere's kiss. That single kiss had been surprising. Anne hadn't realized she was capable of flaunting convention to the extent of putting her lips on the ducal person.

And the surprises didn't stop there. Sedgemere's kiss intrigued, offering contradictions and complexities, like a business opportunity in a foreign culture. His kiss was confident without being arrogant, gentle without being chaste, ardent but respectful, intimate without presuming.

Anne would be a lifetime analyzing one kiss that for Sedgemere had probably been an unremarkable moment in a life of casual privilege and sophistication. He'd not even smiled at her, but rather, had handed her up into the coach, tipped his hat, and wished her safe journey.

"We're coming to the gates," Effie said. "Thank the Almighty, we're finally coming to the gates."

"Effie, you've never traveled in such comfort as you have the past three days," Anne said, for once the Duke of Sedgemere's first team of coaching horses had been put to, the hostlers at subsequent inns had replaced them with further loans of Sedgemere horses. Meals had arrived to Anne's rooms hotter and faster. Her chambers had been the best the premises had to offer.

The woman who became Sedgemere's duchess would have a lovely life, in some particulars.

"Traveling is traveling," Effie harrumphed. "And now we're to deal with the staff of a duke and duchess. Mark me, miss, they'll want their vales and be as high in the instep as the duke himself."

Veramoor's estate lay in the Lakes, snuggled right up against the Whinlatter forest. Anne had enjoyed the scenery, which was unlike even the sweeping green landscape of the Dales. She did not enjoy the prospect of the next two weeks. Communication with Papa would be difficult, for she'd brought only so many pigeons.

And Veramoor had doubtless invited a number of bachelor earls, for he and his duchess fancied themselves matchmakers.

"My, my, my," Effie whispered, gawking out the window. "It's a bloomin' palace, miss. You'll need a ball of twine to keep from getting lost between the bedroom and the breakfast parlor."

The façade was majestic, a massive Baroque structure that put Anne in mind of the Howard family seat in Yorkshire. Two enormous wings projected from a central dome, the whole approached by a long drive that ended in a broad carriageway encircling a fountain.

Thus did dukes live. The grandeur of Veramoor House was a reproach to any banker's daughter who longed for more kisses from chance-met dukes. Papa could afford such a dwelling, but neither he nor Anne would know what to *do* with it.

"I was wrong," Effie said as the carriage drew to a halt. "You'll need six balls of twine, miss. Promise you won't leave without me. If I get lost, there's no chance of anybody finding me in this palace."

"You'll be given a map, Effie," Anne said, as a liveried footman opened the carriage door and flipped down the steps. "And I won't leave without you."

Effie might not be the only person Anne knew, but she'd definitely be the only person Anne could trust here.

Inside the house, Anne was greeted by the duchess, a petite, fading redhead with snapping blue eyes. Despite the grandeur of the entrance hall, Her Grace commanded the entire cool, soaring space, ordering footmen this way, porters the other.

"Oh, my dear Miss Faraday," Her Grace said, taking Anne by both hands. "You are the image of your mama. May I call you Anne? You must not call me Margot, alas, or the other ladies will be scandalized, but your mama called me Margot long ago. She talked me into trying a cigar the year she made her bow, and I—a sensibly married woman at the time—have never been so sick in all my days."

The duchess's tone was welcoming, her grasp warm and firm, and yet, she was warning Anne too. Special favor might be shown, but Anne must not presume.

Not that she would, ever. She'd kissed a passing duke by chance and for three days, been plagued by his memory. Missed him even, when she'd yet to spend more than two hours in his company.

"I had not heard this about my mother," Anne said. "You must tell me more when time allows."

"Harrison will show you to your rooms," Her Grace said, "but before the mob descends, you'll take tea with me, won't you? I'll send a footman to collect you in an hour or so, and your maid can sneak in a nice lie-down. Will that suit?"

The Duchess of Veramoor would not have taken three days to deal with matters at Waterloo. She'd have dispatched the Corsican by noon on the first day and been entertaining callers for luncheon thereafter, not a hair out of place.

"Tea would suit wonderfully, Your Grace. My thanks."

Sedgemere's teams must have made good time, because Harrison, an underhousekeeper, told Anne she was among the first to arrive.

Most of the guests would be along as the day progressed, with more arriving tomorrow.

"And there are always stragglers." Harrison was a tall blonde who moved at a brisk pace, a set of keys jangling at her waist, a touch of Ireland in her words. "Her Grace never plans much for the first day, but we've high hopes for this year's gathering."

Anne had high hopes she'd be allowed to snatch a nap before her tea with the duchess. "I'm sure we'll all have a lovely time."

Until the gentlemen arrived and started bothering the maids, drinking too much, making inane wagers, and ogling Anne's bosom.

"Our record is four engagements," Harrison said, unfastening her keys. "That was three years ago, and one of them doesn't really count because it was Their Graces' youngest. Gave us a start, that one did, but she's wed happily enough and is expecting her second. Do you fancy any particular gentlemen?"

Merciful days. Longing shot through Anne's weariness, yearning for a quiet, fragrant walled garden, and a duke who was brusque, kind, and a surprisingly adept kisser.

"I beg your pardon?" Anne managed.

"Their Graces pride themselves on knowing when a couple might suit," Harrison said, thrusting a key into a lock. "They make up the guest list with the young people in mind, if you take my meaning. Her Grace says I talk too much, but you seem like the sensible sort."

"Thank you, though right now I'm the tired and dusty sort. This is a lovely room."

Early afternoon light flooded a cozy sitting room, one appointed in blue-and-gilt flocked wallpaper, blue and white carpets, blue velvet upholstered furniture, and bouquets of red and white roses. The impression was restful and elegant, and the blue and white decorating scheme carried into an airy adjoining bedroom.

"Her Grace puts her special guests on this corridor," Harrison said. "You have the best views and the most quiet. The bell pull is near the privacy screen, and a tray will be sent along shortly. We'll have a buffet tonight. Guests gather at seven in the blue gallery. Any footman or maid can give you directions."

No balls of twine, alas. Harrison went bustling on her way, Effie disappeared to locate Anne's trunks, and for the first time in days, Anne was in the midst of complete silence.

So, of course, memories of Sedgemere's kiss resonated only more loudly. Of his gloved hand cupping her cheek, his tongue brushing over her bottom lip, his leg insinuated between her thighs.

"If I'm to have only one forbidden kiss in my life, that one will at least linger in memory until I forget my own name," Anne murmured. She twitched a lacy curtain back and cracked open the window. Her room overlooked the side of Veramoor House that faced the stables, magnificent buildings that might well have been lodging for another titled family.

Carriage houses sat beside the stables, and green paddocks stretched behind them up to the slope of the woods. A woman of artistic talent would gorge herself on views like this, while Anne's imagination went to the expense of such a facility.

That too had been in Sedgemere's kiss, a sense of wealth leading back across the centuries, tens of thousands of acres of tradition and stability, not merely a pile of newly minted coins. Sedgemere's kiss spoke of resources so vast, the man with title to them could dispense with time in any manner he saw fit, even if that meant indulging in a pointless kiss with a woman who should not have presumed on his time, much less his person.

"I'm not sorry I did it," Anne said. "I hope he's not sorry either."

Carriages tooled away from the main drive and over to the carriage houses, and grooms bustled about while porters transferred baggage to carts. Papa would need to know of Anne's safe arrival, and he'd doubtless send her dispatches requiring immediate replies.

Anne allowed herself one more moment at the window, one more moment to inhale a breeze scented by the nearby forest, the extensive gardens, and the magnificent stables. This was what a duchess's world smelled like of a summer day, and it was lovely.

Another carriage made the trek from driveway to carriage houses, two horsemen riding ahead. The horses under saddle were beautiful animals, but their heads were down, their legs dusty. Both men dismounted, both took off their hats and gloves, both handed horses off to grooms.

Between one flutter of the lacy curtain and the next, Anne's mind confirmed three things that her abruptly pounding heart already knew.

First, the tall gentleman with the moonlight-blond hair was Sedgemere.

Second, if Anne were prudent, she'd never ever be alone with him again.

Third, if she did happen to find herself private with the duke in the next two weeks, she'd be helpless not to kiss him again—every chance she got.

"I SAY we should have arrived late," Hardcastle groused. "We ought to have tarried an extra day at Sedgemere, so you might have gone calling on a pretty neighbor in Yorkshire. But no, you are Sedgemere, so you heed no counsel save your own, and all creation must align itself for your convenience. You finally meet a woman who's up to your mettle, and instead of bestirring yourself to pique her interest, you lend her the fastest teams in the realm to speed her away from your side."

Hardcastle was nervous. Next he'd be spouting Latin, for that was how Hardcastle coped with the anxieties a bachelor duke must never exhibit before others.

"I say we needed to arrive early," Sedgemere replied, because short of Latin, a good argument settled Hardcastle's nerves. "One wants to scout the territory, befriend the help, study the maps, as it were. Veramoor is all genial bonhomie, but do not turn your back on his duchess."

"One doesn't," Hardcastle retorted, tugging at a cravat that had become dusty hours ago. "Not unless one is abysmally ill-mannered. What are you staring at?"

"Those are my blacks," Sedgemere said as a team of four coach horses was led around to the carriage bays, where the harness would be removed, polished, and carefully hung. "I know my own cattle, and those are my blacks."

"You must own two hundred black horses," Hardcastle said, withdrawing a flask and uncapping it. "One set of equine quarters looks the same as another."

"The heat has provoked you to blaspheming, and I know that team. I bought them from a Scottish earl not a year past, the first transaction I've done with the man. He brews a beautiful, lethal whisky."

"All whisky is lethal. They are a handsome team."

They were, in fact, a gorgeous team, for they confirmed that traveling the length of England with Hardcastle had not cost Sedgemere his few remaining wits. The coach from which the horses had been unhitched looked familiar because it *was* familiar.

When last Sedgemere had seen that coach, his entire being had yet been humming with the pleasure of having kissed the lady he'd just sent on her way at a tidy gallop.

"I do not care for that expression, Sedgemere," Hardcastle said, using a wrinkled handkerchief to bat the dust from his hat. "That expression is *bemused*, as if you're plotting mischief unbecoming of a gentleman. The last time I saw that expression, Headmaster nearly wore out his arm warming our little backsides."

"It was worth it," Sedgemere said. "We agreed the birching was worth seeing Lord Postlethwaite shorn of his flowing tresses for the rest of the term. Besides, what boy of eleven is vain about his hair, for God's sake? Poodlethwaite had it coming."

The nickname had been Hardcastle's stroke of genius. Sedgemere had been the one to cut off his slumbering little lordship's hair.

"Let's greet our host and hostess, shall we?" Hardcastle said. "I'm for a soaking bath and a nap, and I daresay you could use some freshening as well."

"Happens you're right." For as the handsome blacks were led away for a rubdown and some hours at grass, Sedgemere knew three things.

First, he would not present himself to Miss Faraday in all his dirt, though he would find her, and soon.

Second, he was a gentleman, so he must apologize for having kissed her.

Third, he most definitely would kiss her again, every chance he got.

"THOSE ARE CHILDREN," Anne said, half of her weariness falling away. "I didn't realize the house party was to include children."

"Their Graces have thirty-six grandchildren, though the duchess's goal is one hundred," Harrison said. "The children are always welcome at Veramoor House."

Three little boys came to a halt facing Anne in the corridor. Each had flaming red hair, each carried a small valise.

"Ma'am," the tallest said, executing a bow. The other two bowed as well, but as a unit. Twins, then, though their looks were not exactly identical.

"Gentlemen," Anne said, curtseying. "Hello, I'm Miss Anne Faraday."

The shorter two exchanged a look. The tallest switched his valise from one hand to the other. "You're not *Lady* Anne? We only know ladies and servants."

"That was rude, Ryland," one of the twins said. "We know some commoner women who aren't servants. They aren't as pretty you though, ma'am."

The footman who'd been herding the boys along the corridor cleared his throat. Harrison twitched at her keys.

"Thank you for the compliment," Anne said to the shortest boy. "I am a commoner, but I'm also a guest at this house party. I hope you are too?"

The child who'd spoken not a word yet nodded and blushed, and because he was a redhead, his blush was brilliant, right to the tips of his ears.

"We're to help protect Hardcastle from the mamas and debutantes," Ryland said. "His Grace of Hardcastle told us so. I'm Alasdair, and this is Ralph and Richard. They're lords too."

More bows. Anne would explain proper introductions to them some time when two other adults weren't looking pained and impatient, and a duchess wasn't waiting tea on Anne.

"I am very pleased to meet you all," Anne said. "I hope our paths cross again soon. Will you stay for the full two weeks?"

"Oh, yes," Richard replied, "and we're not to get dirty ever, and we're to stay out of sight all the time, and we're to behave, or Papa will make us write Latin until Michaelmas. I don't see how we can help protect Hardcastle if we're doing all this behaving and staying out of sight."

The quiet boy, Ralph, spoke up in tones barely above a whisper. "Richard is l-logical. Papa is logical too."

Alasdair swatted Ralph's arm. "Ralph is our lexicon, when he talks at all."

Something quacked in the vicinity of Ralph's valise. Harrison's keys fell silent. The footman's eyebrows climbed nearly to the molding.

"I daresay you're all three tired and hungry," Anne said. "Best get up to the nursery soonest."

"Of course," the footman said, marching off. "Come along, your lordships."

"A pleasure to have met you," Anne said, curtseying as deeply as if they were three little dukes.

Alasdair, who was apparently burdened with a courtesy title already, bowed, followed by his brothers.

"Likewise, ma'am. Have a pleasant stay. Will you help us protect Hardcastle? Papa says friends look out for one another, and Hardcastle is my god-papa."

"He's quite fond of us too," Richard said. "He said so, anyway, and Papa didn't correct him."

For small children, these three could be quite serious, putting Anne in mind of...

Oh, merciful days. Hardcastle was Sedgemere's friend, and these were Sedgemere's boys. The blue eyes shaded closer to periwinkle rather than frozen sky, the noses were understated compared to His Grace's, but the earnestness, the gravity was already there.

"Assisting you to look out for the Duke of Hardcastle will be my special privilege," Anne said. "Do you see that door there, with the two birds on it? That is my room, and you may seek me there before supper if you have need of me. I'll know I can find you in the nursery."

Another quack issued from Ralph's valise. He clutched his traveling case to his chest, expression panicked. Richard and Alasdair stepped in front of him, the eldest wearing a scowl worthy of a duke.

"Off with you," Anne said, smiling brilliantly. "The Duchess of Veramoor is expecting me for tea, and I dare not disappoint her. Very pleased to have met you, gentlemen, and I look forward to seeing more of you."

When the footman nearly dashed up the stairs, the boys bolted after him, while Anne stood listening to indignant quacking that boded wonderful adventures for the next two weeks.

"I OUGHT to see to the boys," Sedgemere said, though he'd rather accost an underbutler and bribe Miss Faraday's location out of him.

At Sedgemere's side, Hardcastle trudged up the stairs. "You

ought to take a damned bath. Your fragrance is most un-ducal, Sedge-mere. The boys will want a trip to the garden after having been cooped up in the coach all day, and they do not need you spouting lectures about *cave quid dicis* —well, good day, Miss Faraday."

Beware what you say. Excellent advice at all times. Even knowing Miss Faraday was a guest at Veramoor House, Sedgemere wasn't prepared for the sight of her right there on the first landing of the main staircase. He was dusty, disheveled, and, yes, sweaty, while she was comfortably elegant in lavender sprigged muslin.

She was also staring at his mouth and smiling a pleased, naughty smile.

"Your Graces, good afternoon," she said, dipping a curtsey. "I believe I just had the pleasure of meeting your children, Sedgemere, and what delightful gentlemen they are."

Damn and blast. "They are hellions, madam, and don't be fooled by Lord Ralph's quiet either. I'll order them to stay away from you, not that children should be in adult company if it's at all avoidable. Veramoor was insistent that the children be brought along, and his duchess likes children, if you can credit such a thing."

He was babbling, and he stank, and Hardcastle was looking amused. Worse than all that, Miss Faraday's smile had disappeared.

"I like children," she said. "Like them better than most adults, and longed for siblings when I was growing up. I still wish I had a brother or a sister. Your sons are *perfectly charming*, and you should be proud to show them off."

Charm. Why the devil did women set so much store by charm? "If you say so," Sedgemere replied.

"He'll be taking the boys for a romp in the garden in about an hour," Hardcastle said, the wretch. "Perhaps you'd care to join them? This far north, the roses last a bit longer, and the light is lovely."

That was not Latin. That was Hardcastle meddling, though thank goodness, his bumbling had restored Miss Faraday's smile.

"A walk in the garden would be just the thing," she said. "From my window, I can see a fountain in a knot garden. Shall I meet you and the children there in an hour?"

Gardens and Miss Faraday were a lovely combination. "I'm not sure if the children—"

Hardcastle coughed, sounding like Sedgemere's own grandmama, then muttering something that sounded like *ducal dumbus doltus*.

"An hour," Sedgemere said. "Give or take. The boys struggle with punctuality." Also with manners, proper dress, deportment, French, Latin, sums—they were terrible with sums, the lot of them—and with anything resembling civility.

And yet, Sedgemere couldn't bring himself to send Alasdair—Ryland—off to Eton. Not just yet.

"I'll look forward to joining you." Miss Faraday patted Sedgemere's arm and bustled off, sending a whiff of lavender and loveliness though Sedgemere's tired brain.

"*Non admirentur*," Hardcastle said. "And particularly don't gawk at the lady on the main staircase, when anybody might see you."

Sedgemere took the remaining stairs two at a time. "I'm to meet her in the garden in one hour, Hardcastle. That leaves me only thirty minutes to bathe, shave, and change, and thirty minutes to lecture the boys. Ten minutes per boy is hardly sufficient for putting them on their manners."

Hardcastle ascended the stairs at a maddeningly decorous pace. "The point of turning children loose in a huge garden is so they can for one quarter of an hour forget their manners. *You* certainly did."

"I beg your pardon?"

Hardcastle marched right past Sedgemere, heading down the long corridor on the side of the house overlooking the stables.

"You heard me," Hardcastle said. "At The Duke's Arms. I thought to retrieve you from the garden because Miss Faraday's coach was ready to leave the yard, and what do I find, but a peer of the realm accosting an innocent young lady in the shade. I withdrew quietly in deference to the lady's sensibilities *and my own*."

"She gave as good as she got, Hardcastle. You mustn't be jealous."

"I am not jealous," Hardcastle said, counting doors as they strode along. "I am firmly in Miss Faraday's camp, and shall do all in my power to further her interests. I am confident the boys can be won to that cause as well. If your intentions with respect to Miss Faraday are dishonorable, I shall kill you. This is my room. Yours is the one with the rose carved on the door."

"You intrude on one kiss, and you're ready to call me out?" Sedgemere said, oddly touched.

"I'll shoot to kill. I'll take good care of the boys," Hardcastle replied. "You needn't worry on that score. I might marry Miss Faraday too."

Hardcastle was a bloody good shot, and he wasn't smiling, but then, Hardcastle never smiled.

"One kiss does not a debauch make," Sedgemere said. "I must away to my bath."

"Elias, for God's sake, be careful," Hardcastle said, jamming a key into the lock on his door. "You married young, and thus were spared the dangerous waters of infatuation and flirtation. Miss Faraday is decent, and your kisses could ruin her. You don't want the ruin of a young lady on your conscience, particularly not that young lady. Moreover, I do not want to raise your children."

Hardcastle's admonition was appropriate. A desire to kiss a woman wasn't that unusual, but Sedgemere's regard for *this* woman was something altogether more substantial.

"I won't ruin her," he said, fishing his own key from his pocket. "I like her, I like her father, and I have reason to hope she might like me. Let's leave it at that, shall we?"

Because tempus was fugit-ing, and a gentleman was punctual. Sedgemere had told the boys as much on hundreds of occasions.

"Be off with you," Hardcastle said, pushing his door open. "Perhaps later I'll explain to you the peculiar circumstances under which Lord Ralph asked me how to say 'duck' in Latin."

"Ralph is a quiet fellow with two brothers, both of whom are quick with their fists," Sedgemere said, fiddling the key in his lock. "Of course he needs to know how to duck in several languages."

Hardcastle shook his head and disappeared into his room.

The key turned in Hardcastle's lock, an appreciated reminder that cut through Sedgemere's sense of urgency. House-party rules meant bedroom doors stayed locked at all times. He'd make sure Miss Faraday grasped that thoroughly the next time he had enough privacy with her to kiss her senseless.

TEA with the duchess had been forty-five minutes of stories about Anne's mama, stories her own father hadn't seen fit to pass along, or perhaps Papa didn't know them.

Mama had apparently been an accomplished flirt, including foreign princes among her entourage, though she'd been the mere daughter of a baron. The idea that she could have married anybody, but had chosen Papa was... touching.

Anne had barely five minutes to stop by her room for a straw hat before finding her way to the knot garden, which was deserted. She forbade herself to check the time, and instead opened the first of the dispatches from Papa that had been waiting for her at Veramoor House.

The news was not good, but then, Papa was a worrier, taking the welfare of each client very much to heart, though he never, *ever* mentioned clients by name. Anne was mentally composing her reply when a shadow fell across the page.

"The Vandal horde will descend in less than five minutes. If that correspondence is valuable, you'd best tuck it away or they'll use it to start a conflagration and tell you they're re-enacting the burning of Moscow."

Sedgemere stood glowering down at her, though Anne hadn't heard his approach. She stashed Papa's epistle in her reticule and rose.

"Your Grace, good afternoon." Now what to say to him? Papa's stack of letters was a reminder that two weeks in the country was as much time as Anne would ever have for a flirtation with any man, much less the duke. Papa needed her, and always would.

"Hardcastle threatened to call me out for kissing you," he said, offering his arm. "I claim the same privilege. If he imposes his attentions on you contrary to your preferences, I will kill him."

Sedgemere's tone was colder than the Russian winter, and yet, Anne had the sense he spoke in jest. She accepted his escort and let him lead her away from the clipped symmetry of the knot garden.

"I can't imagine His Grace of Hardcastle imposing his attentions on anybody," Anne said. "He seems a shy fellow."

Sedgemere's hand rested over Anne's, probably the courtesy of a man who'd been married for several years. She liked most married men, for they tended to strut less and laugh more genuinely.

"Hardcastle will call *you* out, madam, if you tell anybody else he's shy, but he is. He inherited the title early, and natural circumspection became severe reticence as he matured. I would like to kiss you again, though, so tell me now if my attentions are unwelcome."

Merciful days. Was this how the nobility went about their affairs? Anne was spared from a reply by shrieking from the direction of Veramoor House's back terrace.

"Right on schedule," Sedgemere said, tensing. "I apologize in advance for the noise, the dirt, the lack of manners, the—"

"Over here!" Anne called, tugging off her straw hat and waving it. "Gentlemen, you've found us!"

Three little boys came pelting across the garden, Hardcastle following at a more decorous pace.

"Papa! We said we'd find you, and we did," the oldest called. "We found you in the first instant. Hello, Miss Anne!"

"Hello, Miss Anne!" Lord Richard chorused, elbowing Lord Ralph, who mumbled something.

"Apologize for your noise," Sedgemere bit out. "If a single guest thought to nap after a long day's travel, you've just woken them. You've probably spooked half the horses in His Grace's stables and curdled tomorrow's milk into the bargain. Ryland, I expect better of you."

Three little faces fell, three stricken gazes went to the crushed shells of the walkway. Clearly, Sedgemere himself was in need of a nap.

"But you did find us," Anne said. "And you're exactly on time, and you've brought His Grace of Hardcastle with you, which was very gracious of you. Might I trouble one of you gentlemen to put my hat on that bench by the roses? The sun is lovely after I've been shut up in a stuffy coach for days."

"I'll do it!" Richard yelled.

"I'd be pleased to assist you, ma'am," Ryland said, stepping in front of Richard.

"Perhaps Lord Ralph could tend to this errand for me," Anne said. "While Lord Ryland can find me six perfect daises, and you, Lord Richard, can scout us a patch of clover. I feel the need for some lucky clovers today, and I know just the sharp-eyed boys who can help me find them."

Three gallant little knights flung bows at her, then scampered off on their quests, while Hardcastle appropriated a bench some yards away.

"How did you do that?" Sedgemere asked. "You got them to bow, they're not bellowing, and nobody started a fight."

"We all like to feel useful, Your Grace." In Papa's household, Anne was endlessly useful, which was no comfort at all, weighed against the prospect of Sedgemere's kisses.

"I loathe being useful," Sedgemere said. "I'm useful from the moment I wake to the moment I close my eyes, tending to this estate, that committee, dodging the Regent's subtle requests for money. Usefulness can be wearing."

Out of the mouths of dukes...

"Little boys like to be useful, sir, and they were punctual, and they're very dear," Anne said, towing the duke past delphiniums the same shade of blue as his sons' eyes.

"Are you perhaps late to an engagement, Miss Faraday? We're required by propriety and common sense to remain within sight and sound of the boys. Their nursery maids, whom you will note are only now emerging onto the terrace, will be in a dazed stupor for the next three days. At least one of them will try to hand in her notice before facing the return journey."

Anne slowed her steps, though she'd been hauling His Grace in the direction of some shade provided by a pergola laden with grape vines.

"The boys need to run and make noise, Your Grace, while I, having surrendered my hat, need the shade."

"I am jealous of my offspring," the duke muttered. "For they get to do as they please, while you've yet to give me permission to share further kisses with you."

"You are very persistent," Anne said as they reached the shade. The arbor offered a view of the flowering beds and of three small boys, all crawling around in the grass in search of Anne's luck.

"I am very... interested in your kisses, Miss Faraday."

If Sedgemere opened a discussion of money, of pretty gifts offered as a token of his *interest*, Anne would be sick all over the heartsease.

Though she would be tempted. Papa wouldn't blame her, but the notion of becoming Sedgemere's mistress was... wretchedly tempting. Two weeks abruptly became an interminable sentence to disappointment and awkwardness.

Anne set aside her reticule, which held three fat letters from Papa. "I did not guard my virtue from all the impecunious viscounts and foul-breathed barons so I could sell it to you, Sedgemere. One kiss, no matter how lovely, doesn't earn you that much presumption, duke or no duke."

She took a seat. He remained standing, hands behind his back. Anne expected him to stomp away, taking his consequence, his presumption, and his kisses with him. She had a handkerchief in her reticule, and the vines roofing the arbor meant she could cry here in peace.

"I have insulted you," Sedgemere said. "That was not my intent." Still, he remained by the bench, like the clouds of a summer tempest hung over a valley, hoarding rain while flashing fire in the sky and threatening thunder from a distance.

"Do not loom over me. I'm tired, and I have correspondence to tend to, and surely, we needn't create drama so early in the gathering." Anne had warned Papa a house party was nothing but a waste of time.

"I'm waiting for you to invite me to share that bench, madam, so that we might have a civil discussion regarding your egregious misconception."

His tone said waiting was a significant imposition too.

"Do sit," Anne said, waving a hand. She'd forgotten her gloves in her haste to meet Sedgemere in the knot garden. The house party wasn't formal, so no great scandal would result from her oversight.

Sedgemere came down beside her like a hot air balloon drifted to earth, all slow, inexorable shadows, growing larger as he came closer. He chose to sit *quite* close to her.

"You have been propositioned by royalty," he said. "My apologies for creating the impression that—hell. I meant you no insult, Miss Faraday. I'm out of the habit of being attracted to a woman, any woman, and your kiss took me by surprise."

"As yours did me, Your Grace. Are you attracted to men?" Anne had two good male friends who escorted her regularly to the theater or the opera, though her primary function in their company was to quell gossip and enjoy the outing.

"You're not even supposed to know of such goings-on," Sedgemere said. "I will speak directly, because any minute, Ralph will bloody Richard's nose, Ryland will pummel Ralph, or Richard will black Ryland's eye."

"If you proposition me, I will do worse than that to you, Your Grace."

The look he gave Anne was appraising, or just possibly, approving. "I am forewarned. Please recall that Hardcastle must shoot me when you're done thrashing me. Wooing you will be exciting."

CHAPTER FOUR

"*Wooing me?*" Anne retorted. Pleasure, incredulity, and despair wafted on the fragrant breeze. "You barely know me, sir."

She and his grace sat side by side, nearly touching, though in the next moment Anne realized that the warmth covering her knuckles was Sedgemere's hand. Nobody would see him taking such a liberty, but Anne felt that touch everywhere.

"I like what I know of you so far," he said, "which is unusual enough that I'm interested in getting to know you better. Notice, I am not propositioning you, for which you'd beat me, and I am not proposing, for which you'd laugh me to scorn. I am suggesting that we use the next two weeks to become better acquainted. I've never met such a violent woman. Your passionate nature attracts me, if you must know."

Sedgemere's fingertips traced along the back of Anne's hand, the opposite of violence, his touch warm in contrast to his cool tone of voice.

"I've never been accused of having a passionate nature," Anne said. "Quite the contrary, until I met you." Papa used to call her his little abacus. Now she was stealing kisses in gardens, and nearly holding hands with Sedgemere in broad daylight. "I am not interested in marriage, Your Grace. My father's household is my home."

Though lately, that home had felt more like a prison.

Sedgemere's fingers paused, then wandered to the underside of Anne's wrist and from there to her palm. His touch was neither presuming nor hurried, and yet, all of Anne's attention was riveted to the question of where his fingers would travel next.

"Then perhaps," he said, "over the next two weeks, I can change your mind, hmm? Perhaps you'll consider your options, and include me among them. Or perhaps you won't."

A breeze stirred the vines above, bringing the scent of the stable and forest beyond. Beneath those hearty, earthy scents was the fragrance the duke wore, which Anne would ever associate with tender, surprising kisses.

"I won't change my mind," Anne said. "I might..."

Sedgemere's fingers laced with hers, like vines embowering a bench beneath a trellis, lovely to look at, but strong enough to tear down stone edifices, given enough summers.

"Yes, Miss Faraday?"

"I will not marry you, and I will not be your mistress."

Across the garden, a boy yelled about having *found one.*

"Those parameters exactly define the bounds of a thorough wooing," Sedgemere said, leaning close. "If you think you've dissuaded me from further kisses, you are daft."

He kissed her cheek and rose just as Lord Ralph came churning into the arbor.

"I found one!" he bellowed. "Miss Far Away, I f-found one."

"Her name—" Sedgemere began as Anne shot to her feet and approached the boy.

"Lord Ralph, you must show me. It's been an age since I've even seen a four-leaf clover, and you've brought this one straight to me."

Anne knelt and admired a big, perfect four-leaf clover. "Come," she said, taking a blushing Lord Ralph by the hand. "We must show your papa."

"But your name—" Sedgemere said as Anne led the boy to his father.

She glowered at the duke, brandishing her lucky clover. Her smile promised that if Sedgemere tromped on Lord Ralph's accomplishment, there'd be no more shared kisses, not on any terms.

"This is the most magnificent clover I have ever seen," she said, shoving it before Sedgemere's eyes. "Don't you agree, Your Grace?"

Sedgemere closed his hand over Anne's, more warmth, more strong, sure wrapping of his fingers around a part of her person. She kept hold of the boy with her other hand, which left her no means by which to hang on to her wits.

"That is..." Sedgemere's brows drew down, brows very like those on little Ralph. "That is a fine clover. I'm sure it's redolent of good luck."

"It's green," Ralph said.

"Redolent is not a color," Sedgemere began. "The word comes from the Latin verb *redolēre*— "

Because Anne was out of hands, she nudged Sedgemere's boot with her toe. "Of course it's green. Your papa means that this clover reeks of luck." She took a sniff, then held the clover under the ducal nose. "It's lovely, wouldn't you agree, Your Grace?"

Sedgemere took a cautious whiff. "I have never smelled a luckier clover, Miss Faraday."

Ralph's smile was bashful. "I found it myself."

"Then you must keep it," Anne said, dropping the boy's hand. "This is the most special lucky clover I've ever seen, and you found it."

Anne could feel Sedgemere's lectures ready to rain down, about gentlemanly generosity, *trifolium whatever-um,* and grass-stained knees, of which Ralph had two.

"You must keep it, Miss Faraday," Ralph said. "I found it for you."

Anne fluttered, she gushed, she sniffed at the clover, then thanked Ralph from the bottom of her heart, while Sedgemere shifted from boot to boot. When Ralph had galloped back to the clover patch, Anne fetched her reticule off the bench and tucked the clover between the folds of one of Papa's letters.

"Don't you dare," she said to His Grace, "tell me Ralph is a silly little child. He's a fine boy, and he brought me a lovely clover. He got my name wrong the first time only because he was excited, you see, and if you must inflict Latin on him, then you make it special, a secret he shares only with you. He's a small boy, not a duke, so you must speak English to him, not duke-ish."

"Miss Faraday."

Anne jerked the strings of her reticule closed. "Thank you for a lovely outing, Your Grace. I will take my leave of their young lordships before I go in."

"*Miss Faraday.*"

Anne had to get away. Had to answer Papa's letters before she tore them to bits. Sedgemere wanted to woo her, while she wanted... children, a husband, a home of her own. Mundane blessings every girl was raised to treasure.

"*Anne.*"

She looked around for her hat, then realized the tongue-tied Lord Ralph had left it halfway across the garden at her request.

"Your Grace?"

He drew her to the back of the arbor, a shady, private place where a lady could gather her composure.

"My son, my Ralph, who barely says a word if his twin is in the same room, is now standing a full two inches taller because of you and your silly clover. He spoke to you in sentences. I heard him, and if you only knew how long... he's shy."

Sedgemere's words were entirely understandable, but he'd again acquired the quality of a storm cloud, billowing with emotions, raising the wind, lightning visible, thunder threatening, and yet not a drop of his finer sentiments hit the earth.

Insight struck like a thunderclap. "You worry about him," Anne said. "You're smart enough as a parent to worry about the child who's quiet."

"*I* was quiet," Sedgemere said, jamming his hands into his pockets. "A ducal heir cannot *be* quiet. He must be studious, though practical. Intelligent, but not academic. Well-read, without being bookish. He must command the respect of all, while trusting none."

"He sounds like a very dull creature," Anne said slowly, "a miserable creature. Lord Ralph is three removes from the title, though." In the next instant, she knew, simply from the set of Sedgemere's jaw, that *he* had been three removes from the title too, and the progression from younger son or nephew to duke had been miserable and dull indeed.

Also lonely.

"Oh, Sedgemere." Anne wrapped her arms around him and hugged him as tightly as she'd wanted to hug Ralph when he'd brought her his clover. "I'm sorry."

Hugging Sedgemere was like hugging a surveying oak, like trying through weightless emotion to sway a landmark valued for its very immobility. Anne hugged him anyway, grateful for the sheltering privacy of the grape arbor.

Sedgemere was not a monument to ducal consequence and titled self-importance. He was a papa consumed with worry, and trying, by Latin and lectures, to safeguard children who'd someday have to muddle on without him.

"My mother taught me numbers," Anne said, resting her cheek against Sedgemere's lacy cravat. "She was desperate for me to learn numbers, because Papa is a banker, and without numbers, I'd have no way to understand him. I don't hate the numbers, but I'd rather have more memories of my mother, not my math teacher."

A hand landed on Anne's hair, gentle as sunbeams. "Hardcastle says the same thing. He lost his parents, and wishes not that his father had had more time to show him how to be a duke, but rather, had had more time to show him how to go on with the present ducal heir.

Little children come without instructions. A grievous disservice to those raising them."

And to the small boys and girls.

Sedgemere's arms had stolen around Anne, and she remained in his embrace, the benevolent breeze whispering through the greenery around them, honeysuckle gracing the moment. This was not kissing, but Anne most assuredly felt wooed.

"They'll be back," Sedgemere said, "and not a four-leaf clover will survive in Veramoor's gardens."

"We must treasure the ones we come upon today," Anne said, "or over the next two weeks, for they might be all the lucky clovers we shall ever find."

Sedgemere stepped back, a trailing vine of grape leaves brushing his crown. "You'll give me two weeks, then? Two weeks to win your friendship, and whatever else I might entice from you?"

Dalliance was the name for what lay between the mercenary interest of a mistress and the marital commitment of a wife. Temporary passion, stolen moments, lovely memories.

Bearable heartbreak.

More than Anne had ever thought to have, much less than she wished for, and probably far less than Sedgemere intended.

"A ducal dalliance," she said. "Those must be the best kind."

His gaze cooled, suggesting Anne had disappointed him. That hurt, but leaving him at the end of two weeks would hurt more. Never kissing him again, never tasting his passion, or hearing his confidences again, would have hurt most of all.

SEDGEMERE CHATTED, socialized, and was amiable, in so far as he was capable of such nonsense, all the while intercepting debutantes intent upon making off with Hardcastle's bachelorhood. The job was taxing, when what Sedgemere preferred to do was spend time with Miss Anne Faraday.

The boys, oddly enough, provided the means to achieve that end, for Miss Faraday liked children.

Because Sedgemere liked *her*, that meant he too spent time with the baffling, energetic, worrisome trio who called him Papa.

"I would never have suspected you of such kite-flying abilities," Miss Faraday said, linking her arm through Sedgemere's. "Your boys will brag about you for weeks."

All three, even Ralph, had bellowed their encouragement when Sedgemere had taken over from Ryland to rescue a kite flirting with captivity in the boughs of a pasture oak. Their cries of "Capital, Papa!" and "Papa, you did it!" should have been audible back in Nottinghamshire.

"They will brag about you, my dear," Sedgemere countered. "The known world expanded when they saw you skipping rocks."

Miss Faraday walked along with him companionably, her straw hat hanging down her back like any goose-girl on a summer day. Sedgemere had come to the astounding conclusion that Miss Faraday enjoyed touching him. Simply enjoyed touching him.

She hugged the boys—fleetingly, in deference to their dignity, but good, solid squeezes. She patted their heads, she took their hands, and she sat right next to them on benches and picnic blankets.

She linked arms with Sedgemere, took his hand, tidied his cravat, and even—he'd nearly fainted with disbelief—brushed a hand over his hair when the breeze had mussed it. She'd done so in the walled garden of The Duke's Arms, but that very morning, she'd done the same thing within sight of all three boys.

And that too, had apparently fascinated Sedgemere's progeny.

"I was skipping rocks before I could write my name," Miss Faraday said. "My father wanted sons, of course. What man doesn't? But he got me. He calls me a great, healthy exponent of the winsome gender, and made do with me as best he could."

Hannibal Faraday was a shrewd, cheerful soul, but what was wrong with the banker, that he couldn't treasure the daughter he'd been given? Anne was lovely, practical, kind, and indifferent to the typical insecurities and machinations of single young women.

"So your papa taught you to skip rocks?" Sedgemere asked. They were strolling around Veramoor's ornamental lake, the hour being too early for the other guests to be out of bed, and too late for rambunctious boys to remain imprisoned in the nursery.

"My papa taught me to skip rocks," Miss Faraday said, as the path wended into the trees bordering the lake. "Also to shoot, to ride astride—my mother intervened when I was eight—and generally gave me a gentleman's education."

How... lonely, for a young girl. How isolating. "The term gentleman's education is a contradiction in terms," Sedgemere observed. "Young boys go off to school to learn bullying, gossiping, flatulence, and drinking. Had it not been for Hardcastle—"

"Well done, Richard!" Miss Faraday yelled. "I counted four bounces!"

Sedgemere had used the word flatulence in the presence of a lady. A gentleman, regardless of what passed for his education, ought not to do that.

"Well done!" Sedgemere called. "Excellent momentum!"

"Papa says you have a good arm," Ryland shouted.

Richard saluted, grinning, then squatted along the lakeshore, likely searching for another rock. Ralph was tempting the ducks closer to the bank with toast pilfered from a breakfast tray, and Ryland threw sticks as far out into the lake as he could.

"You are such a good papa," Miss Faraday said. "The boys will recall this house party for the rest of their lives, and they'll remember these mornings with you."

Sedgemere would recall these mornings for the rest of his life. As much as he wanted to kiss Anne Faraday again, he'd mustered his patience the better to study her. What single woman of common birth disdained a ducal husband?

Why did Anne look skeptically upon him as a possible husband, when apparently, she found him physically appealing, enjoyed his company, and *even* enjoyed the company of his children?

As a result of his caution, Sedgemere had spent time with the lady apart from the other guests, and in the presence of the children. He still wanted very much to kiss her—at least to kiss her—but his attraction was growing roots and leaves, blossoming from respect into admiration, from liking into warmth.

He'd spoken of becoming better acquainted, but he'd envisioned becoming better acquainted with her kisses, with the feel of her hands in his hair. He'd not realized that watching her teach Ralph to skip rocks might also be part of the bargain.

"I am on to your tricks, miss," Sedgemere said. "You have the knack of finding something agreeable about the boys and praising them for it. They, who have perhaps two percent praiseworthy behaviors by natural inclination, double their efforts in benevolent directions, and thus their demeanor improves."

"It improves exponentially," she said. "My mother took the same approach with me, the servants, and, I suspect, Papa."

Exponentially was an interesting, academic, and appropriate term, also accurate when applied to the increase in Sedgemere's regard for Miss Faraday. He patted her bare hand, kite-flying being a bare-handed undertaking.

"You take the same approach with me, madam." And it was working. The boys had been so much troublesome baggage when Sedgemere had arrived. Now this hour with them was the most enjoyable of the day. He'd learned to notice and enjoy his own sons.

Better still, his boys were enjoying their papa. Ralph had gone so far as to snatch Sedgemere by the hand and drag him to the lakeshore for Miss Faraday's rock-skipping demonstration.

"I think you should round up the other children in the nursery and challenge them to a raft-building contest," Miss Faraday said, as she accompanied Sedgemere deeper into the trees. "The lake isn't three feet deep at the center, and the weather is obligingly hot."

The lake was five feet deep at the center, but only at the center.

"Will you kiss me if I propose a raft-building contest to our host and hostess?"

"I will probably kiss you regardless," the lady replied. "If the adults undertake boat races, you must be sure to assign Mr. Willingham to the same boat as Miss Cunningham."

"Of course." Sedgemere would be equally sure to assign Miss Faraday to the boat *he* captained. "Do I take it you can swim, Miss Faraday?"

"Like a fish, though there isn't much call for swimming in the management of Papa's household. This shade feels divine. If we picnic later today, we must picnic near these trees."

Sedgemere had positive associations with picnics. Hardcastle would chaperone, of course, and any picnic was hours of bowing, chatting, and amiability away.

"Might I look forward to a kiss at this picnic, madam?"

"You may look forward to a kiss this very moment, Your Grace."

THE LAKE HAD EXPANDED the longer Anne had wandered its shore with Sedgemere. Once she and his grace reached the tree line, they'd be out of view of the house, the stable, the children, and out of reach of Anne's common sense and her conscience. The tree line, alas, seemed to recede with each step Anne took toward it, until she and her escort finally gained the cool privacy of the woods.

Sedgemere had played the pianoforte with casual competence when Miss Higgindorfer had needed an accompanist the previous evening. At dinner, he always sat well up the table from Anne and kept all the titled ladies tittering and smiling, though Anne had yet to see him smile.

And he'd made no move whatsoever to kiss Anne again.

They were wasting days, and nights, and Papa's letters already anticipated the happy moment when Anne would be back, *"where she belonged."*

Here was where Anne belonged, beside Sedgemere on a wooded path in the Whinlatter forest.

"I am to look forward to a kiss this very moment?" His Grace asked. "Or am I to enjoy a kiss this very moment?"

The air smelled different in the woods, earthier. The lakeshore was ferns and rocks right up to the water rather than the pebbled beach constructed closer to the house. Birds flitted overhead, and across the lake, a duck honked indignantly.

"You are waiting for me to kiss you?" Anne asked.

Sedgemere's hand trailed down her arm, a simple caress through the muslin of her sleeve.

"Matters seem to go well when we kiss each other, Miss Faraday." The duke bent his head as Anne leaned toward him, and the morning transformed from pretty to transcendent.

Anne had seen such a transition before, when a young lady of her acquaintance had been proposed to at a formal ball. The smitten gentleman had gone down on bended knee, flourished a big, sparkly ring, and made his intended the toast of the evening with his gallantry. The young lady had been transfigured for the evening, not merely pretty, but luminous.

And so the simple act of Sedgemere's lips brushing Anne's changed the day from a summer morning in the Lakes to a moment of heaven. He kept her hand in his, folded her fingers against his heart, and threaded his free hand into her hair.

"God, the taste of you," he muttered against her mouth. "The feel of you."

The feel of him, solid and familiar, but *terra incognita* too. Anne roamed Sedgemere with her hands, hungry to learn his contours. He was hard angles, solid muscle, and fine tailoring, until her explorations ventured from his shoulders and jaw to his hair.

His hair was warm, spun sunshine. The boys, being redheads, didn't have this silky, swan's-down hair. The duke's cravat was more frothy pleasure, sartorial exuberance in its exquisite blond lace edging and in the sheer abundance of fabric.

Sedgemere's tongue made entreaties against Anne's lips, and she let him have her weight, the better to focus on the intimacies he offered. He tasted of toothpowder and of the sprig of lavender he'd stuck between his lips when he'd crossed the garden.

Sedgemere shifted, and Anne's back was to a sturdy tree. The squirrels and birds had gone quiet. The water lapped rhythmically against the rocks, in time with the desire beating through Anne's veins.

"The boys—" Sedgemere said, bracing a forearm near Anne's head.

"I want—" Rather than waste time with words, Anne showed him what she wanted: him, snug against her, the evidence of his arousal a reassuring reality against her belly. She hooked a leg around his thigh and got a fistful of his hair.

This was not a tame, unplanned garden kiss. This was a kiss she'd anticipated for days and nights, a kiss that could lead to wicked pleasures and glowing memories.

Sedgemere's mouth cruised down Anne's throat, the sensation maddeningly tender, then he changed direction, nuzzling a spot beneath her ear that conjured heat in her middle. Anne clutched his shoulders, lest her knees buckle, or her fingers busy themselves unfastening his clothing.

When she found Sedgemere's mouth, she offered him a kiss of wanton, reckless desire, for a taste of Sedgemere was a treat both luscious and bitter. She could not have him. She could only sample him, and the sheer fury of that frustration gave her desire a desperate edge.

"Papa! I found a frog!"

Ralph's voice. Anne had found a handsome prince, but she must throw him back.

"He found a toad!" Ryland, ever the knowledgeable older brother.

"Anne, love, you mustn't be upset," Sedgemere whispered, kissing her brow. His thumb traced the side of her face, his breath whispered across her cheek. "Plead an indisposition tonight, and I'll come for you."

She managed a nod. Sedgemere straightened, and a shaft of sunlight smacked her in the eyes. She let him go when she wanted to grab his hand and disappear with him into the forest for the next hundred years.

By the time the boys came pelting into the woods, Anne had jammed her straw hat onto her head and slapped a smile on her face. She even admired the toad, a grand warty creature whom the boys named Wellington.

And then she made them turn him loose, because a duke, even an amphibian duke, must be allowed to go about his business, as Sedgemere would go about his when the house party ended.

"IF YOU LOOK at the clock one more time," Hardcastle muttered as he took the chair beside Sedgemere, "the entire assemblage will know an assignation awaits you."

Miranda Postlethwaite, sister to the shorn poodle of long ago, barely hid her frustration at Hardcastle's choice of seat, for she'd apparently taken it into her head to become Sedgemere's duchess.

Across the room, the poor Higgindorfer woman commenced an aria about death being the only consolation when true love proved fickle. Her voice was lovely, though her accompanist was some clod-pated earl or other.

"I'm still fatigued from watching my sons ride Veramoor's sheep," Sedgemere whispered back. From laughing so hard his sides had nearly split. Even Ralph had been overcome with merriment, though Miss Faraday—instigator of the impromptu sheep races—had bellowed the loudest encouragement.

"You're fatigued from an excess of ridiculousness," Hardcastle mused. "One never would have guessed utter frivolity required stamina. Have you proposed to Miss Faraday yet? You're a hopeless nincompoop if you haven't. It's all very well to affix your boys to the backs of hapless ovines, and allow the children to charm the lady with their foolishness, but you won't find her like again, Sedgemere."

No, he would not. "For your information, I have the lady's permission to embark on a wooing."

Hardcastle crossed his legs, a gesture he alone managed to make elegant instead of fussy. "A wooing that involves sheep races. Subtle, Sedgemere. You'll start a new fashion at Almack's, I'm sure."

The wooing involved kisses too. In the woods along the lake and later in the day, behind the stable while scouting a proper course for the sheep races—not that the sheep viewed a racecourse as anything other than more space to graze.

"Are you jealous, Hardcastle?"

"Terribly. I've always wanted to throw a leg over a sheep and hang on for dear life while the crazed beast did its utmost to fling me into the dung heap."

Anne's observation about Hardcastle being shy came to mind. She'd described the upbringing of a young duke as dull and miserable, and she'd been right. The upbringing of a *shy* young duke would also be... lonely.

"You don't fancy any of the young ladies here, do you?" Sedgemere asked. "Miss Higgindorfer seems nice enough, and you'd have all the Italian opera you'd ever want."

"She fancies Willingham, and I do not fancy opera."

Hardcastle loved music. He'd been teased for it by the other boys at school and hadn't been heard to play the pianoforte since. Did the prodigy of a governess enjoy music? Could she play, even a little?

A glance at the clock revealed that four entire minutes had elapsed since Sedgemere had last checked the time.

"I thought Miss Cunningham had set her cap for Willingham," Sedgemere said. "One can see how Veramoor and his duchess would find such gatherings amusing. Rather like several chess games in progress at once."

"Propose to Miss Faraday, Sedgemere. Other fellows have

remarked the warmth of her laughter, the affection she showers on the children."

Other fellows including... *Hardcastle?*

"I believe she is testing me, Hardcastle. She's been pursued by men of high degree, fellows whose intentions were not flattering to anybody. You're right that Anne is an heiress—her papa has mentioned specifics to me—and she's right to be skeptical of any man's advances."

"Anne. You refer to the lady by her first name. Hmm."

Polite applause followed, for true love had finally accepted its bitter fate and faded to a wilting minor cadence.

"You will make my excuses," Sedgemere said, rising. "Too much sun, the press of business, neglecting my correspondence, et cetera."

"Take care, Your Grace. Amor et melle et felle est fecundissimus."

Love is rich with both honey and venom. "Pleasant dreams to you too, Hardcastle."

Sedgemere quit the music room without allowing a single lady to catch his eye, for Hardcastle's observation had been too close to the mark. Anne kissed with a fervor that delighted and intrigued, she was unstinting in her affection for the boys, and she showed every appearance of welcoming a dalliance from one of the most eligible bachelors in the realm.

She also disappeared to her room by the hour, pleading a need for rest, or to pen a letter to her distant papa. She avoided any topic that related to the future, and she disdained the notice of every eligible young man, attributing even courtesies solely to an interest in her father's wealth.

Not without justification, apparently, for her father was obscenely wealthy.

Sedgemere stopped by his rooms to make use of his toothpowder and change out of formal attire. When a gentleman bent on wooing intended to take his lady swimming, the fewer clothes, the better.

CHAPTER FIVE

The tap on Anne's door was expected. The conflict about whether to heed Sedgemere's summons was not.

Anne planned to dally with Sedgemere, then send him on his way. His Grace's intentions were honorable, and Anne dreaded the day when she saw disgust in his keen blue eyes.

She opened the door anyway. "Your Grace. Good evening."

The duke was in riding attire, though of course he wouldn't go riding when the hour was nearly midnight. Never had snug breeches, tall boots, and a billowing shirt beneath an embroidered waistcoat looked so attractive. He carried a hamper in one hand. His jacket was slung over his other arm.

"Miss Faraday, you are invited to a stroll by the lake. I'd bow, but that would look silly with my present encumbrances."

"Can't have you looking silly," Anne said, snatching a shawl and joining him in the corridor. "I was half expecting you to have a go at riding Veramoor's ram earlier today."

"Your hair is down," Sedgemere said. "I've never seen your hair down."

Anne's hair was tidily braided. "Nobody save my lady's maid has seen my hair *down*, Your Grace. Are we in a footrace?"

"Nobody?" Sedgemere paused with one hand on the doorway to the servants' stairs. "I would like to be the first, then. Also the last."

He went bounding down the stairs, leaving Anne to follow at a more decorous pace. Sedgemere still hadn't precisely proposed, which was fortunate. For when he proposed, she'd have to refuse him.

They emerged on the side of the house that faced the lake, away from the thumping of the pianoforte, away from lights and applause and curious eyes. The water reflected the silvery moonshine, a slight breeze riffled the surface.

"I've been reconnoitering all day," Sedgemere said, striding off, "looking for the perfect spot: Close to the house, for the less time spent hiking in the dark, the better. Far enough away from the house that nobody would hear us talking if they left a window up. Near the lake, because the lake is beautiful, but tucked beneath the trees, because privacy is of utmost concern. Then too—"

Anne hauled him up short by virtue of yanking on the handle of the hamper he carried. She took the hamper from him, draped his jacket over it, then stepped into his arms.

"I've missed you, Sedgemere. All through dinner—"

Through every moment. When he'd roared with laughter at the boys on their wooly steeds, when he'd picked Ralph up and tossed him into the air as the victor, when he'd sauntered into the blue gallery in his evening attire. Anne could not lay eyes on Sedgemere without her heart aching.

She'd accosted him beneath one of the many oaks that dotted Veramoor's lawn. They would not be visible from the house, so she indulged in the need to kiss him.

Sedgemere obliged with delicate, patient, maddening return fire, until Anne's thigh was wedged between his legs, and she was clinging to him simply to remain upright.

"About that perfect spot," Sedgemere said.

Anne leaned into him, his heartbeat palpable beneath her cheek. When she was with him, her awareness of the natural world was closer to the surface. The breeze swaying through the boughs of the oak, the water lapping at the shore, the rhythm of Sedgemere's life force, all resonated with the desire raging through Anne for the man in her arms.

"No spot can be perfect," Anne said, and all house parties came to an end.

"Your kisses are perfect," he said. "Shall we sit for a moment and pretend to admire the moon?" Sedgemere withdrew a blanket from the hamper, and Anne grabbed one edge of a quilt worn soft with age.

The quilt bore the scent of cedar, a good blanket for making memories on. Sedgemere backed up a few steps, so the frayed edge of the fabric lay directly at the foot of the oak. The shadows here were deep, while the forest rose in a great, black mass behind the lake. Above it, stars had been scattered across the firmament by a generous hand.

"If I proposed tonight, would you decline my suit?" Sedgemere asked.

"I admire persistence," Anne said, folding down onto the blanket. "I'm no great fan of badgering."

Sedgemere ought to have flounced back into the house. He instead came down beside Anne, undid his waistcoat, and tugged off his boots.

"You're stubborn," he said. "Stubborn is a fine quality. You're also not wearing stays."

"I expected we'd go swimming," Anne said.

He arranged his boots, waistcoat, and stockings at the edge of the blanket. "So did I, but have you any idea, madam, any notion, what the image of you in a wet chemise does to my thought processes?"

As a result of that last embrace, Anne had some idea what such an image did to his breeding organs.

"Probably the same thing the image of you naked to the waist in sopping wet breeches does to mine, Your Grace. The water will be warm too, because the lake is shallow and the sun has been fierce."

In the next instant, Anne was on her back, fifteen stone of half-dressed duke above her.

"The sun has been fierce, indeed. You made Ralph laugh, my dear. You made *me* laugh. I've every confidence you made the sheep laugh too."

Sedgemere's kisses bore no laughter. They were all dark wine, billowing wind, and honeysuckle moon shadows.

Anne wiggled, she squirmed, she yanked on the duke's hair and shoved at him, until Sedgemere was lying between her legs, his weight a necessary but insufficient complement to the desire rioting through her.

"You needn't be noble," Anne panted between kisses. "I'm not a virgin, though once upon a time, I was a fool."

She took a risk, telling him that, but Sedgemere didn't pull away. Instead, he shifted up, so Anne could hide her flaming face against his throat. His hand cradled the back of her head, and he pressed his cheek to her temple.

"I'm sorry," he said, his grip fierce and cherishing. "Whoever he was, he was not worthy of your regard, and you are well rid of him. We'll speak of it if you like. I'll ruin him for you, I'll even call him out, but please, my love, not now."

My love. Anne could be Sedgemere's love, for a span of days. She wrapped herself around him, yearning and frustration turning the cool evening hot.

"I want you," she said, trying to get her hands on his falls. "Sedgemere, I'm tired of waiting, of being patient. We have only days, and I can't stand the thought that—"

The duke reared back and pulled his shirt over his head. In the moonlight, he was cool curves and smooth muscles. Anne wanted to nibble on his shoulders, and lick his ribs, and—

He got to his feet, peeling his breeches off and kicking them to the grass, so the entire, magnificent naked whole of him stood before her.

"My name is Elias," he said. "Given my state of undress, I invite you, and you alone of all women, to call me by my name."

He wanted to give her his name, in other words. Anne could accept only part of his proffer.

"Elias, I'll need help with my chemise." Not because she couldn't reach the bows. Anne had chosen her attire for this outing carefully. She needed her lover's help because her hands shook too badly.

His, by contrast, were competent and brisk, untying each bow in succession, until Anne's chemise was undone, her treasures guarded only by Sedgemere's consideration and her own lack of courage.

"Leave it on if you like," he said, kissing Anne onto her back. "I don't need to see you to know that you're glorious."

He was glorious, finding the exact right balance between haste and leisure, between boldness and delicacy. With maddening gentleness, he caressed Anne's breasts through the cotton of her chemise, until she was the one to shove the fabric aside and arch into his hands.

She loved that he'd be naked with her, loved that every inch of him was available for her delectation. Memories, of clothing shoved aside while somebody slogged through an endless Schubert sonata on the next floor down, tried to intrude.

Anne figuratively threw those memories in the lake. Sedgemere was not a presuming earl, trying to get his hands on her dowry by virtue of hastily fumbling beneath her skirts. Sedgemere was, in fact, in no hurry whatsoever, for which Anne was tempted to kill him.

She bit his earlobe. "If you do not apply yourself to the task at hand with more focus, Your Grace, I will toss you into the water."

He glowered down at her, his hair tousled, his chest pressing against her breasts with each breath.

"Call me Elias, by God. You'll not be Your-Gracing me when I'm inside your very body, woman."

Anne lifted her hips against him. "Your Grace, Your Grace, Your Gr—oh, *my*."

His aim was excellent, his self-restraint pure torment. Slowly, by teasing advances and retreats, Sedgemere joined their bodies, while Anne's grasp of words, intentions, everything but Sedgemere unraveled.

"Say my name," he growled, bracing himself on his forearms.

He could keep up this rhythm all night, Anne suspected. All summer. For the rest of eternity. Her mind knew he expected some response from her, words of some sort. The rest of her was incoherent with relief to have him inside her, and with yearning for yet more of him.

She ran her foot up his calf, then locked her ankles at the small of his back. The ground was hard beneath her, and that was good, because she needed the purchase to push into Sedgemere's thrusts, to love him back.

"Say my name, Anne."

She tried to harry him, to say what she needed with her body. "Sedgemere, *please*."

He kissed her, a quick smack when she wanted to devour his mouth. "Good try, but you'll have to do better, my dear."

Perhaps to inspire her, he sped up for the space of five breath-stealing thrusts, then returned to a slower tempo.

"Dammit, *Elias*."

He laughed and showed her how much he'd been holding back. The starry sky reflected Anne's pleasure, in fiery streaks of desire and surprise, and then more and more pleasure, as if the entire lake had left its bounds to deluge her in sweet, sweet satisfaction. Cool fire and moonlit water, then the solid comfort of the earth beneath her, and the lovely stirring of a breeze over her heated skin.

Sedgemere gave her long moments to simply glory in the experience, and to recover. Anne stroked his hair, kissed his shoulder, and wished she had words instead of fleeting caresses to offer him.

Then he moved again inside her lazily, teasing her into another brief, blinding moment of gratification that helped Anne hold back the regret stalking her joy. When he kissed her temple, then gathered her close and simply held her, she yet managed to savor the sheer pleasure, and keep the tears at bay.

When Sedgemere withdrew, however, and spilled his seed on her belly, she told herself his consideration was for the best, even while she wept.

SEDGEMERE BRACED himself on one elbow, the effort of withdrawing from his lover having resulted in a combination of relief—he'd done the impossible in tearing himself from her, after all—and rage. Everything in him rebelled at his caution. His body had spent itself in a confused torrent of pleasure and dismay, his mind refused to function, and even the natural wariness of the wealthy, powerful duke was looking on in bewildered disbelief.

What would Anne think of him, nearly proposing one instant, then protecting his freedom in the next?

Fortunately, his gentlemanly honor had maintained the upper hand, for Anne's freedom had been protected as well.

She passed him a handkerchief.

"You do this part," she said, her hand falling to the blanket in languid surrender. "I can't move."

"I can't think," Sedgemere muttered, wiping the evidence of his passion from her pale midriff. "God above, Anne Faraday."

Should he propose again now? Hold her? Leave her in peace? Being a duke did not prepare a man for being a lover, much less a fiancé on offer.

"We ought to go for a swim," Anne said. "Though we might set the lake aboil."

Her voice was different, not so crisp, not so... confident.

"You aren't going anywhere," Sedgemere said, finishing with the handkerchief and tossing it in the direction of his boots. He'd wash that handkerchief himself and treasure it all his days. "I will expire if you abandon me for the pleasures of a brisk swim, for any pleasures save those available in my embrace."

Anne rolled to her side, giving him her back. "You would have to carry me to the lake, Elias. Even a dozen steps are beyond me. What a formidable lover you are."

Elias. Freely given, affectionately rendered. The last of the frustration resulting from their truncated joining slipped away. Sedgemere tucked himself around his lady and flipped the quilt over them.

"When I think of the days I've wasted flying kites and skipping rocks," he said, nuzzling her nape. "Stewarding sheep races, for pity's sake."

"Every duke needs a talent to fall back on when the title pales," Anne replied, kissing his forearm. "You will be the foremost steward in all the realm for sheep races."

Anne had explained to the boys how to jockey a sheep, waved her hat madly to inspire the sheep to complete the racecourse, and hoisted Ralph into Sedgemere's arms at the conclusion of the contest. From there, Sedgemere had naturally put the boy on his shoulders and lost the last remaining bit of his heart into Anne Faraday's keeping.

Her inherent kindness extended even to taking care of male hopes and dreams, to nurturing the tender male ego.

"Stewarding sheep races is indeed a demanding and much sought-after profession," Sedgemere said. "Might I also aspire to become the steward of your heart, Anne?"

Her posture remained the same, sprawled on her side, her bum tucked into the lee of Sedgemere's body, her cheek pillowed on his biceps, her feet tucked between his calves.

The moment changed, nonetheless, and Sedgemere wasn't quite sure how. Did that stillness mean he had her full attention, or that she was poised to march off into the night?

"You already have my heart, Sedgemere. You had it the moment you noticed that Helen Trimble regards me as if I were the evidence of a passing goose on the bottom of her shoe. You had it when you lent me your teams all the way up from Nottinghamshire. You had it when I saw how protective you are of Hardcastle, though he hardly needs protecting. You had it when you realized your boys are in want of encouragement."

Sedgemere was encouraged, for this litany had nothing to do with his title, or with his consequence. He'd merely behaved as a gentleman toward... well, as a besotted gentleman.

"You imply that my lovemaking did not impress you," he said, his hand finding its way to a warm, abundant breast. "Shall I address that shortcoming?"

She lifted her cheek from his arm. "Somebody has lit the lamps in the nursery."

Against Sedgemere's palm, flesh ruched delicately. "One of the boys had a nightmare or started a pillow fight."

He'd like to have pillow fights with Anne, also formal dinners, house parties, holidays, quiet breakfasts, afternoon naps...

And babies.

"Sedgemere, your boys have that bedroom just before the corner. Why would they be awake at this hour?"

"They should be cast away with their labors, you've kept them so active," Sedgemere said, withdrawing his hand. "I suppose you want to investigate?"

Anne scrambled to sitting, and gathered up her chemise. "What if one of the boys has fallen ill? Feeding a great herd of people can mean the kitchen is less careful to keep hot food hot and cold food cold. Bad fish can carry a grown man off, or bad eggs. Mutton can turn, and if the sauces are heavy, and a boy is hungry, he might not notice."

Oh, how Sedgemere loved her, loved her fierce protectiveness of the boys, her ferocious passion, her laughter.

Her hesitance to accept his offer of marriage was not so endearing.

"Anne, calm yourself. They are robust boys, and nobody in the entire gathering has shown a single symptom of ill health. They know not to eat anything that tastes off, because a duke's heir might be drugged and kidnapped."

Her head emerged from her chemise. "Gracious, Sedgemere, you lead an exciting life. Hadn't you best get dressed?"

He did not want to get dressed. He wanted to tackle Anne and ravish her and tickle her, and then make love with her in the warm, shallow waters of the lake.

"Anne, will you marry me?"

"Now is not the time, Sedgemere. Your children might be ill, fevered, dyspeptic. One of them might be injured, or might have gone missing. One must always be aware of risks, and with children, the risks are limitless."

Not a *yes*, but also not a *no*, and she was right. Now was not the time. Sedgemere found his shirt, then pulled on his breeches.

"It's probably nothing. Ralph still occasionally wet the bed as recently as last summer. His brothers helped him hide the sheets and get new ones from the linen closet. I wouldn't have known if I hadn't overheard the housemaids discussing it."

The dress went on next, a loose, high-waisted smock with short sleeves and a lace-edged bodice. Of all Anne's dresses, including her dinner finery and ballroom attire, this one would always be Sedgemere's favorite.

"You should be proud of the boys for sticking together," she said. "Not all brothers do. I can't find my—"

Sedgemere passed her a pair of low-heeled slippers. "I am proud of the boys, and lately, I've started telling them that. I do hope Ralph hasn't wet the bed. He'll be mortified."

"Perhaps his duck has got loose," Anne said, kneeling up to help Sedgemere with his cravat. "Any duck would grow restless, living in boxes and closets."

"His *what*?"

"Josephine, his duck. I come out before breakfast for a walk around the lake, and Ralph is often in company with Josephine, whom he has brought clear from Nottinghamshire. She's a very well-traveled duck. Hold still, Sedgemere."

Anne finger-brushed his hair into order, fluffed his cravat, and passed him his jacket.

Because she was studying him, Sedgemere had a moment to study her. The moon had risen higher, and thus more light was available, and he could see what she doubtless hoped was hidden by the darkness.

Despite her brisk tone, despite her obvious concern for the children—and this damned traveling duck— Sedgemere's intimate attentions had moved Anne Faraday to tears.

Now was not the time, she'd said, but as Sedgemere took her hand and led her back to the house, he vowed that they would find the time, and he'd have an answer to why his lovemaking had made her cry.

And an answer to his proposal of marriage.

THE MAIDS WERE IN AN UPROAR, Richard and Ryland were pacing about in their nightshirts, a footman hovered, and two governesses in nightcaps and night-robes were arguing about whose job it was to evict rogue ducks.

Sedgemere stood in the middle of this pandemonium as if nursery riots were simply another duty on the endless list of duties dukes took in stride, while Anne could not find a useful thought to think or a helpful deed to do. Three older boys from the room across the corridor lingered in the doorway, and a small red-haired girl peeked around the jamb as well.

"The lot of you will please settle down." Sedgemere hadn't raised his voice, and he'd hoisted Ralph onto his hip. "Lord Ralph, when did you last see the duck?"

"She was in her b-box after supper," Ralph wailed, "but some-body let her out. I'll never s-see her again, and Josie was my only d-duck."

Two of the boys hovering in the door slipped away, the footman took to bouncing forward and back on his toes, and everybody else fell silent.

"You," Sedgemere said to the footman, "please follow the two fellows who departed and search their quarters. If you require my aid in that endeavor, I'll happily lend it, and I'm sure the boys' parents will too. You two," he went on, addressing the governesses, "are excused with my apologies for the uproar. If you maids would see the other children to their beds and search the playrooms for any stray ducks, I'd appreciate it."

"But my Josephine is lost," Ralph moaned. "My only d-duck, and she won't know her way around, and the other boys are mean, and the cook will kill her and feed her to the guests."

"Anne," Sedgemere said, "in the morning, you'll have a word with the Duchess of Veramoor if Josephine remains truant. Please instruct Her Grace to modify the menus so no duck is served until Josephine has been returned to her owner's care."

One did not instruct the Duchess of Veramoor, but that wasn't the point. "Certainly, Sedgemere. I'll speak with Her Grace before breakfast."

"Can you do it tonight?" Ralph asked. Tears streaked his pale cheeks, and he didn't even raise his head from his papa's shoulder.

"Morning will suffice," Sedgemere said. "Nobody is awake in the kitchen to wield so much as a butter knife at this hour, my boy, and duck is never served for breakfast. It isn't done."

A great sigh went out of the child as Sedgemere sat on the edge of a low cot, arranging Ralph in his lap.

"You lot," he said, gesturing to Ryland and Richard. "Get over here. We have a mystery to solve. Miss Faraday, your powers of deduction are required in aid of our task."

Anne took a seat on the opposite cot, because Ryland and Richard had tucked in on each side of their papa. The picture they made, three handsome little redheads clustered around their blond papa, all serious focus on a missing duck, did queer things to Anne's heart.

She had no powers of deduction, but her predicament didn't call for any. She was not simply attracted to Sedgemere, she loved him. This slightly tousled fellow was the true man, not the wealthy aristocrat, but the conscientious parent, Hardcastle's devoted friend, Anne's lover—her wooer. Sedgemere's passion was a sumptuous pleasure Anne would never forget, but the devotion to his children, to finding a missing duck, would hold her heart captive forever.

"Now," Sedgemere said. "We've cleared the room of spies and spectators. If you wanted to hide a duck somewhere that would cause a great commotion and embroil the duck's owner in terrible trouble, where would you boys stash the duck?"

"Not in my rooms," Richard said. "Maybe in the governess's rooms?"

"The governesses would be shrieking the house down by now," Ryland observed. "Josie's not the quietest duck."

"We have to find her," Ralph said. His hand came up, thumb extended as if headed for his mouth, but Sedgemere gently trapped Ralph's hand in his own.

"Miss Faraday," Sedgemere said, "where would an errant duck cause the staff or guests the greatest disruption? Where would a duck be the worst possible surprise?"

Four sets of blue eyes turned on Anne as if she knew the secret to eternal happiness and how to remove an ink stain from a boy's favorite shirt. If she failed them—

"The linen closet on the floor that houses the young ladies," Anne said, rising. "I know exactly where it is too, because it's around the corner from my own rooms."

"You fellows stay here," Sedgemere said, depositing Ralph on the bed. "If Josie should come waddling home, she'll be upset, and only

Ralph will be able to catch her. We'll report back shortly. Miss Faraday, lead on."

Sedgemere extended a hand, and Anne took it. She ought not to
have, not in front of the boys, not without an adult chaperone. But all
too soon, she'd have to tell Sedgemere they could never be married,
and so she took what she could, and clasped his hand.

CHAPTER SIX

"A damned duck," Sedgemere groused, though he wanted to howl with laughter. "A damned duck has attached itself to my nursery retinue and I had no idea. A damned female duck."

"Josephine sounds like a boy to me," Anne said. "The lady ducks have the louder, more raucous voices, rather like fishwives or alewives."

Anne's voice was soft, tired, and determined, and her grip on Sedgemere's hand secure. He could hunt ducks with her all night, all year, for the rest of his natural days. Voices came from around the corner, and Sedgemere pulled Anne into an alcove inhabited by a pair of Roman busts.

Miss Higgindorfer and Miss Postlethwaite went giggling past, extolling the virtues of *His Grace's* manly physique and lovely dark hair.

"Poor Hardcastle," Sedgemere whispered. "You check the corridor."

Anne did, her stealth worthy of Wellington's pickets. She gestured Sedgemere out of hiding, but he first tugged her back into the alcove and stole a kiss.

"For luck," he said. "My son's happiness and his entire regard for his papa rest upon locating this prodigal duck."

"The linen closet is just down here," Anne said.

And the damned closet, as it turned out, was locked. "Boys can't get into a locked closet, and I doubt—"

A soft, plaintiff quack sounded from the other side of the door. Anne's lips quirked as she fished at the base of her braid and produced a hairpin.

"One carries extras," she said, "in case another lady might have need, or a duck might be trapped behind a locked door." She applied the hairpin to the lock, and the latch lifted easily.

They couldn't leave the door open, lest the duck fly off, so Sedgemere wedged himself through the door and towed Anne in after him.

"Gracious, it's quite dark," she said.

Sedgemere looped his arms around her. "And the blasted duck has gone quiet, but we did find her, so perhaps another kiss for luck will produce complete victory."

He had not the first inkling how to find a duck in a tiny, pitch-dark room, but finding Anne's mouth with his own involved no effort at all, only pleasure. He kissed her and kissed her and kissed her, until her back was against the shelves of sheets, towels, and bedclothes, and the scents of lavender and laundry starch had become Sedgemere's favorite aphrodisiacs.

He was on the point of opening his falls when a soft quack sounded near his left boot.

Anne's sigh feathered past his cheek. "I told you I think he's a boy duck. He just sniffed at my ankle."

"There'll be none of that," Sedgemere said, stooping to pick up the duck. "The only fellow who'll be sniffing at your ankles is me, madam. This is not a small duck."

The bird snuggled into Sedgemere's grasp as if weary of being at liberty. Sedgemere, however, was not weary of kissing Anne, so he leaned in for more, kissing her around the duck.

"We should go," Anne whispered, her hand framing Sedgemere's jaw. "It's late, and the boys will worry."

"We should be married," Sedgemere said, as Josephine quacked her—or his—agreement. "Even the duck agrees."

"I cannot marry you, Your Grace." She kissed him lingeringly. "I am needed in my father's house, and you should marry a woman of some consequence."

The duck quacked again, not as softly.

"Do you think I'm after your money?" Sedgemere asked. "I have no need of it, Anne. I need only you. The boys love you, you will make a fine duchess, and I—"

The door opened as the Duchess of Veramoor's crisp voice rang out. "I knew I heard something quacking. It appears, though, that we've found ourselves a duck and a duke—among others. I must say, this is most irregular. I do not recall a duck on my guest list."

ANNE ENDED up holding the duck, stroking her fingers over Josephine's soft, smooth feathers, while the Duchess of Veramoor paced the boundaries of a private sitting room.

"Sedgemere, you are found in a linen closet kissing the stuffing out of an unmarried woman of good birth, *at my house party*. A duck is no sort of chaperone, and I'll not be able to keep the Postlethwaite creature quiet."

For Miss Postlethwaite had been at Her Grace's elbow when the linen closet door had been opened. Josephine had honked a merry welcome, and Anne's future had been destroyed.

More destroyed, which was semantically impossible.

"I was in the act of making Miss Faraday an honorable offer," Sedgemere said. "She had yet to fully explain her response."

Anne had been on the verge of explaining her way right into His Grace's breeches. She cuddled the duck, who bore that indignity quietly. They'd both had a challenging evening, after all.

"Sedgemere, you do me great honor," Anne said, gaze fixed on Josephine's bill, "but I cannot marry you. I have explained that I'm needed at my father's side."

The duchess sat, so Sedgemere had room to pace. "You think I'm in want of coin," he said. "That's the only explanation I can fathom. You are confused by the events of the evening, and your normal common sense has deserted you. I do not care that much,"—he snapped his finger at Anne, and Josephine made as if to nip at him —"for your wealth."

If only it were that simple. "Sedgemere, I am old enough to know my own mind, and we would not suit."

A great, big, fat, quacking falsehood, that. Even the duchess looked impatient with Anne.

"We won't sort this out tonight," Her Grace said. "I will speak to the Postlethwaite girl tomorrow. A maid outside Miss Postlethwaite's door will ensure my guest does not roam before breakfast, but that's as much as I can do."

Sedgemere paused at the window and twitched back a lacy curtain. From this side of the house, he'd have a view of the moonlit lake.

"You might remind Miss Postlethwaite," Sedgemere said, "that if she speaks a word against Miss Faraday, nothing I could say or do would stop Hardcastle from offering Miss Postlethwaite and her entire set the cut direct."

Anne took heart from that observation, because Hardcastle would also cut anybody who spoke a word against Sedgemere.

"Do you love another, Miss Faraday?" the duchess asked.

What an appalling question. "I am not *in* love with anybody save Sedgemere."

Ah, God, a mistake. A mistake brought on by the lateness of the hour, forbidden passion, and stray ducks.

"Are you with child by another?" Her Grace's tone brooked no dissembling, but her gaze was kind. "Young ladies can be taken advantage of, and you are honorable enough not to put a cuckoo in the Sedgemere nest."

Sedgemere's gaze was stricken. He dropped to the sofa beside the duchess like a rock flung into the lake.

"*Anne?*"

"Sedgemere is the first man to turn my head in more than five years. I have not behaved well, and I do apologize for abusing your hospitality, but that is the extent of the situation. I'll leave in the morning, and you may put it about that I enticed the duke to a dalliance, for that is the truth."

Anne had no experience enticing anybody to do anything, though, so the truth was unlikely to be believed.

"Sedgemere, do not try to hector the woman into becoming your wife," the duchess said, getting to her feet. "Miss Faraday's mother was equally resolute once her mind was made up, else she would never have married Hannibal Faraday. No family wants to see a daughter married off to an impecunious banker, but Fenecia was smitten. Miss Faraday has her mother's pretty looks, I'm told she has her mama's aptitude for numbers, and apparently, she has her mother's independence too. Off to bed with you two—separate beds, if you please."

Her Grace swept out, a small, forceful woman, who hadn't been surprised or even disappointed to find lovers in her linen closet kissing over a stray duck. If Anne were ever, through some miracle, to become a duchess, she'd aspire to such savoir faire.

In the present situation, however, it was all she could do not to cry.

"Give me the damned duck," Sedgemere said, "and do not think to hare off in the morning, like a naughty schoolgirl. If you run, the Postlethwaite creature will set the dogs of gossip upon you, but her aspirations in Hardcastle's direction will keep her quiet for the duration of the gathering."

They had a small wrestling match over the duck, mostly because Anne wanted any excuse to brush hands with Sedgemere. She'd apparently achieved the goal of rejecting his suit. Now all that remained was to survive a few more days, enduring the fruits of her victory.

~

AFTER ESCORTING Miss Faraday around the lake, Hardcastle bowed the lady on her way. This involved ignoring the despairing glance she sent toward Hardcastle's oldest and dearest pain in the arse, for Sedgemere was on his full ducal dignity on the far side of the terrace. His Grace of Sedgemere's excuse for spying on Miss Faraday —this time—was that most pressing of errands, accompanying a duck on its constitutional.

"I know not which of you is the more pathetic," Hardcastle said, crossing the terrace. "The house party ends tomorrow, and you're reduced to taking the air with an anatine companion. Where is your courage, Sedgemere? Storm the castle walls, sing the die-away ballads beneath the lady's window, muster a bit of derring-do."

Hardcastle had been introduced nearly two weeks and an eternity of tedium ago to Josephine. She waddled about in the grass below the terrace and would likely be as glad as Hardcastle to quit the party.

"How is Anne?" Sedgemere asked.

"Miserable. The only topics about which I can inspire her to discourse are canal projects and housing developments." The lady was also willing to listen to anything, anything at all, related to Sedgemere. His upbringing, his antecedents, his impatience with foreign languages, which Hardcastle attempted to redress by constant references to Latin.

"Then she and I are both miserable," Sedgemere said, lowering himself to the top step, as if he were a small boy, willing to sit anywhere on a summer day, provided he sat *outside*. "The only hypothesis I've concocted is that Anne fears I'm seeking her hand to gain control of her dowry. This is patently false, of course, also insufficient to explain her behaviors."

Hardcastle's delicate ducal ears were not equal to hearing the details of those behaviors. He'd attempted a late-night stroll around the lake several evenings ago, and had had to change his route not far from the house.

"You might try asking Miss Faraday why she's refused a life basking in your cherishing regard," Hardcastle suggested. "At least on the topic of compound interest, she's blazingly articulate."

"Hardcastle, have you been at the brandy this early in the day? Anne is not a solicitor, to be bored with your talk of business."

Josephine quacked, flapped her wings, and went strutting across the grass in the direction of another duck who'd come wandering up from the lake.

"Anne is a banker's daughter," Hardcastle said. "Can you imagine what the dinner conversation with her dear papa is like? Prinny's debts, Devonshire's racing wagers, the latest gossip on 'Change?"

"She's humoring you, Hardcastle," Sedgemere snapped. "Tossing conversational lures that will tempt you away from your pettifogging Latin aphorisms. What are those ducks about?"

The other duck was craning its neck and flapping its wings. Josephine carried on like a fellow who wanted to cut in partway through a waltz but couldn't attract the dancers' notice.

"Miss Faraday was not humoring me, Sedgemere. She waxed eloquent about a gentleman's education including the basics of finance, for hers certainly did, and she made a strong case for allowing children from a young age to—"

A furious quacking commenced from under the tree as Sedgemere shot to his feet. "That's *it*. That's what she's afraid of. Hardcastle, watch that duck and bring her inside with you, or Ralph will have a fit of the vapors. By God, Hardcastle you have your moments."

Hardcastle rose more slowly. "Whatever are you going on about,

Sedgemere? Perhaps you're having a fit of the vapors." For which his grace was long overdue, in Hardcastle's opinion.

"Ryland told me Anne had explained multiplication to him, when the boy's barely grasped addition and subtraction. He's keen for math, though, so I thought Anne had simply humored a boy's interests. Then there's *exponentially*, and her mama marrying an impecunious banker who's now a damned nabob. I must talk to the duchess."

"While I wrangle quarreling ducks."

"Hardcastle, I do worry about you. Those ducks are not quarreling, and we'll have to change Josephine's name to Joseph."

Hardcastle risked a glance beneath the tree. "One shudders at the company you've dragged me into, Sedgemere. This house party has turned into a debauch for ducks. Why I ever agreed to chaperone you here escapes my traumatized mind. Be about your wooing, and plan to quit this den of iniquity at first light."

"I LOVE HIM," Anne said, "but Sedgemere is a duke. His duchess will be in the public eye, and Nottinghamshire is so very far from London, where Papa must bide."

"Your mama would not like to see you in this state," the Duchess of Veramoor said, passing Anne a plate of French chocolates. They were making Anne sick, these chocolates, but she could not stop eating them.

"Mama's the one who made me promise I'd look after Papa, no matter what." Chocolates deserved a cold glass of milk, or perhaps a tot of fine brandy, not a pot of tepid gunpowder. "I've kept my promise, but Papa shows no signs of retiring, and he can't exactly take on a partner or sell the banks."

Anne had hinted enough in recent years to know he wouldn't. Papa loved the idea of leaving his little girl a stinking fortune, as if a fortune ever sent a lady on a duck hunt in the middle of the night, or loved her witless beneath the Cumbrian moon.

A knock sounded on the door of Her Grace's private parlor. This was the same room where Anne had rejected Sedgemere's proposal, though by day, it was a cheery place. Sunshine poured in the west-facing windows, and beyond the windows, the green expanse of the forest marched up the hillside behind the lake.

The knock came again, louder.

"Enter," the duchess said.

Sedgemere sauntered in, breathtakingly handsome in his country gentleman's attire, not a blond hair out of place and not a hint of warmth about his demeanor. Anne wanted to throw the entire box of chocolates at him and leave in fit of weeping.

And she wanted to have his children.

"Sedgemere, do stop glowering," Her Grace said, thumping the place beside her on the settee. "Your timing is awful. Anne was about to explain to me why she's being so dunderheaded, but I suppose that explanation is better given to you."

To Anne's horror, the duchess rose, helping herself to a chocolate. "Your mother married for love, Anne Faraday. She would not want to see you trapped beneath a heap of money." Her Grace departed, patting Sedgemere's cheek and munching on her chocolate.

"Miss Faraday, will you object if I close the door?" Sedgemere asked.

They were alone and she was no longer *Anne* to him. "You can't close the door," she retorted. "Any passing gossip will note that I'm private with you, *again*, and then all of Hardcastle's attempts to quell the rumors will be for naught. Let's take a final walk around the lake."

"No more perishing perambulations around the lake, if you please. Hardcastle is at this moment presiding over a duck orgy, though a brush with debauchery will do the old boy good. We'll visit the stable."

A duck orgy? Had Anne's rejection cost Sedgemere his reason?

"Come along," Sedgemere said, pulling Anne to her feet. "We

have much to discuss, such as your mendacity, and your lamentable tendency to protect the fellows who give their hearts into your keeping."

That comment made no sense, for Anne had been telling the absolute miserable truth: She loved Sedgemere, and she could not become his duchess. Not ever.

THE PUZZLE PIECES ADDED UP, so to speak, the longer Sedgemere rearranged them in his mind. Anne came along quietly as Sedgemere escorted her to the Veramoor horse palace—many tenant cottages were not so comfortable, even on Sedgemere's estates—and then beyond, to a winding path through the trees.

"If you need privacy to berate me," Anne said, "the stable would have sufficed, Your Grace."

"I would needlessly upset the livestock, did we tarry in the stable, though I do need privacy for what must be said."

"You're a duke, sir. You understand about duty, and your duty is to find a duchess who can look the part and dance the part. She must host your political dinners, endure court functions with you, socialize at the very highest levels, while I've merely been propositioned at the very highest levels, and—Sedgemere, stop."

She untangled her arm from his and stood in a slanting beam of light like some fairy creature who'd disappear if Sedgemere blinked.

"*I love you*," Sedgemere said quietly, though he wanted to bellow the words to every corner of the realm. "And because I love you, madam, you will do me the courtesy of granting me a fair hearing."

His words were intended to capture the lady's attention, but she turned away.

"Unfair, Your Grace. Mortally unfair." Her shoulders were rigid with emotion—also graceful and pale.

Sedgemere wanted to shake her by those elegant, sturdy shoulders. Instead he stepped closer and spoke close to her ear.

"Give me five minutes, Anne Faraday. If after five minutes, you never want to see me again, I will do my utmost to oblige you."

She turned abruptly and gave him such kisses as ought to have set the woods ablaze. Even when they'd made love, Anne hadn't surrendered herself into his embrace with quite this much abandon, this much desperation. She kissed Sedgemere as if she would, indeed, send him packing.

Which would not do. Sedgemere picked his lady up and carried her to a fallen tree, one at the perfect height for a passionate embrace. Anne hauled him closer by the lapels of his coat and spread her knees so Sedgemere could stand between them.

They needed to talk, to sort their future out, but what *they* needed must, for a few moments, yield to what *Anne* needed.

"Anne, we needn't rush," Sedgemere whispered as she started unbuttoning his falls.

"We have no more time," she retorted. "I will miss you until the day I die, but we still have these moments, and Sedgemere, you must not make me beg."

Anne's kisses rather prevented anybody from begging for anything, at least verbally, so Sedgemere pleaded his case with warm caresses to those shoulders he'd admired earlier, and soft murmurs of appreciation for the turn of her knee, the elegant curve of her throat.

"You expect me to make love with you here and now?" Sedgemere whispered before she finished with his falls. "In the forest primeval, not ten yards from—God save me."

Anne's hands went diving beneath layers of expensive Bond Street tailoring, her grip both careful and determined.

"I want you," she said. "If this is all I can have of you, then please oblige me."

"I'm not the condemned prisoner's last meal," Sedgemere said, frothing skirts and petticoats up around the lady's waist. "I'm your intended, and the man who loves you."

He settled the argument with one sure thrust—or at least silenced Anne's reply—and then desire took over, until the far branches of the fallen tree upon which Anne perched were swaying to the give and take of Sedgemere's passion.

With Anne so desperate and silent, Sedgemere's desire became driven by a need to relieve her fears for their future. He slowed the pace and gentled his kisses, until the quiet of the woods, the stillness of the lake became a part of his lovemaking.

"I do love you," he said. "I will always love you."

"Elias, you must not—" Anne didn't finish that thought, which was prudent of her, because Sedgemere *would*, all afternoon if necessary. He'd caress her lovely breasts, kiss her beautiful shoulders, and silence her remonstrations with pleasure.

She allowed him enough time that his thighs eventually burned, the discomfort a small testament to a lover's devotion, and then his heart ached, when Anne seized the initiative and surrendered to satisfaction.

"You think I'll leave you now?" he said, stroking a hand over her hair. "You think I'll withdraw and abandon you, because your place is running your father's households as a dutiful spinster daughter?"

"You must," she said, though her arms remained lashed about his waist. "Tomorrow morning, Elias, you must return to Nottinghamshire, and I'll away to York."

Tonight, he'd announce their engagement, but first, Sedgemere undertook to give his lady the rest of the pleasure due her. He let his love for her fly free, let it show in every caress and thrust and kiss and moan, until Anne was again clinging to him, and whispering his name. He held off long enough to be sure she'd found satisfaction, and then he joined her in that place where nothing—not duty, not time, not fear or even worry—could crowd past the love he shared with her.

LOVE AND HATE were not opposites, they were... close cousins, for the more Anne loved Sedgemere, the more she hated what her life had become.

A fortune in lies and deceptions, a wearying farce that had no end. She loved her papa, of course, and she understood that a banker had obligations, a sacred duty based on trust. Far more depended on the trust placed in Papa than Anne's mere happiness.

A bank's good health could uphold that of a nation or a monarchy. A bank failing could be the ruin of many innocent lives. Her mother had taught her that almost before Anne could stitch a straight seam.

"Your bottom cannot be comfortable," Sedgemere said, scooping Anne off the tree trunk and setting her on her feet. "The rest of you is woefully unmussed."

Her mind was mussed. In moments, Sedgemere was buttoned up, his shirt tails tucked in, every evidence of their recent lovemaking gone, while Anne...

"I need your handkerchief, Your Grace."

A square of white linen appeared on Sedgemere's palm, held out to Anne as if on a tray. "So you do."

She didn't bother turning her back, but reached under her skirts and made use of the handkerchief, while Sedgemere hiked himself to sit on the fallen tree, an oak, from the looks of the wilting leaves.

"I'll take that," Sedgemere said, when Anne had finished.

He was so matter-of-fact about such earthy intimacies. Anne would not have predicted this about him, any more than she would have predicted his abilities as a steward of sheep races.

"I'll miss you," she said, folding the cloth carefully to hide evidence of its use. "I'll miss the boys too, but I think Hardcastle has been largely effective quelling any gossip about our kiss in the linen closet."

"You were right, you know," Sedgemere replied, tucking the handkerchief into a jacket pocket. "Josephine is a drake. You're also quite wrong, about missing me. You will have little occasion to miss me, when we're married. You might, however, miss very much being the brains behind your papa's vast financial empire. As your husband, I'll see that you remain at the helm of his fortune to the extent that's where you'd like to be."

SEDGEMERE CURSED himself for a henwit when Anne silently braced herself against the tree trunk, as if she'd been informed of a great loss. He slid to his feet and pulled her into his embrace rather than risk her leaving him alone in the forest.

"Your mother had the same gift, I'd guess," he said. "It is a gift, you know, to be able to grasp finances, to see possibilities where others see only boring figures and limitations."

She was light in his arms, no more leaning on him than a beam of sunshine would lean on a breeze.

"From a young age," Sedgemere went on, "probably before your mama died, you've carried the burden of your father's banking enterprises on your own shoulders. You've chosen the investments, the projects, the risks, while he's gossiped at the clubs and signed the documents."

She shook her head, a curl coming loose from her bun. "You must not say such things. Papa is the banker. His grandfather started the bank, and Papa knows every customer, every account, every balance."

"But he doesn't grasp *money*," Sedgemere said. "He was struggling badly when your mother took him in hand, and he'd have lost several fortunes by now if you hadn't kept him from unwise investments. You read the papers voraciously, you correspond with him several times a day, and you've advised Hardcastle on his finances without His Grace even realizing it."

Anne began to shake, like a fading leaf in a strong autumn wind. "Sedgemere, you cannot believe that I, a mere spinster daughter, could hold the reins to some of the greatest fortunes in the realm. I manage the household, I deal with squabbling housemaids. I don't even know the names on many of the accounts."

Sedgemere tucked that stray curl back in its place when he wanted to undo her coiffure entirely.

"You make it a point not to know the names, to insist your father speak to you in hypotheticals and exercise what discretion he can. Nonetheless, the bank and all its titled, arrogant clients rely on you to increase the wealth in its coffers. That's what the flock of pigeons and platoon of special messengers are about. That's why you can explain multiplication to a boy who disliked addition and subtraction. That's why you will marry me."

She tore from his embrace and stomped off, deeper into the woods. "Don't you see, Sedgemere, Papa will fail without me. He nearly failed when Mama died, but she'd warned me I'd have to step in. He was about to invest in tulips—tulips, of all the cautionary tales! —and I could not keep silent. Once he realized that I was as capable as Mama had been, he expected that I'd sort matters out."

"And you've been sorting them ever since," Sedgemere said, resisting the urge to haul her back into his arms. "You've done so well that his business has grown *exponentially*, and now you dare not take your hand off the tiller for even a few weeks."

She swung around to face him and crossed her arms, a feminine citadel of exasperation. "Not even for a few days. Papa takes odd notions and gets ahead of himself, and while I would love to be your wife, Sedgemere, I cannot have the fate of royal dukes and presuming earls on my hands. Papa could ruin them, especially now when they all trust him to produce such excellent returns. The Postlethwaites were courting ruin until two years ago. The Cheshires cannot afford another Season for both daughters. You see my predicament."

Sedgemere saw her brilliance, her frustration, her predicament, and her honor.

He also saw his future duchess. "My love, you have needed a partner. Your father was sensible enough to accept your help when it was offered. Will you be as wise? All that's wanted is a duke at your beck and call, a fellow somewhat wanting for charm, but well-endowed with consequence and devoted to you."

He took another step closer, for he had her attention. "I'll simply tell your dear papa that he's to dine with us once a week without fail, and that he's to hire the manager of your choosing, who will report to you. Hannibal will not sign a document without your permission, will not commit to an investment unless you've discussed it with him. I will further bruit it about that the ducal finances, including your dower funds, will be entrusted to his bank for safekeeping."

As Sedgemere stalked closer, Anne unfolded her arms. "You'd have me manage my own fortune?"

"Mine too, if you have time. I'll be too busy loving my wife and creating trouble in the Lords. Or keeping kites from disappearing into trees, stewarding sheep races, dandling our babies on my knee. If you enjoy finances, it's my duty to see that you may have as much diversion in that regard as you please—and as little burden. A duke knows all about duty, my dear, but he needs the right duchess to teach him about happily ever afters and true love."

A DUCK QUACKED SOMEWHERE OUT on the lake, and a breeze presumed to tease at Sedgemere's hair. His tone was very stern, but his eyes were no longer an arctic wilderness to Anne. His eyes held promises, and challenges, and such a steady regard her heart warmed to behold him.

That he'd puzzled out her situation didn't surprise her that much, though he'd found her out much more quickly than she'd anticipated. She had not, however, expected that his reaction would be to... solve her dilemma.

"I like money," she said, lest he mistake the matter. "I like making money grow like that magical beanstalk, and grow with the slow inexorability of the moonrise, grow every which way in between." Grow like her feelings for Sedgemere. "I like interest calculations, and formulas, and ledgers that balance to the penny. I can chase a missing penny for hours."

Sedgemere stood very close. "I can make love with you for hours."

Anne had enjoyed a taste of that, when she'd nearly torn his clothes from his body, and he'd met her frantic overtures with slow, steady, relentless desire. Sedgemere's self-control had taken her breath away, and driven her nearly to Bedlam at the thought of having to give him up.

She smoothed her fingers over the lock of his hair sent amiss by the wind. "I like money, I do not like being its slave, Sedgemere. You must keep your hand in the finances, help me manage Papa, and ensure I have time to hunt for lucky clovers."

She longed, not only to be rescued from her inherited burdens, but also to have all the happiness life as Sedgemere's wife and mother of his children could dream of. Wealth mattered not at all without somebody to share it.

Anne had learned that lesson four hundred thousand pounds ago. She had never learned how to beg, though. Sedgemere held her heart in his hands, and all she could do was await his decision.

He gazed out over the lake, his expression inscrutable. "Will you search for those treasures in the locations of my choosing? The lucky clovers and such? A few might be stashed in the places you've yet to thoroughly inspect."

Relief and gratitude, sweet and profound, coursed through Anne. She need not be her papa's abacus ever again—Sedgemere would intercede when she felt overburdened—and she need never carry another burden in solitary misery either.

"You are all the treasure I will ever need, Elias. You and the boys, and Joseph too, of course."

Sedgemere's arms came around her, Anne leaned into him, and before they returned to the house, she did, indeed, find an entire bouquet of lucky clovers in some very unlikely places.

EPILOGUE

"Anne looks different to me," Hardcastle said as he and Sedgemere sat down to the obligatory rare beefsteak and undercooked potato featured in London's most exclusive gentlemen's clubs. On a blustery late autumn day, the place at least had a roaring fire in its dining room. "She seems... happier."

Though how taking Sedgemere in hand could add to a woman's happiness, Hardcastle did not know. Sedgemere seemed happier too. He swore less frequently, reduced fewer presuming earls to quivering wrecks in the Lords, and no longer plagued Hardcastle night and day about finding a bride.

Tedious business, bride hunting, but Hardcastle's own grandmama had taken up the cudgels, and seeing Sedgemere and his duchess billing and cooing restored a man's faith in miracles. Thank goodness, Hardcastle had a nephew in the nursery to prevent Grandmama from declaring outright war on his bachelorhood. Finding the right duchess would require care and planning, nerves of steel, and a well-developed sense of martyrdom.

"Please pass the damned salt," Sedgemere snapped. "Are you quite well, Hardcastle? I'm not in the habit of repeating my requests."

"Yes, you are," Hardcastle replied, passing the salt cellar. "Until you get exactly what you want. When is the blessed event?"

The delicate silver spoon Sedgemere had been dredging through the salt paused. "Did Anne tell you?"

Well, damn. "You told me. Your step is lighter, you bring up the boys more often than you mention whatever scheme you're hatching with Moreland regarding the Corn Laws. You dragged me to a shop that sells kites last Tuesday. Marriage agrees with you. Ergo, a blessed event becomes likely."

Sedgemere sprinkled salt just so over his beefsteak. The potatoes were hopeless, but Hardcastle passed the butter anyway.

"I should become a papa again in the spring," Sedgemere said. "I'm shamelessly hoping for a daughter, and so are the boys. Don't think you're safe though."

Sedgemere was safe at last. A man at risk of becoming a stodgy old duke had been rescued by a banker's daughter and a few weeks of duck hunting, as it were. Hardcastle congratulated himself on having played matchmaker with no one the wiser.

"I am a duke," Hardcastle said, taking a sip of a red wine more hearty than delicate. "No one would dare harm my person. Ergo, I am safe. Grandmama would kill the matchmakers for even trying to usurp her right to plague me herself on the matter of matrimony."

"As would I, as would Anne, and the boys too. You are not safe, however, from the Duchess of Sedgemere's latest ambition. Aren't you having anything to eat?"

Ambitious duchesses ought to be outlawed by royal decree. Hardcastle poured himself more wine.

"I'd rather hear about these ambitions you've allowed your wife to develop, for I sense they do not bode well for your oldest and dearest friend." Also, possibly Sedgemere's loneliest friend, though a duke became inured to loneliness.

"Anne has your happiness in mind," Sedgemere said. "I'm mentioning her plans because you're owed a warning. Once the baby arrives, Anne will turn her attention to organizing a house party.

She's been in correspondence with Her Grace of Veramoor, and your days as a single duke are numbered, my friend."

"This is the thanks I get for finding you a wife?" Hardcastle retorted. "For presiding at a duck orgy, and becoming godfather to no less than five waddling little god-ducklings? Now your own duchess is plotting a house party, and my name is on the guest list? Sedgemere, you disappoint me."

Though the betrayal was sweet. Sedgemere's duchess had him firmly in hand. Probably regularly in hand, too. Envy tried to crowd its way onto Hardcastle's dinner menu, but he fended it off by focusing on the threat immediately before him.

"When is this bacchanal to take place?" Hardcastle asked.

"You have plenty of time, not until summer, when all the best bacchanals take place. You might consider spending the summer in France."

Not again. France, Ireland, Scotland... Weariness joined envy as additions to the evening's menu.

"Grandmama will never allow me to decline an invitation from Sedgemere House," Hardcastle said. "I suppose we'll have sheep races at this gathering too?"

Sedgemere sat back, crossing his knife and fork over his mostly empty plate. Marriage must have given Sedgemere an appetite, for Hardcastle had found the food utterly ignorable.

"You're just jealous," Sedgemere said, which was true enough. "I'm the better sheep-race steward, and you know it. We probably will have sheep races, because the boys are insistent that Christopher come along with you to the house party."

Christopher, the nephew who grew three inches every time Hardcastle visited the nursery.

"What do we have to do to get some trifle in this establishment?" Hardcastle muttered. "You'd have me drag an innocent child the length of the realm so he might be inducted into the royal order of sheep jockeys. My upbringing was deprived, I see that now."

His upbringing *had* been deprived, of course, so had Sedgemere's.

They'd been ducal heirs from too young an age, not allowed to be boys much less rascals or sheep jockeys. Christopher deserved better, though hauling him from Kent up to Nottinghamshire would also mean...

"Hardcastle, that expression does not bode well for the king's peace."

"The poor king sired fifteen children," Hardcastle replied, signaling the waiter. "He'll never have peace again. If Christopher is to attend this house party—assuming it ever takes place—his governess will have to travel north with us and join the assemblage for the duration."

"Ah, the trifle arrives," Sedgemere said, as one waiter removed the dinner plates, and another set a frothy, fruity confection before each duke. "Eat up, Hardcastle. For nothing you can say or do, promise or threaten, will tempt me to get your name off Anne's guest list."

"Don't be needlessly puerile," Hardcastle said, taking a spoonful of creamy, delectable heaven. "I know my duty. Eat your trifle, Sedgemere. If Christopher and I are invited to this house party, to this house party we will go."

Though they would not go without Christopher's devoted governess, of that, Hardcastle was most certain.

Read on for Hardcastle's happily ever after...

MAY I HAVE THIS DUKE?

by Grace Burrowes

Originally published in the novella anthology
Dancing in the Duke's Arms

Dedicated to the care givers

CHAPTER ONE

"You wished to see me, Your Grace?"

Gerard Juvenal René Beaumarchand Hammersley, Eighth Duke of Hardcastle, pretended for one more moment to study his list of tenants, because he emphatically did not wish to *see* Miss Ellen MacHugh. The woman destroyed his focus simply by entering a room, and when she spoke, whatever remained of Hardcastle's mental processes came to an indecorous, gaping halt.

An indecorous, gaping, *sniffing* halt, because Miss MacHugh had the great temerity to carry about her person the scents of lavender and lilacs.

The duke rose, for Miss MacHugh was a lady, albeit a lady in his employ. "Please have a seat, Miss MacHugh. I trust you're well?"

They'd perfected a system, such that they could dwell in the same house for much of the year, but go for days without speaking. Weeks even. Hardcastle's record was thirty-three days straight, though admittedly, he'd been ill for part of that time.

She, by contrast, had the constitution of a plough horse. She never lost her poise either, while he fumbled for words in her presence or prosed on about the weather.

Or some other inanity.

"I am well, Your Grace. Thank you for inquiring. Christopher is well too."

"If he were unwell, and you had failed to notify me, you'd be without a post, madam."

She dipped her chin, a rather stubborn little chin. Her hair was dark russet, and her height was sadly wanting, but that chin could be very expressive.

Miss MacHugh was not willowy, she was not blond, she was not subservient, she was not—oh, her faults were endless. She wasn't even entirely English, her mother hailing from the Scottish region of Peeblesshire.

"Did you summon me for a reason, sir?"

Hardcastle clasped his hands behind his back, marched to the library window, and attempted to recall what lapse of sense had prompted him to summon—ah, yes.

"I'm to attend a house party up in Nottinghamshire," he said. "Christopher will accompany me, and you will accompany the boy."

"When do we leave, Your Grace?"

"We leave Tuesday. Please ensure Christopher has everything he might require for a two-week stay in the country. You and he will share the traveling coach, and I will go on horseback. Thank you, that will be all."

She rose to her inconsequential height, and yet, such was Ellen MacHugh's presence that Hardcastle remained by the window, yielding the rest of the library to her.

"Has Your Grace considered tutors to take over Christopher's education?" she asked.

What queer start was this? "He's barely six years old, Miss MacHugh. Unless I mistake the matter, the boy is learning what he needs to learn from you. I hadn't any tutors until I was eight."

She flicked a gaze over him that nearly shouted: *And look how well that turned out.* "Christopher is exceedingly bright, Your Grace, and eager to learn."

"As was I. Unless you believe a six-year-old boy's education to be beyond you, this conversation has reached its conclusion."

More and more often, when Hardcastle spoke, his grandfather's voice emerged, condescending, gruff, and arrogant. Had Robin lived, he'd have laughed himself silly at his older brother's metamorphosis into a curmudgeon-in-training.

"I'll take my leave of you then, sir. I'd like to call one other item to Your Grace's attention, though."

Hardcastle knew that tone and knew what it portended. Miss MacHugh was preparing to scold her employer.

The woman excelled at scolding her employer. She'd been in the nursery for nearly three months before Hardcastle had realized what her gentle, polite, well-reasoned discourses were. He'd been slow to catch on, because a duke of mature years had little to no experience being scolded.

By anyone.

"Unburden yourself, Miss MacHugh. What item remains for us to discuss?"

She had the most beautiful complexion. All roses and cream, with a few faint, delicate freckles across her cheeks. Hardcastle knew better than to stand within freckle-counting range, because when he got that close to her, his thumbs ached to brush over her features.

Aching thumbs on a duke were the outside of absurd.

"I'm giving notice, Your Grace, of my intention to quit my post. I thought you might like some warning. If we leave on Tuesday, and the house party lasts two weeks, you should expect my departure from your household at the end of the house party. I leave it to you to explain the situation to Christopher at the time and place of your choosing. Good day, sir."

She offered him a graceful curtsey and bustled off toward the door.

Hardcastle strode to the door as well, and because his legs were significantly longer, and his resolve every bit a match for Miss MacHugh's, he was first to reach their destination.

"Miss MacHugh, after living under my roof for three years, caring for my heir, and otherwise functioning as a member of this household day in and day out, you simply announce an intention to leave?"

Of course she'd want to leave *him*. He was a demanding, ill-tempered, patently unfriendly employer. Hardcastle could not fathom how she'd leave the boy, though.

"This is how it's done, Your Grace. The employee gives notice, the employer writes a glowing character. You wish me well, and I thank you for all you've done for me."

She peered at him encouragingly, as if willing him to repeat that sequence of disasters back to her.

"All I have done is pay the modest wages you tirelessly earn, madam, but this giving of notice will not answer. In Nottinghamshire, I'll be expected to socialize morning, noon, and night. The entire region is infested with dukes, thus its unfortunate style, the Dukeries. Because I myself am a duke—lest you forget that detail—I am obligated to exchange courtesy visits with half the shire."

He kept his hand on the door latch, in case she took a notion to flee before he'd made his point. "How can I find a replacement for you if I'm dodging the hopeful young ladies?" Hardcastle went on. "Shall I interview your successor when I'm playing cards until all hours with the fellows? When I'm rising at dawn to ruin good boots tramping about in the fog, shooting at pheasants, drunken viscounts, or other low-flying game?"

Miss MacHugh turned her smile on Hardcastle, proving once again that she had no conscience. Her smile would make small boys confess to felonies and large boys long for privacy, preferably with her, a freshly made bed, and a few bottles of excellent spirits.

"Your Grace is an eminently resourceful fellow," she said. "If you turn your mind to locating a successor for me, then I'm sure a parade of candidates will materialize in the servants' parlor in an instant."

Ellen MacHugh was a temple to mendacity, pretending to compliment him, while instead mocking his consequence.

"My agenda for this house party, Miss MacHugh, is to locate a candidate for the position of Duchess of Hardcastle. Her Grace, my grandmother, claims I have forgotten to tend to this task and must address the oversight before I'm a pathetic, graying embarrassment, falling asleep over the port and importuning the housemaids. I'm to parade myself before the debutantes and matchmakers, sacrifice myself once again on the altar of duty, and for good measure, be a good sport about surrendering my bachelorhood."

And in the depths of the ducal heart, Hardcastle suppressed a plea as honest as it was dismaying: *Don't let them take me.* Ellen MacHugh wouldn't deride him for that sentiment either, for she was a woman who treasured her independence fiercely.

The corners of her serene smile faltered. "Her Grace is a formidable woman. I can understand why you'd make her request a priority. But tell me, sir, how does one *forget* to get married?"

One became a ducal heir at age seven, a duke at thirteen, and arrived to the age of three-and-thirty with one freedom, and one freedom only, still intact.

"I expect, Miss MacHugh, I neglected to marry the same way you did. I occupied myself with other, less disagreeable matters. Doubtless, you will now admit that your departure from the household would be most inconsiderate, particularly at this juncture. I will regard the topic as closed until further notice."

Russet brows twitched, a gratifying hint of consternation from a woman who was the soul of self-possession.

"You have my leave to return to the nursery, madam." They stood near the door, within freckle-counting range. The fragrance of lilacs and lavender, like a brisk, sunny morning, provoked Hardcastle into opening the door for his nephew's governess, as if he were a common footman.

"Your Grace, I do apologize for the timing of my decision, but this once, I cannot change my plans for your convenience. I have reason to believe another situation awaits me. You have just shy of a month to replace me, sir. If you do find a lady willing to be your duchess, she will certainly take an interest in choosing Christopher's next governess."

Then Miss MacHigh-and-Mighty was gone, gently pulling the door closed behind her.

The voice of the previous duke nattered on in Hardcastle's head, about good riddance to a woman who'd never known her place, and governesses being thick on the ground, and small boys of excellent station needing to learn early not to grow attached to their inferiors.

The seventh duke had been an arrogant old windbag. With a couple of bottles of port in him, he'd had the verbal stamina of a Presbyterian preacher amid a flock of adulterers.

The eighth duke didn't care for port. He liked Ellen MacHugh's self-possession, her good opinion of herself, her boldness before her betters, and her infernally alluring freckles.

Hardcastle had never admired *or desired* a woman more than he did Miss Ellen MacHugh. She had no use for him, though, so perhaps he'd best find a replacement for her after all.

"HE'S GROWING WORSE," Ellen said, hems whipping about her boots in the confines of the housekeeper's sitting room. Two days after her interview with the duke, she was still upset with him. "I didn't think Hardcastle could grow worse. He informed me that accepting a post in the north would not suit his convenience. 'Doubtless,' sayeth the duke, 'you will now admit that your departure from the household would be most inconsiderate.' God help the poor woman who must conceive children with him. She'll suffer frostbite in a delicate location."

"Ellen, that is unkind and unladylike."

Dorcas Snelling had been housekeeper to the Duke of Hardcastle since the present titleholder had been in dresses. She was the closest thing Ellen had to a friend, but when it came to ducal infallibility, Dorcas might as well have been a papist discussing an especially virtuous pope. Dorcas was at that moment embroidering golden flowers on the hem of a curtain that would hang in the ducal dressing closet, for pity's sake.

"I barely exaggerate Hardcastle's sangfroid," Ellen rejoined. "He can't even bring himself to look down his nose at me, and he has a deal of nose to look down."

On the coal man such a nose might have been unfortunate; on Hardcastle, it was splendidly ducal. Shoulders broad enough to do a Yorkshire ploughman proud were also ducal on Hardcastle. Dark eyebrows that put Ellen in mind of a pirate prince were—on Hardcastle—ducal.

His stern mouth was ducal, and his silences were nearly regal. The only feature that defied the title was Hardcastle's hair, which was as curly and unruly as Christopher's, albeit much darker.

"You're determined to leave?" Mrs. Snelling asked, knotting off a gold thread.

"I never meant to stay this long, but Christopher has wrapped his grubby paws around my heart. Now His Grace is determined to marry, and Christopher will have an aunt to look after his welfare."

To be fair, Hardcastle was a conscientious guardian. Christopher's material needs were met in every particular, and when the head footman had raised his voice to the boy for sliding down the front banister, His Grace had sent the man to a lesser estate in East Anglia.

Christopher had been denied any outings on his pony for a week. Only a duke would fail to see that the governess was the one punished by such a scheme. Christopher's abuse of the banister had happened on Ellen's half day, but she'd made sure his unruly behavior hadn't reoccurred.

"Miss MacHugh!" The boy himself came charging into the housekeeper's sitting room. "I've found you. Nurse says I mightn't have to come in if you're willing to walk with me in the garden, but I had to come in to ask you. I found a grasshopper, and eleven ants, and four butterflies. That's a lot."

"It's a pretty day," Ellen said, extending a hand to Christopher. "A walk in the garden will help us settle to our French when we come in. How many insects did you see in all, Christopher?'

"A lot?"

"Let's count, shall we?"

While Ellen walked the child through a basic exercise in addition, she also tried to memorize the garden where she'd spent many peaceful hours over the past three years. The roses were beyond their glory, but the perennials—daisies, hollyhocks, foxglove, salvia, verbena, lavender—were still in good form.

Come Tuesday, Ellen would leave this place, despite His Grace's fuming and pouting.

She'd miss Hardway Hall, miss the routine and orderliness of it, miss the child she'd come to love ferociously, and even miss the duke. He was predictable in his severe demeanor, he paid punctually, and he didn't intrude into the nursery. Without intending it, Hardcastle had provided Ellen a place to heal her wounds and mourn her dreams.

Many women hadn't even those luxuries.

"Why do roses have thorns?" Christopher asked, sniffing a rose without touching it anywhere. He was a careful boy, but not a worried boy. Ellen would miss him until her dying day.

"Thorns protect the roses from being grabbed carelessly," Ellen said, "from being eaten by passing bears, from being handled without respect."

Would to God young ladies were given a few thorns before the young men came sniffing about.

"I like daisies better," Christopher said. "They aren't the color of blood, and they don't make you bleed if you touch them. Daisies are happy."

Christopher was happy, curious, and full of energy. He ran down the length of the rose border, made a turn past the end of the laburnum alley, and was pelting back in Ellen's direction when he came to an abrupt stop.

Where an exuberant little boy had stood, a ducal heir appeared, suggesting His Grace was approaching from the stables. Christopher drew his shoulders back, swiped a hand over his hair, and drained all animation from his features in the time it took for a breeze to set the laburnum leaves dancing.

In other words, Christopher was trying to be good.

"Christopher, greetings," said the duke, striding along the crushed-shell walk. "Shouldn't you be at your studies?"

Christopher shot Ellen a look, a plea for intervention. Soon enough, she would be unable to intercede for the boy. Perhaps the new duchess would be kind, though. Ellen could hope for that.

"We are at our lessons, Your Grace," Ellen said. "What better place to learn botany than in a garden?"

The duke treated her to one of those reserved, slightly annoyed perusals, as if from one day to the next, he forgot who Ellen was and how she'd come to be in his household.

"Miss MacHugh, good day."

"We're taking a walk," Christopher said, making a grab for the duke's glove, but stopping short and tucking his own little hand behind his back, much as his uncle often did. "I'm counting bugs, and Miss MacHugh was explaining about thorns."

"Who better to discourse on the topic of thorns? Perhaps I'll walk with you."

Christopher was so enthralled with this prospect, he spun in a circle. "Please, sir! I know lots of flowers, and birds, and how each bird sings differently so his friends and family will hear him. I know I must never, ever, ever touch the laburnum, anywhere, and don't let anybody or anything eat any part of it."

"My garden is apparently full of hazards," Hardcastle remarked.

Was the duke waiting for Ellen to invite him to join them? And why was he going on about thorns and hazards?

"Your garden is beautiful, sir," Ellen said. "Please share it with us."

He stared at the laburnum as if it too, were some sort of interloper he didn't recall hiring. "I knew the laburnum was poisonous. I got the same lectures as a boy Christopher did, but I'd forgotten."

The duke winged his arm, a courtesy he'd rarely shown Ellen before. She took it, because that was what a lady did when a gentleman was on his manners.

"Many other plants are equally dangerous," she said, "but we admire them, carefully, for their beauty or other properties. Then there's foxglove, which can help at the proper dose and kill at an improper one."

"You are not a governess," Hardcastle said. "You are a professor in disguise. How am I to replace you?"

"Please don't wheedle, Your Grace. My nerves couldn't bear it."

"Nor mine, alas," he said, in perfect seriousness.

Christopher had galloped off toward the heartsease, which enjoyed a shady bed near the fountain. Even in high summer, they were doing well, for temperatures in recent weeks had remained moderate.

"I have a rehearsed apology," the duke said, leading Ellen to a wooden bench. "I can't seem to recall it now that the moment to recite has presented itself. I planned to summon you to the library so I could express my remorse for our last conversation."

"No such expression is needed, Your Grace." Though even for him, he'd been high-handed—or nervous? "I will leave my post at the end of this house party, nonetheless. I suggest you explain the situation to Christopher so he'll have time to adjust."

"He won't adjust," Hardcastle said, taking off his gloves and using them to bat imaginary dust from the bench. "Will you sit with me, Miss MacHugh?"

Ellen wanted to refuse Hardcastle, for the simple, contrary novelty of thwarting him, but also because a duke in an apologetic mood upset the balance between them. She was not, however, a recalcitrant schoolgirl overdue for an outing, so she took a seat.

"I was seven when my parents died," Hardcastle said, coming down beside Ellen, and stuffing his gloves in a pocket. "My grandfather had been traveling on the Continent, and it took him some months to return to England. He came swooping into our lives like the wrath of King George, and nothing was ever the same."

"Losing our loved ones is hard." Losing just this pretty, peaceful garden would break Ellen's heart.

"I was managing," Hardcastle said, "as was Lord Robin, mostly because we had a fine governess. Miss Henckel maintained order and routine for us, let us have our tantrums and sulks as we adjusted to the loss of our parents. She knew when to discipline and when to look the other way. Miss Henckel alone took on the burden of explaining to us what was afoot when Papa's coach overturned. I was... attached to her."

Ellen suspected the duke's disclosure was a revelation even to him, but she couldn't afford to waver.

"Not fair, Your Grace. Christopher's parents died three years ago, and he's a happy little boy. He has the staff wrapped around his finger, he has every comfort, and you will not make me responsible for his happiness and well-being. He has *you* for that."

"I hardly know the boy."

His Grace regretted this state of affairs, apparently, but for the first time, Ellen realized why the duke had kept his distance from Christopher, another orphan thrust into the role of ducal heir at a tender age.

"What happened to Miss Henckel?" Ellen asked.

"She was replaced with tutors, of course, and then public school and university. Grandfather and the trustees he chose for me did not believe in coddling a ducal heir."

"I'm sorry," Ellen said, though offering condolences to Hardcastle was an odd turn in their dealings. "The one adult you loved should not have been taken from you when the rest of your life was in chaos. Christopher's life is not in chaos."

At the other end of the fountain, Christopher experimented with passing a stick through the spray and momentarily re-directing the flow of the water. A green maple leaf came drifting down to land on the duke's muscular thigh, a bright contrast to his fawn riding breeches.

He took the leaf in his fingers, twirling it by the stem. "I was fond of Miss Henckel. In any case, I acknowledge that you have the right to abandon your post with proper notice. I do not like it, but I could have turned you off without a character at any point, and you would not have liked that."

"Your Grace is a scrupulously fair man," Ellen said. "You would not have treated me thus." He wouldn't treat anybody with such disregard for common decency, though his version of the civilities and fair play was frosty, at best.

"I want to treat you badly," he said, tossing the leaf into the fountain. "I'm quite wroth with you, madam." He didn't sound angry. He sounded rueful, like a small boy who must abandon the garden for his French lessons.

In the quiet end of the fountain's pool, the leaf spun slowly this way and that as the breezes and currents shifted.

"We have, from time to time, been out of charity with each other," Ellen said. "I'm sure we'll muddle through this as well. I'll help look for a replacement." She could not say more, not with the boy at the other end of the fountain.

She patted the duke's hand—his bare hand—and abruptly was hit with a faint, cool mist across her cheek.

"Sorry!" Christopher bellowed, chortling merrily. "I'm trying to water the flowers!"

"Trying to get a birching," the duke muttered, rising and extending a hand to Ellen. "He's nearly as bad as I was at his age. Have I apologized for my brusque demeanor adequately, Miss MacHugh?"

He'd explained more than apologized, but the explanation was the greater gift. Ellen put her hand in his.

"Your apology is accepted, sir."

He stood for a moment peering down at her, their hands joined. They hadn't touched like this before, bare-handed, casually. Or rather, Ellen hadn't touched His Grace. Had he been waiting for that overture before presuming himself?

"My objective is accomplished then. Find a way to accidentally knock the boy into the fountain. He'll love you for it." The duke bowed and marched off through the laburnum alley, while Christopher shrieked something about having found a great, brown warty toad.

PRIDE, even ducal pride, could carry a man only so far.

Hardcastle's pride had carried him three miles beyond the coaching inn, three miles of wet verge, muddy road, and relentless rain. Three miles of cold trickling down the back of his neck no matter the angle of his sodden top hat and no matter how many times he adjusted the collar of his great coat.

Ajax bore it all stoically—he was the personal mount of a duke, after all—but when thunder rumbled to the north, and lightning joined the affray, Ajax's equine dignity threatened to desert him.

Hardcastle signaled John Coachman to pull up, tied Ajax to the back of the coach, and climbed inside.

"Uncle! We're playing the color game. You're very wet!"

"Miss MacHugh, your charge is a prodigy." Where did one sit when one was a large, sodden duke who reeked of wet horse, muddy boots, and disgust with this entire outing? Hardcastle shrugged out of his great coat and hung it on a peg on the back of the coach door.

"Christopher is a bright boy, Your Grace," her governess-ship replied. "I tell him that frequently."

Miss MacHugh sat on the forward-facing seat beside Christopher, both of them dry and cozy, the boy having the audacity to smile.

Nothing for it then.

A gentleman did not drip indiscriminately on a lady or on a child. Hardcastle took the backward-facing seat and silently cursed all house parties.

"My grandmother will answer for this," he muttered, taking off his hat and getting a brimful of frigid rain water across his *lap* for his efforts. "If it's not the blazing heat, the flies and the dust, it's the mud, the rain, and the cold."

"I'm not cold," Christopher said. "Would you like to play our game with us, sir?"

Hardcastle would rather have throttled his dear grandmama. "A duke, as a rule, hasn't time for games."

The child's face fell, which was durance vile for the uncle sitting across from him. Christopher wasn't to blame for the weather, or for the queasiness that had already begun to plague Hardcastle. Worse, Miss MacHugh's expression had gone carefully blank, as if once again, Mr. Higginbotham had arrived at Sunday services tipsy.

Farmer Higginbotham was probably still tipsy on a Wednesday afternoon, also warm and dry by his own hearth.

"I find," Hardcastle said, "that the luxury of time has been afforded me by the foul weather, the execrable roads, and the boon of present company. What is this color game?'

"Does that mean he'll play?" the boy asked his governess.

"Not everybody has the skill to play the color game, Christopher," Miss MacHugh said, brushing her hand over the child's golden curls. "We've had plenty of practice, while His Grace will be a complete beginner."

"You are no great respecter of dukes, are you, Miss MacHugh?" Hardcastle asked.

"I respect you greatly, sir, but the color game requires imagination and quickness, and Christopher is very good at it."

"Alas, then I am doomed to defeat, being a slow, dull fellow. How does one play this game?"

The coach swayed and jostled along, Hardcastle's belly rebelled strenuously against traveling on a backward-facing bench, and across from him, governess and prodigy exchanged a smile that was diabolically sweet. For a moment, they were a single entity of impish glee, delighted with each other and their circumstances.

For that same moment, Hardcastle forgot he was cold, wet, and queasy, and nearly forgot he was a duke.

"It's simple, sir," Christopher said. "One person picks out an object, then we take turns naming as many colors as we can that describe the object. The person with the most colors wins. I'll give you an example," the boy went on, his manner as patient and thorough as any duke's. "Your breeches are brown, gray near your boots, and buckskin. Also... sort of umbrage where the mud has splashed on them."

"Umber," Miss MacHugh corrected gently—smirkingly. "Umbrage refers to indignation. Umber is a rusty, sienna, orange-y dark brown."

"The game seems simple enough," Hardcastle said. Also tedious and pointless, but not entirely without possibilities. "Let's describe the colors in Miss MacHugh's hair."

"Keen!" Christopher chortled. "Miss MacHugh's hair is ever so pretty, but she's wearing her bonnet."

"She might be willing to part with her bonnet," the duke replied, stretching out his legs and taking care not to let his boots come near her pristine hems. "For the sake of my education regarding the pressing topic of colors, of course."

Sitting backward did not agree with Hardcastle, being damp and cold did not agree with him. Ruffling Miss MacHugh's feathers was unworthy of him, but agreed with him rather well.

"The difficulty," Miss MacHugh said, "is that I cannot assess my own hair as thoroughly as the other players in the game. I will oblige by removing my bonnet, but cannot participate in this round."

She managed to get her bonnet off without disturbing a single tidy hair on her head, then looked about for a place to stash her millinery. Hardcastle took the hat from her and put it on the seat beside him. A hopelessly plain, straw bonnet, but also a prize surrendered into his keeping.

"I'll go first," Christopher offered, turning a serious expression to his governess. "This is a good opening round, sir."

Miss MacHugh smoothed a hand over her skirts. No rings, not even a touch of lace at her cuffs, and yet she did have very pretty hair. Casual observation would call it red, and thick, and plagued by an unladylike tendency to wave and shine.

Hardcastle put a hand over his belly, for the horses were managing a good pace, despite the ruts, and his digestion was suffering accordingly.

"I'd say Miss MacHugh's hair is auburn," Christopher announced, "but I don't know the words for the colors the coach lamps put in it. Fire-colored and the color of laughter."

"Thank you, Christopher," Miss MacHugh said, beaming at the boy. "You pay me such compliments, my bonnet will never fit on my head again."

They shared another moment of complete accord, while the ale and cheese Hardcastle had partaken of miles ago intruded on his awareness most disagreeably.

"Miss MacHugh's hair is auburn," he said, "also red, russet, gold, blond, and *sienna* and the color of having the right answers even when not asked for them."

Christopher's brows twitched down. "You've won, sir. I'd forgot sienna even when Miss reminded me of it. We must play again, or it's not sporting of you."

What did a six-year-old know of sporting behavior? Miss MacHugh's arched eyebrow—Titian, with a hint of amused chastisement—suggested Christopher knew a good deal.

"Very well," Hardcastle said. "My turn to choose, and in the spirit of the opening round, I choose Miss MacHugh's lips."

"You must go first because you won the description of her hair," Christopher said, as earnestly as if the rules of fair play had been devised by Wellington and Napoleon on the eve of Waterloo. The child was very dear in his good sportsmanship. Hardcastle peeled off his damp gloves and tousled Christopher's hair.

"I have set myself up for failure," the duke said. "For I gaze upon the challenge before me, and all I can think is Miss MacHugh's lips are... pinkish."

"They are pinkish," Christopher allowed, "but if they're pinkish, they're also reddish, and maybe with a hint of... well, pinkish and reddish. Do I win?"

Hardcastle made a production of studying Miss MacHugh, who bore his scrutiny with patient indifference. By the light of the coach lamps, he could not quite count her freckles, thank heavens, but he could admire the clean line of her jaw, follow the swoop of dark brows, and mentally trace the shape of a mouth more full than ought to grace a governess's physiognomy.

"I concede, Christopher," Hardcastle said. "My descriptions are apparently in want of color. Shall you play the next round, Miss MacHugh?"

Fourteen thousand rounds later—Hardcastle's muddy boots, Christopher's storybook, Miss MacHugh's beaded reticule—Christopher was yawning hugely and the duke was ready to cast up his accounts. The prospect of riding Ajax in the continuing downpour guaranteed an ague, but that was preferable to a loss of dignity.

"Perhaps I'll ride a few more miles," Hardcastle said, peering out the window at a sopping, green expanse of central England. "Or perhaps we should put up at the next coaching inn, rather than risk the horses in this mud."

His teams were prime cattle, and they'd negotiate any footing handily. His bellyache had been joined by a throbbing head, though.

"Christopher, time to rest your eyes," Miss MacHugh said. "We must ask His Grace to switch seats with you, so you can stretch out on the cushions."

"The boy can sleep in the coach?"

"So I arrive fresh and on my manners," Christopher explained, extricating himself from Miss MacHugh's side. "Miss sometimes rests her eyes too."

The child pulled off his boots as if napping in the coach was simply part of his routine.

Hardcastle shifted to the forward-facing seat, and immediately his head thanked him and his belly quit threatening outright rebellion.

Miss MacHugh folded the opposite bench out, so the boy had the width of a trundle bed to sleep on—they were in a ducal traveling coach, after all—but this left not as much room for Hardcastle's legs.

"I don't bite, Your Grace," Miss MacHugh said, when she'd tucked a wool blanket around Christopher and settled back on the forward-facing seat. "Conditions in even your coach will be crowded when three of us are in here."

"Quite."

Hardcastle abruptly had nowhere to put his arms, his legs, his muddy boots, his anything. He wasn't facing backward, but tumult of another variety assaulted him. He smelled of wet horse, even miles later, while Miss MacHugh smelled of... governess. Lilacs and lavender, sunny gardens, and... happy memories.

They rocked along for another mile, the child falling into a relaxed slumber. The movement of the coach swayed him gently amid the blankets, while Hardcastle felt his own eyes growing heavy.

"You were very kind to let Christopher win half the rounds," Miss MacHugh said, nudging her bonnet way from the boy's feet. "He's sensitive and wants badly to have your approval, though he also has an excellent appreciation for sportsmanship."

"Which he must have acquired from you," Hardcastle concluded. "I certainly haven't spent enough time around the boy to be much of an influence."

Not something to be proud of. He and Christopher were the last surviving Hardcastle males, after all.

"Christopher will recall today fondly," Miss MacHugh said, patting Hardcastle's hand. She'd done that once before, in the garden by the fountain. Very few people presumed to touch a duke, and yet, when Miss MacHugh took liberties, she was relaxed and confident about it.

"You will recall today less than fondly," Hardcastle observed. "I had no idea how tedious traveling with a small child could be."

Miss MacHugh twitched the blanket up over Christopher's shoulders. The boy had to be exhausted to be sleeping so soundly, but then, children did sleep soundly, while dukes rarely did.

"You will recall today miserably," she said, settling back. "If I'd been asked to describe your complexion, sir, I would have started with green, followed up with bilious, and concluded with shroudly pale."

Shroudly wasn't a word, suggesting the governess was teasing the duke.

"Why thank you, Miss MacHugh." Had she suggested Christopher's nap out of consideration for her employer? "If I had to describe the color of your lips, I'd say they were the vermilion glory of sunset at the end of a beautiful summer day spent in the company of good friends whom one has longed to see for ages. They bear the rosy tint of the tender mallow flowers at the height of their bloom, the fresh hue of ripe strawberries glistening with morning dew, and the tantalizing delicacy of raspberries nestled in their thorny, green hedges."

Those vermilion, rosy, strawberry, raspberry lips curved up. "Very good, Your Grace. I know where Christopher gets his aptitude for the game. Very good indeed."

She didn't pat his hand again.

Well.

Hardcastle put an arm around the lady's shoulders to steady her against the jostle and sway of the coach.

"Rest your eyes, Miss MacHugh. We've miles to go before we reach an inn up to my standards of accommodation, and the boy will waken all too soon."

She startled minutely at Hardcastle's forwardness, a reaction he detected only because they were in close proximity. An instant later, she eased against his side, tentatively, then more heavily as sleep claimed her. Hardcastle's belly had quieted entirely, and his headache had departed, but his mind went at a dead gallop down a muddy road indeed.

He did not want to go duchess hunting amid the great houses of the Dukeries, neither did he want to allow Ellen MacHugh to leave his household. He was a duke, however, and those wretches were doomed to a lifetime of marching out smartly, intent on accomplishing tasks they truly did not care to complete.

Hardcastle was damned sick and tired of being a good duke. Perhaps the naughty boy in him should be allowed some long overdue attention.

Only as sleep stole over his mind did Hardcastle admit to himself that he would always strive to be a good duke, and Ellen MacHugh would have little interest in a naughty boy—but perhaps she'd spare a lonely man a bit of company, under the right circumstances.

CHAPTER TWO

"Uncle likes you," Christopher said, passing his pencil to Ellen for a sharper one.

"I respect His Grace greatly," Ellen replied, accepting the dull pencil and passing over a fresh one. Something in Christopher's observation was not entirely innocent. He was six, and children at his age matured rapidly and in unexpected directions.

"No, I mean Uncle *likes* you," Christopher said again.

They'd settled in at Sedgemere House late the previous night, among the last of the guests to arrive.

After being confined in the coach for three eternities—one of them with His Grace—Ellen was happy to be out of doors, sketching on a blanket in the Duke of Sedgemere's sunken garden. The morning was spectacularly beautiful, and the governess responsible for Sedgemere's three boys had suggested this quiet retreat.

"I like His Grace as well," Ellen said, fishing a penknife from the sketching box and getting to work on the pencil.

She did not like Hardcastle. Her situation was worse than that. She *could have* liked him and was only now realizing it. He cared for

Christopher mightily, had a sense of humor, was kind in a gruff avuncular fashion, and was...

Lonely. That insight had devastated her.

Hardcastle had tucked his arm around her as if daring her to protest, and she should have, but hadn't been able to. He knew exactly how to wrap a woman in his embrace, so she was protected without being confined, and without implying the least impropriety.

Ellen had slept deeply against his side and awoken feeling safe, warm, and content—also resentful, for the duke had offered her a comfort she would not know again.

He couldn't understand that, of course. When Ellen had touched Hardcastle, he'd looked a little bewildered, as if a hummingbird or a butterfly had lit on his sleeve. He couldn't know that his touch, so casually offered, bewildered her the same way.

"Uncle kissed you," Christopher said, his tongue peeking out of the side of his mouth. "When we were in the coach."

The penknife slipped, and Ellen came within a whisker of cutting herself.

"Christopher, you must not say such things. His Grace conducted himself with utmost propriety at all times, given the situation."

Christopher looked up from the owl he was drawing. In the fashion of small boys, he was fascinated with owls lately, a welcome change from the frogs and toads of earlier in the summer.

"You say I mustn't tell lies," he replied. "Uncle kissed your hair. That's not a lie. You were asleep and I was too, mostly, but I opened my eyes and saw him. He kissed your hair. You kiss my hair sometimes."

The child was asking a question Ellen hardly knew how to answer. "Lies always get us in trouble, but in this case, the truth could also get the duke in trouble. If he kissed my hair, I'm sure it was simply the same sort of gesture of affection as I've shown you. Or perhaps my hair was tickling his nose."

The truth if misconstrued could get Ellen ruined—again. A

woman permitting her employer kisses while a child looked on was a sorry creature.

Ellen would rather have been an *awake* sorry creature, though.

"I won't say anything," Christopher allowed, getting to work on the complicated task of drawing feathers on his owl. "Uncle is very dignified. Unless you want me to tell him not to do it again?"

The offer was so gentlemanly, tears threatened.

Ellen put the penknife back in the box, the pencil being adequately sharpened. "What would you say to him, Christopher?"

"I'd say to him that when a gentleman likes a lady, he should tell her that, so she knows, not sneak kisses to her hair. Ladies like fellows who are honest. You say that."

"I'm a font of useful notions. That is a very handsome owl, Christopher." A very knowing sort of owl.

"His names is Xerxes. I wish I had a real owl."

"When you are grown, you can have a mews, a real mews, with falcons in it." Ellen would not see him learn to fly his falcons, though. The realization nearly had her weeping outright.

Why had she allowed herself to grow so attached to this boy? Not well done of her at all.

"Who's that lady?" Christopher asked, sitting up. "She looks worried."

No less a personage than their hostess, the Duchess of Sedgemere was crossing the grass. She was a pretty woman perhaps five years Ellen's senior. The same governess who'd told Ellen about the sunken garden had confided that Her Grace had been the daughter of a banker and was quite approachable when the Quality weren't looking.

"Good morning, Your Grace," Ellen said, rising to curtsey. Beside her, Christopher scrambled to his feet and bowed.

"Miss MacHugh, good day, and hello to you, young sir. Christopher, isn't it? May I borrow your governess for a moment?"

Ellen's first thought was that the duchess had somehow learned of the kiss in the traveling coach and had come to see Ellen escorted to the foot of the drive, bag and baggage. Hardcastle would never have allowed that—if he'd kissed her—and as Christopher had noted, the duchess looked a trifle anxious.

"May I be of assistance, Your Grace?" Ellen asked.

"Let's admire the dratted roses, shall we?" Her Grace suggested, moving briskly along the crushed-shell walk, while Christopher went blithely back to feathering his owl. "Sedgemere's gardener was in a taking because the roses were blooming too early. Imagine the effrontery of roses blooming on their own schedule. I'm babbling."

Ellen liked this woman already. "You're worried about something."

"I'm almost too tired to worry, Miss MacHugh. I'm not very good at this duchessing business. Think of me what you will, but I need your help."

The roses were passing their prime, alas, though a few late bloomers were yet in bud. "What can I do to help, Your Grace?"

"Lady Amelia Marchman has decided not to attend my gathering. It's my first house party as the Duchess of Sedgemere, and she has one scheduled for later this summer. I do believe she's trying to sabotage my Come Out, so to speak, by making the numbers on my roster uneven."

"Ah." The warfare of women. Ellen had skirmished on these fields at finishing school, and her aunt had attempted to equip her for the greater battles to come during a London social Season.

"Miss MacHugh, I am in danger of becoming silly," the duchess went on, "and His Grace is nearly out of patience with me. I don't know many women whose consequence would make them appropriate guests at a duke's house party, and I certainly can't call on the few I do know to cover Lady Amelia's defection. I will become the first duchess in the history of duchesses to hold a house party at which the numbers do not balance."

Ellen sank onto a bench, because this request—did a duchess issue requests?—was enormous.

"You might dissuade one of the gentlemen from attending," Ellen suggested as the duchess took a seat beside her. The bench faced a small pond, in which a half-dozen serene white ducks drifted on the water.

"Brilliant notion, Miss MacHugh, but His Grace refused to countenance it. These are his school chums, his cronies from the House of Lords or their sons and younger brothers. They've already started placing bets on the Dukeries Cup race, which event is the main reason the men were willing to come. Some guests will decamp early, when they've played too deeply or grown bored, but I must at least start with an even number of ladies and gentlemen on the roster I circulate before dinner."

Such was friendship among the aristocracy that one could not ask for a favor?

"I hardly have suitable attire, Your Grace." Ellen had the manners though, as well as the French, the literature, the pianoforte. Mama and Papa had had high hopes for her, despite the costs.

"I've inquired of my housekeeper, Mrs. Bolkers, who knows everybody in the Midlands. She claims you come from an old Derbyshire family, and your uncle is an earl," the duchess replied. "I asked Hardcastle after breakfast this morning, and he left it up to you: If you'd like to be a guest at the house party, then he won't object. Nobody saw you arrive last night because you came in so late, and my sons' governess can easily handle one more little fellow."

If Hardcastle had already capitulated, there went Ellen's last, best defense against this folly.

"I should refuse you, Your Grace. Ellen MacHugh left Derbyshire under a cloud of gossip, and now she turns up five years later at your house party?"

Her Grace was not classically beautiful. Her hair was dark rather than fair, her features dramatic rather than pretty. She gazed out across the pond, just as the lead duck tipped down into the water, his tail pointing skyward. Several other ducks followed suit. The prospect was utterly undignified, but thus did ducks find sustenance.

"I'll be the duchess who returns you to the place in society you should never have abandoned," Her Grace said. "Don't steal a fellow from any of the other young ladies, don't be too witty, don't drink too much, and if you can manage to plead a headache for half the waltzes, we'll both get through this, Miss MacHugh. I will be ever in your debt, and you might even enjoy yourself."

Oh, right. Moving in society—even rural society—had gone so well the last time Ellen had attempted it.

"Are you enjoying yourself, Your Grace?"

"Endlessly, Miss MacHugh. Was the gossip serious?"

"I was seen kissing a fellow I was not engaged to." A lie, but such an old, necessary lie that it no longer felt like one.

"What a shameless wanton you are. I was seen kissing a duke I was not engaged to, and look what a miserable fate has befallen me. Let's get you upstairs, then. I have enough clothes for eighteen women, though my gowns will at least need to be hemmed if they're to fit you."

The duchess rose, while across the garden Christopher had taken to watching the ducks.

"I must report my decision to Hardcastle," Ellen said, "and gain his permission to entrust Christopher to your staff."

"Stroll with him after luncheon then. No fewer than five young ladies were eyeing him at breakfast as if they'd love to end up accidentally napping in his bed. His Grace is in for a long two weeks, as am I."

One of those young ladies would likely conclude the gathering as a prospective duchess.

"I'm in for a long two weeks as well, ma'am. A very long two weeks."

"THIS HOUSE PARTY was the most confoundedly inane notion my grandmother ever bludgeoned me into," Hardcastle muttered. "Now you tell me your uncle is an earl? Will I next learn the Regent has abdicated and winged hedgehogs grace the skies of Notting-hamshire?"

Hardcastle hadn't adjusted to the notion of Miss MacHugh leaving his employ, and now he was to accept that she was niece to the Earl of Dalton?

"I did not want to embarrass my family by my decision to go into service," Miss MacHugh said. "I had already embarrassed them enough, you see, so I took a position in Cornwall."

No, Hardcastle did not *see*.

Beneath the window of the duchess's sitting room, on a back terrace festooned with potted salvia, sat a small regiment of beauties who were little more than half Hardcastle's age. Each one was possessed of a devious mind and a large settlement, and collectively, they were plotting his downfall. They'd formed ranks at breakfast and had spent the morning going at him, like French cavalry charging a British infantry square.

Sooner or later, his lines would break, and he'd be compromised into taking a duchess not of his choosing.

In Kent, the idea of acquiring a duchess had seemed inevitably sensible. Somewhere on the Great North Road, that scheme had become anathema, while another idea—a daft, delightful idea—had taken its place.

Hardcastle quit the window before one of the enemy generals spotted him. "Explain this embarrassment you caused your family, madam. Have I harbored a bad influence in my nursery?"

A damned attractive bad influence, at that. In borrowed deep green finery, Ellen MacHugh's figure showed to excellent advantage, and her complexion was perfection itself. Her hair was severely contained, for now, and the result was feminine elegance of an order Hardcastle was not accustomed to withstanding.

"You have harbored an innocent young lady who allowed a man to kiss her," she replied. "That young lady was seen by idle gossips, which might have been the young man's intention. I left rather than let the talk grow. Nothing more, Your Grace."

With that degree of composure, she'd be a terror at the card tables. Nobody would be able to predict when she was bluffing.

"You're pretty," Hardcastle said, stepping closer. "Damned pretty."

Miss MacHugh smoothed a hand over silk skirts. "Should I apologize for that transgression, Your Grace?"

"You'll regret it," he said, trying not to stare at the simple gold locket nestled just above her breasts. "For every female pursuing me, two fellows will pursue you, and men cannot be relied upon to behave honorably, as you already know."

Hardcastle could endure the simpering females, but the notion that the strutting cocks and squealing stud colts would be sniffing around Ellen MacHugh—*his* Ellen—was unsupportable.

"I am to be the duchess's personal guest," she replied. "The gentlemen will behave themselves."

Worse and worse. "My dear Miss MacGoverness, the duchess herself is on trial here. This is her maiden attempt at managing a major gathering, and the other women will sabotage her personal guest's reception by sundown. I've met these women, and they're enough to give me an ague starting immediately."

For the first time, Miss MacHugh looked uncertain. "I told the duchess this would not work."

Hardcastle put his hands behind his back rather than find out for himself if the gold of Ellen's locket was warm from her body heat.

Perhaps he was suffering from an ague in truth. "Duchesses are formidable women and difficult to gainsay," he allowed. "I have a suggestion."

Miss MacHugh touched the locket, reminding him that he'd seen her do that before, at Sunday services when the weather was temperate.

"I will not like this suggestion, sir."

"You'll loathe it less than you'd loathe being mashed up against the wall of the linen closet when young Mr. Greenover takes a notion to acquaint you with his charms. I've yet to see him sober, but he's in line for an earldom and already controls a large fortune. Perhaps you'd like him to propose?"

She appeared disgusted, bless her. "When this house party has concluded, I will return to my family in Derbyshire."

Well, damn. If she'd been leaving him for another post, he could simply have raised her salary. Returning to the loving arms of the family daft enough to allow her into service posed a conundrum, for what could compete with family?

"So you'll tolerate my attentions for the duration of this house party?" Hardcastle asked. This strategy had come to him as he'd beheld the forces of marital inevitability gathering on the terrace below. He did not want just any duchess, and he certainly did not want a duchess who schemed to get her hands on a tiara regardless of the duke involved.

He wanted a woman who...

"Your attentions, sir?"

"I'll act as your swain," Hardcastle said, though he had no experience *being* a swain. "You'll be my damsel. We don't have to be smitten. A few glances, the occasional sighting of us walking too closely together, a waltz or two. Nothing compromising. If you see a fellow you'd like to pursue, simply tell me, and I'll do the same if one of the ladies should catch my eye."

Miss MacHugh's expression was severe indeed, as if Hardcastle were her charge and he'd just broken his slate over his knee.

"I do not like falsehoods," she said. "They grow and tangle, and become hurtful."

"My entire life is a falsehood," Hardcastle rejoined, coming near enough to study the highlights the afternoon sun put in Miss MacHugh's hair. He knew the texture of her hair, had stolen a nuzzle of it in the traveling coach. Knew the silk of it against his lips, knew the lilac and lavender scent. He knew she had seventeen freckles on her left cheek, fourteen on her right.

Hardcastle also knew his time was up. No more idle musing, no more tacitly comparing every other woman to her, no more telling himself infatuation was normal even for a duke. If he failed to woo Ellen MacHugh in the next two weeks, she'd march out of his life forever.

"My life is a study in falsehood," he said, taking up the reins of the conversation. "I'm to wear my title as if it's a great privilege, as if running twelve estates and doing what I can to keep the Regent from bankrupting the country is an endless honor. I'm to be honorable and gentlemanly without ceasing, perfectly attired at all times, never say the wrong thing, never do the wrong thing. No human man can live up to that standard."

Miss MacHugh smoothed a hand down his lapel. "But you do, sir. You are a good man and a good duke. I've recently come to the conclusion that I like you."

What in the perishing damned hell was a man to say to that?

"Then I'm not asking you to perpetrate any falsehoods, am I, Miss MacHugh? Simply act as if you like me. My name, by the way, is Gerard."

She leaned close enough to sniff the rose affixed to his lapel, then stepped back. "Gerard Juvenal René Beaumarchand Hammersley, Eighth Duke of Hardcastle," she recited. "I'm simply Ellen Ainsley MacHugh."

She was simply driving him to distraction, fingering that locket.

"My brother called me Rennie," Hardcastle said. "My father called me the despair of the house of Hammersley, though he occasionally smiled as he said it."

Miss—Ellen—peered at the gathering below, her expression disgruntled. "I will be complicit in your scheme, sir, but I foresee it ending in great scandal. Those young ladies will learn that I was governess to your heir. They will not deal kindly with me when they do."

"They will not learn of it, and in two weeks you and I will be free to quit this house and move on to happier pursuits."

Though what could be more enjoyable than pursuing her? For Hardcastle would.

He'd vowed this as she'd stepped away from him, and his every instinct had thundered at him to kiss her. She was an earl's relation, she wasn't interested in the dandiprats frolicking around the men's punchbowl, and she loved Christopher.

A tidy solution to several problems, including the predictable insurrection in Hardcastle's breeches every time she drew near.

"Very well, sir, we have a bargain." Ellen held out her hand, an elegant, freckle-free appendage.

Hardcastle took it and pressed his lips to her knuckles. "We have a bargain," he replied, keeping her hand in his.

"You're being a swain already," she said, half-amused, half-exasperated. "Am I to sit next to you every evening over cards? Give you all my waltzes?"

"You are to adore the very ground upon which I strut," he said, patting her hand. "I'll enjoy that part rather a lot. Do you even know how to bat your eyelashes?"

"You're to worship the ground I mince about on too, sir," she said, retrieving her hand. "And no, I did not acquire the ability to bat my eyelashes when I was learning French and Italian."

"Call me Hardcastle, please, or perhaps you might judiciously slip and use my name, then blush becomingly at your lapse." He'd like to make her blush. She was a redhead, and they did not blush subtly.

"And you shall slip and call me Ellen," she retorted. "What have I got myself into?"

"You have got yourself *out of* a lot of spotty boys and leering husbands drooling down your bodice, because you have me to keep them from such impropriety. You may go to sleep at night knowing you have preserved the sanity of at least one deserving duke. One question, my dear."

She glowered at him. "Yes, *dearest* Hardcastle?"

"What's in the locket? It's pretty and suits you in both its simplicity and elegance."

He'd confused her. Ellen's expression said she could not tell if

Hardcastle's compliment was sincere, or swain-ly balderdash. She took the locket off over her head and opened it.

"This is a miniature of my sister. She has one of me. We're twins, though I am the elder by a few minutes."

Hardcastle dutifully took the locket, not because he needed to see a small, inexpert likeness of a younger version of Ellen, but because she'd offered to show him of her own accord. The painter, however, had been skilled with miniatures, catching the beauty of a young girl whose poise hadn't yet eclipsed her innocence.

"She's very like you, very fetching," he said, wanting to hold the locket in his palm, but giving it back anyway. "You'll see her again soon."

Drat and damn the luck.

"We're not identical," Ellen said, "but the resemblance is quite strong. I've missed her terribly."

Hardcastle knew what it was to miss a sibling. Why hadn't he realized that even governesses had family, and would miss that family? If he could have had one more day with Robin, with his parents, with even his grandfather...

"We're expected in the back gardens for Italian ices, my dear," he said, winging his arm.

Ellen dropped the locket over her head and wrapped her hand around his sleeve.

"For another two weeks, we can support this farce. Lay on, Hardcastle, and do try to look adoring."

"BLESS YOU, Hardcastle! You've found my Miss MacHugh," the Duchess of Sedgemere gushed. Ellen stifled the urge to duck behind the duke, for every pair of eyes on the terrace had turned to her.

"Your Grace." Ellen curtseyed deeply, while beside her, Hardcastle bowed. "Thank you so much for excusing me from the morning's activities. Won't you introduce me to the other guests?"

"But of course," the duchess said, and then Ellen was led away from the safety of Hardcastle's escort and introduced to at least thirty thousand other people, some couples, some family groups, far too many single young men, and at least one gorgeous blond duke. She encountered pleasant, welcoming smiles, leers, and from the young women intent on winning Hardcastle's notice, *un*-pleasant *un*-welcoming smiles too.

"Are you one of the Derbyshire MacHughs?" one young lady asked.

"Ellen's uncle is the Earl of Dalton," the duchess supplied. "His countess and I are fast friends, and Ellen has ever been a favorite of her aunt's. She is already a favorite of mine too."

And thus did trouble begin, as Miss Tamsin Frobisher's baby-blue eyes narrowed, and she twirled a fat, golden sausage curl around her finger.

"I seem to recall—" Miss Frobisher began.

"You will have to excuse me," the duchess said. "I am so sorry, but I must oversee the serving of the ices. Miss Frobisher, perhaps you'll assist me, and Ellen, I'll leave you in the care of my dear husband."

His Grace of Sedgemere had been silently accompanying them through the introductions. He was not a handsome man, his Nordic features were too severe for that, but when his gaze lit on his duchess, his expression softened.

"Come, Miss MacHugh, we've only the last of the bachelors yet to go," Sedgemere said, seizing Ellen's hand and positioning it on it arm. "They'll be on their best behavior or I'll kill them."

Ellen wrapped her hand around his sleeve as they traversed the steps to the lower terrace, but she already felt the flames of gossip licking at her back.

"How considerate of you, Your Grace. I'm sure Hardcastle would assist you to dispose of the remains."

"Hardcastle had better be on his best behavior too, or you need only apply to me, madam. This scheme of Her Grace's is demented, and you're either a saint or a fool for accommodating it."

"In either case, you're most welcome, Your Grace. Are all dukes so fierce, or do you and my—Hardcastle have a rivalry of some sort?"

"I consider Hardcastle among my very few friends, Miss MacHugh. Now, attend me, for my recitation will be sufficiently tedious that I don't care to repeat it. The fop on the left is Jermand Hunslinger, sot and wastrel at large, but decorative. The dandy to the right is Harold Schacter, Viscount Ormandsley, whose besetting vice is horse racing. The imbecile in the middle is Greenover. He's heir to the Earl of Moreton, has already accosted two chambermaids, and will likely not survive the next week."

Neither would Ellen. "You'll kill him, sir?"

"My duchess will turn Miss Frobisher and Miss Pendleton loose on him. Poor sod won't know his top from his tail by Sunday afternoon."

"What a ruthless duchess you have, sir."

"They're the best kind."

SEDGEMERE STOOD ACROSS THE ROOM, impersonating a Viking guardian angel at Ellen MacHugh's side, looking quite severe, and probably laughing his arse off. Sedgemere had perfected silent mirth before leaving Eton. Hardcastle had no doubt it had served Sedgemere well through an interminable dinner too.

Miss Frobisher's pale, quivering bosom had occupied Hardcastle's attention on the left, or tried to, while Miss Pendleton's more modest attributes had been jiggled at him from the right through at least ninety-seven exquisitely presented courses.

Hardcastle had declined the blancmange and would likely never enjoy that particular dish again.

"You might smile, Hardcastle," the Duchess of Sedgemere said. "My housekeeper has been asked by four different lady's maids for a map of the guest wing, ostensibly to prevent the young misses from getting lost."

"If you gave any of them—"

She patted his hand, but the gesture conveyed none of the comfort, none of the soothing, that the same touch from Ellen would have.

"You're in the family wing Hardcastle, and so is your Miss MacHugh. Does she know you're smitten?"

"Anne, for shame. Dukes are not smitten." Though Sedgemere was. Clearly, at some point, a man who'd never been known to dance with the same woman twice had given all his waltzes to the banker's daughter. "What do you know of Miss MacHugh's family?"

"I've done a bit of research, thanks to Mrs. Bolkers's unfailing memory regarding the Quality. Ellen MacHugh never made her bow. She went to the right sort of finishing school, her auntie the countess was all ready to sponsor her Come Out, but then something happened, and into service Ellen went, far to the south, nobody knows exactly where."

"Cornwall." Literally the ends of the earth. "Her references were from Cornwall when she joined my household. Good God, now we're to endure the caterwauling and cooing."

For nothing would do, but Miss Frobisher must have Lord Ormandsley turn pages for her at the pianoforte. She played competently, she displayed her bosom for the viscount more competently still. Hardcastle's head was beginning to pound, and he was thinking fondly of rainy miles in his traveling coach, when Miss Frobisher concluded her piece and aimed a vivacious smile at Ellen.

"Won't you play for us, Miss MacHugh? I'm sure one of the gentlemen would be happy to turn pages for you."

Ellen's gaze met Hardcastle's for an instant, an *I told you so* rather than a plea flung across the parlor. A chorus of "I'd be pleased to assist," and "I'd love to oblige" rose up from amidst the puppies, and Hardcastle's headache migrated to the region of his heart.

This was his fault. What if Ellen couldn't play? What if she played badly? What if—

"I can play from memory," she said, rising gracefully and crossing to the piano. "I'm a bit rusty, but it's a beautiful instrument, and I do love music. I'll play one of my mother's favorites."

She took her place on the bench, the lamplight dancing fire through her auburn hair.

Hardcastle braced himself for some sprightly, repetitive Mozart rondo, or a crashing Beethoven first movement.

As she started to play, a collective sigh eased from the room. She'd chosen a ballad from Mr. Burns's work, "My Love Is Like a Red, Red Rose." The key was major, but the words of the poem were of farewell to a dearest love. She mercifully declined to sing, though Hardcastle knew each verse by heart.

Ellen's playing featured not showy virtuosity, but instead, a sweet, leaping melody over lilting accompaniment and sentimental harmonies. Every dissonance was quickly resolved, while every phrase spoke of loss and regret.

When the piece concluded, the room remained silent for a moment, bathed in the peace of a tender melody. The duchess led the applause and prompted another young lady to play as Hardcastle edged around the room and took Ellen by the arm.

"You play very well," he muttered, as Miss Pendleton went thumping into a tormented rendition of "Charlie, He's My Darling." "My head will soon be killing me. Might we admire the croaking of the nearest frog or the moon's reflection on a mud puddle, or some blasted thing where it's quiet?"

"I'd like that, Your Grace," Ellen replied, fluffing the folds of his cravat.

"Do that again, please, while the Frobisher creature is goggling at us, and the Sheffield heiress is for once not tossing her curls. It's a wonder the woman hasn't dislocated her neck."

Ellen obliged, rearranging lace at the same time she settled Hardcastle's nerves. "Some fresh air would be welcome, sir."

They left through the open French doors, the terrace offering relative cool and quiet compared to the crowded parlor. Hardcastle found a bench on the lower terrace, seated the lady, came down beside her, and stifled the urge to check his watch in the ample moonlight.

If he sought his bed this early, talk would ensue.

"I am ready to strangle my grandmother for insisting I attend this gathering," Hardcastle said, "and I'm ready to leave at first light, but Sedgemere is a friend, and I'd not disrespect his hospitality. Say something."

"The piano will need tuning by morning," Ellen remarked. "Miss Pendleton enjoys a very confident touch at the keyboard."

The damned chit could have drummed for a Highland regiment, but at least out here, her chopping at the hapless "Charlie" was at a tinkling distance.

"You enjoy a confident touch when your hands are on my person, Miss MacHugh. I like that."

The lady ceased fussing her skirts. "I beg your pardon, Your Grace?"

A conversational commonplace had never worn as much starch. "I said, you enjoy—"

"I heard you, Hardcastle. If you think for one moment that a casual gesture between people who've known each other for years—"

Hardcastle cradled her jaw against his palm, and Ellen fell silent. He leaned nearer, close enough to catch her scent, close enough to whisper.

"Don't scream." Then he kissed her.

ELLEN'S HEART was breaking about once every fifteen minutes. She saw Hardcastle teasing the duchess, a woman he clearly considered a friend, and was struck with the realization that in the past three years, she'd never once seen Hardcastle teasing anybody.

But then, nobody had teased him either.

He'd compliment a trio of companions on their embroidery and march away, oblivious to the envy directed at the companions by the young ladies they were supposed to attend.

Hardcastle was lonely, and Ellen was leaving him. He was such a good man, in his way, and after this house party, she'd never see him again.

She'd played for him, of course. Offered him Mr. Burns, a comfort in her younger years, a piece she'd be playing from memory decades hence. *I will love thee still, my dear, till all the seas gang dry...*

Hardcastle would love like that, relentlessly, deeply, nigh reverently. He'd love like a duke—

"I am ready to strangle my grandmother for insisting I attend this gathering," he said as he and Ellen gained the blessed peace of the terrace. "And I'm ready to leave at first light, but Sedgemere is a friend, and I'd not disrespect his hospitality. Say something."

Don't go, sir. Please, don't go. Not yet.

They were mere yards from the rest of the gathering. Ellen searched for a prosaic response and came up with an inanity.

"The piano will need tuning by morning," she said. "Miss Pendleton enjoys a very confident touch at the keyboard."

Her playing had sounded desperate to Ellen, as if by bombarding Hardcastle with notes, Miss Pendleton might decimate His Grace's indifference.

"You enjoy a confident touch when your hands are on my person, Miss MacHugh. I like that."

Ellen could not possibly have heard him correctly. "I beg your pardon, Your Grace?"

"I said, you enjoy—"

When in doubt, when in an utterly confused quandary, a governess always had a good scold ready.

"I heard you, Hardcastle. If you think for one moment that a casual gesture between people who've known each other for years—"

Ellen had not even begun to know this man. She'd misjudged him for years, hidden from him, in fact.

Hardcastle cradled her jaw against his palm, the warmth of his hand startling, for this was an informal house party and he wasn't wearing gloves.

"Don't scream."

His mouth settled over hers, the way calm settled in her heart when a solution arrived to a thorny problem, bringing with it rightness, relief, and a sense of revelation.

Yes, this. Exactly and emphatically, this. Hardcastle's kiss was rivetingly sweet, not a presumption, but an invitation, a fragrance that beckoned Ellen into a garden of blooming pleasures. His arm encircling her shoulders, his warmth and nearness, his hand cradling her cheek, his tongue—

Exotic orchids joined the sensual bouquet that was the duke's kiss. Heat from no apparent source glowed inside Ellen, light filled her mind where thoughts should be. The texture of his hair pleasured her fingers, and the taste of him—lavender and sweetness, from the last round of tea cakes—made her hungry in her soul.

Hardcastle could tease with kisses, drat him. Could nuzzle Ellen's ear and send all her questions and protestations begging. She tried to tease back, by nibbling on the soft flesh of his lower lip, by stroking a hand over his chest, inside the warmth of his evening coat.

That effort was hopeless. The more she touched him, the more muddled *she* became.

When the duke desisted, Ellen's heart was banging against her ribs as if a dozen unruly schoolgirls were leaping about inside her. When she would have traced her finger over his lips, he gently pushed her head to his shoulder.

"Your kisses want practice, my dear."

Indignation should have had Ellen drawing back, but a note in His Grace's voice stopped her. He was *pleased* that she had no idea how to kiss a man. He approved of her lack of experience, the wretch. As if she were the last tea cake on the tray, saved just for him.

"Yours is my first kiss, Hardcastle, and you provided me no warning." She ought not to have admitted that. He'd be impossible now, not merely an impossible man, but an impossible *duke*.

"You can't read up on how to kiss a fellow, Ellen. Not even in Latin. The business wants practice, and I'm sure you'll be a quick study." He kissed her again, a light smack on the lips. "Gets easier with practice, you see?"

He was entirely too smug about this venture, while Ellen had yet to locate her wits. She instead maneuvered artillery in place that ought to at least puncture Hardcastle's self-satisfaction.

"Are you trifling with the help, Your Grace?"

"The help isn't exactly leaping off the bench and calling for the gendarmes, is she?" he asked, his tone cooling.

"And ruin what's left of my reputation?"

The question sobered him. Ellen could feel Hardcastle's attitude change even before he withdrew his arm.

"Nobody is out here," he said, "and a simple kiss between adults does not a reputation ruin. You're not a giggling twit."

"I am an earl's granddaughter with a questionable past. Why did you kiss me, Hardcastle?"

He pushed off the bench and lounged on the balustrade a few feet away. Over his shoulder, the gardens were limned in moonlight, a fairy world suited to Christopher's owls. Behind Ellen, inside the parlor, the bashing about of poor "Charlie" came to a merciful final cadence.

"The demented women at this house party are out to capture themselves a duke," Hardcastle muttered. "You are my sole defense against their schemes, particularly now that His Grace of Wyndover has left the field, pleading the equivalent of a bachelor's megrim. It may be necessary for me to pay you marked attention, and I can't have you rebuffing my overtures."

Hardcastle's logic was a kick in the belly to Ellen's fancies. "So that was a rehearsal kiss? A theater production for the leering masses we're likely to face at tomorrow's picnic?"

His expression shuttered, and he became not Ellen's duke, not Hardcastle who'd steal a kiss to her hair, but a statue of a man, a fixture of the moonlit, fantastical garden.

"That kiss was not entirely a fiction, madam. Not on my part. If you're offended by my honest regard, I apologize. I presumed, and it needn't happen again."

Laughter spilled from the parlor. The hordes would soon descend, all smiles and sly glances. Ellen abruptly wanted to cry, but because she was not in her governess attire, she had no handkerchief tucked into her sleeve.

Hardcastle pushed off the wall and strode toward the house, pausing only long enough to gently squeeze Ellen's shoulder before he left her alone in the moonlight.

CHAPTER THREE

"If you importune Miss MacHugh like that again, I shall call you out, Hardcastle, and I will shoot to wound your pride, at least."

The evening was mild, and no fire had been lit in the library's hearth, so Sedgemere's threat cracked across the darkness like a pistol shot.

"If you call me out, I'll choose swords," Hardcastle replied, turning two glasses on the sideboard right side up. "You're no kind of swordsman, while my skill is indisputable. May I offer you some of your own brandy?"

"That decanter's full of whiskey," Sedgemere said, rising from a wing chair near the windows. "Anne has connections in the north who obligingly keep me supplied. The brandy's on the desk."

Hardcastle poured himself a brandy, for his nerves wanted soothing, not more passion. He passed Sedgemere a serving as well and touched his glass to his host's.

"To victory in battle," he said, reciting one of their toasts from boyhood. They'd both had ducal expectations foisted upon them too soon and at too great a cost, and that toast had covered a host of challenges.

"To honor in victory," Sedgemere replied, ambling over to the window. "What could you have been thinking, Hardcastle? Ellen MacHugh is your nephew's governess, and you were on her like a bear at a honey tree."

"I rather was." And she'd returned the compliment. "Miss MacHugh has agreed to be the object of my apparent affection for the duration of this gathering, and I shall be hers. A certain familiarity between us lends credibility to that fiction."

"Any more credibility, Hardcastle, and the woman would be having your child. I opened the French doors to my library thinking to gain some fresh air without joining the throng in the parlor, and I find a pair of minks on my terrace."

Two minks, two eager, thoroughly enthralled minks. Hardcastle took comfort from that.

"I became more enthusiastic than I intended, Sedgemere. I planned delicate forays, tactful overtures, not... not the complete surrender of my dignity." Or the complete surrender of Ellen's, for that matter.

When it came to kissing, she was a deuced fast learner, though, dignity be damned.

Sedgemere settled on the arm of the chair, moonlight glinting off the glass in his hand. "People think I married Anne for her money. Her papa is filthy rich, of course, and the settlements were indecently generous."

"People are idiots," Hardcastle shot back. "You could no more be bought by a banker than you could by the Empress of Austria." Though not for lack of trying in the latter case.

"You are an idiot too, Hardcastle, if you think by indirection to test the waters with Miss MacHugh. Go down on damned bended knee and give her the pretty words. At the very least, stop accosting her within earshot of half the gossips in London. Or leave her alone. Those are your options."

Thank God the library was without illumination. "She's leaving me in two weeks, Elias. Has given notice, and was most insistent on rejoining her family. Leaves a fellow rather..."

"At a loss," Sedgemere said gently. "Anne led me quite a dance. You'd think it's the duke who longs to be pursued for himself, rather than for his consequence. Anne stands to become wealthier than most dukes can dream of being, and I finally understood what she needed besides my passionate kisses and handsome escort."

The brandy helped. Sedgemere's company helped more. "You're uglier than a donkey's back end on a muddy day. Anne felt sorry for you, I'm sure."

Sedgemere saluted with his glass. "You're the one who set me straight, Hardcastle."

"I was half drunk, and exhausted by your violent pouting. You, a duke, sulking about like a college boy avoiding his creditors. I was on the point of proposing to Anne myself, rather than put up with more of your wallowing."

"Were you really?" Abruptly, the temperature in the library had dropped twenty-odd degrees, though at least Sedgemere had stopped handing out maudlin advice to the lovelorn.

"No, but Grandmama would have liked Anne, and Christopher adores her. What am I to do about Ellen MacHugh?"

Sedgemere, with the aplomb of a true friend, only guffawed rather than going off into whoops.

"You must charm her. The dictionary is on the table behind you, if the word is foreign to your experience. Convince her you want her in truth, despite her wild hair and advancing age, despite her humble origins."

"Her hair is perfect, and she's not a scheming twit. She's the granddaughter of an earl."

Another guffaw, followed by a snort, but Sedgemere should be allowed his diversions. He hadn't kissed Ellen MacHugh on the moonlit terrace, hadn't felt the fire and eagerness in her, hadn't endured the wonder provoked by her sheer female lusciousness and starchy retorts.

"Charm," Sedgemere said. "C-h-a-r-m. If you reach chicken, you've gone too far."

"If I reach chaste, I've gone too far. Maybe I should compromise her."

"I wouldn't advise it," Sedgemere said, swirling his brandy. "She'll be forever haunted by the thought that you had to marry her, that you married far beneath yourself. Society will never let her forget that your proposal was forced too."

"Blast you and your good sense." If Hardcastle compromised Ellen, he'd be haunted by the thought that she had married *him* out of necessity as well, not because she wanted to. "I'm taking this decanter upstairs with me."

"Better the decanter than the governess. Wedge a chair under your door when you're in your bedroom alone."

"Right. House party rules." Did Ellen know the house party rules? "Thank you, Sedgemere, and good night."

Hardcastle had reached the door, feeling silly for pilfering the brandy, when Sedgemere's voice drifted across the room.

"Compromise her, and I will thrash you, Hardcastle. Hard enough to hurt."

Sedgemere might not emerge victorious, but he'd give a good account of himself, which notion comforted on Ellen's behalf.

"I'd let you land a few blows for old time's sake, because you do so love it when Anne kisses your hurts better."

Hardcastle pulled the library door closed behind him amid more mirth from His damned perishing Grace, though what did it say about Hardcastle's ducal consequence that he envied his friend a lady to kiss his hurts better?

LETTERS TO EMILY always took a long time to write, and Ellen knew better than to attempt them when tired. Her mind would not settle, though, so she got out of bed and labored for half a page.

Hardcastle had kissed her, and his boldness hadn't been merely insurance against an awkward moment, when the fiction of interest in each other must be supported with a display of affection.

"I cannot fathom His Grace's motivation," she muttered, dipping her pen again and waiting, waiting for the excess ink to form a droplet, then fall back into the inkpot. "He is a surpassingly intelligent man, and more than capable of expressing himself clearly."

But Hardcastle was reserved too, possibly even shy.

Ellen was watching another droplet gather on the sharp end of the quill when a soft knock sounded at her door. By the standards of a social gathering, the hour wasn't that late. She set the pen aside, rose, and opened her door two inches.

"Your Grace?"

"No, it's Greenover, come to make violent love to you before his over-imbibing renders him entirely insensate. Let me in, madam, if you please."

The duke was, for the first time in Ellen's experience, less than perfectly turned out. His cravat had gone missing, his jacket with it, and the top button of his waistcoat was undone. His cuffs were turned back, and his rebellious hair had defeated decorum entirely.

He looked tired, disgruntled, and altogether delectable.

"Come in, Your Grace, though I'm hardly decent."

"You're covered from your pretty neck to your equally pretty toes, though the appearance of your toes must remain a matter of conjecture on my part, as I have never made their acquaintance."

Though only half dressed, Hardcastle still sounded every inch the duke. Ellen would miss even his voice, miss the clipped, ironic energy, the euphony of Oxford learning, and the confidence of bred-in-the-bone leadership.

"If you stare at my mouth like that much longer, madam, I will be forced to return the compliment, and then we'll get nothing discussed."

She'd kissed that arrogant mouth of his, been ensnared in its tender promises and bold overtures.

"You've interrupted my correspondence, sir, and the hour is late. What might I do for you?"

He locked the door, a sensible precaution, one Ellen should have seen to. "I was reminded by Sedgemere that you might not have attended many house parties. There are rules."

The first of those rules ought to be: Never allow a duke you've kissed into your bedroom late at night. Candlelight shot fire through the duke's tousled hair, and his shirt—the finest lawn—revealed the musculature of his arms in intriguing detail.

"You need not trouble yourself, Your Grace. The duchess reviewed the rules with me: Don't over-imbibe, don't steal anybody's beau, sit out half the waltzes."

He prowled over to the escritoire and capped the bottle of ink, then swept up the parings from Ellen's last efforts with the penknife and upended them into a dust bin near the hearth.

"You will not sit out waltzes if I'm on hand to dance them with you. You may also dance with Sedgemere, or with Oxthorpe, if he's joined the gathering with his duchess. I'm not referring to those rules, I'm referring to the rules of self-preservation."

Ellen knew all about self-preservation. She was leaving Hardcastle's employ partly in pursuit of that very aim.

His Grace had stopped prowling and tidying and was peering at Ellen's unfinished letter.

"A gentleman does not read another's correspondence, Your Grace." Her observation was intended to carry the whip-crack of an offended governess, not the plea of a besotted spinster.

"When you print your sentiments this large," he said, studying the half sheet of writing, "one can't help but read them from halfway across the shire. Who's Emily?"

"My twin sister. I showed you her miniature."

Hardcastle moved a branch of candles, the better to snoop into Ellen's private sentiments. "Her eyesight must be wanting, and she hasn't your gift for scholarship." He peered at the letter more closely, and Ellen's lungs refused to breathe. "*I am sad to leave my duke,*" he quoted. "*He is, in his way, very dear.*"

"Right now, you are not dear at all, sir. I will scream if you do not quit my room this instant." And then Ellen would cry, because the last treasure a woman ought to be able to keep for herself was her privacy, and Hardcastle had just trodden that right into the carpet.

"Am I dear?" he asked, setting the letter down. "From you, that is quite flattering. You will be pleased to know—"

He fell silent as voices sounded in the corridor. When the footsteps faded, Ellen marched to the window and yanked the curtains closed lest the fool man silhouette himself in her window for half the guests to see.

"I will be pleased to know what, Your Grace? That you have no respect for my dignity? That you are amused by my efforts to maintain a connection with my only sibling? That you—"

Strong hands settled on Ellen's waist and turned her to face her guest. "You will be pleased to know, madam, that *in your way*, you are dear to me as well."

Ellen wanted badly to touch Hardcastle's cheek, also to throw him out of her room, for the conversation was doomed.

"In my way, Your Grace?"

"You brook no foolishness, you don't fraternize with the footmen, you cannot be intimidated, though you are never rude, and you are unfailingly kind to my nephew. You have a sense of humor, which one sees in plain sight as rarely as a falling star in a summer sky. You are pretty, damn you, and hide your beauty more assiduously than your smiles. You kiss exceedingly well for a beginner. In your way, Ellen MacHugh, you are dear."

He growled his sweet sentiments begrudgingly. His hands remained at Ellen's waist, and she covered them with her own, not to dissuade him, but to hoard his touch.

"You are ill-tempered much of the time because you are tired," she retorted. "You take your responsibilities seriously, and you are almost afraid to love Christopher, lest he be taken from you too. You are very brave, Your Grace, and protective of all for whom you're responsible. For a duke, your kisses are surprisingly beguiling."

His hands slid around her to the small of her back. Ellen's fingers rested on his muscular biceps. "How many dukes have you kissed, Miss MacHugh?"

"Only the one, and him not nearly enough to speak knowledgeably."

So Ellen kissed him some more.

SOMEWHERE BETWEEN KNOCKING on Ellen's door and realizing that he'd never before seen her hair down, Hardcastle lost track of which rules he was intent on lecturing her about. Something about wedging a chair under his chin lest he gawp the night away. Her braid was a thick skein of auburn secured with a bright green bow she would never have worn when governessing in Kent.

Keep your door locked at all times, he wanted to tell her as her lips grazed his. *Admit no one*, he thought, as her tongue took a delicate taste of him. *Never drop your guard for an instant*, his brain shouted, while his hands cupped the lady's derriere and brought her flush against him.

She let him *in*, let him taste and beg and tease and beg some more even as he tugged the infernal bow free of her braid and slipped the scrap of silk into his pocket.

"You've used your tooth-powder," he muttered, walking her back until she sat on the bed.

"You've used yours."

Then she was at him again, pulling him over her, until he was crouched above her on the bed. Some dim, despairing corner of his mind knew he was behaving badly, but being a paragon was damned hard, *lonely* work.

Being a swain apparently had much to recommend it. Who knew?

Hardcastle gently palmed a breast through Ellen's nightclothes. "I want to devour you, and you're not telling me to stop."

"I've wanted to devour you for three years, which is why—"

Three years? Three years they'd wasted with civilities and fine manners and thirty-three-day silences?

"Which is why you're not stopping me now," Hardcastle said, unbelting the homeliest quilted dressing gown ever to enshroud a man's dearest dreams. "You can stop me, Ellen. If you order me from your room, I will get off this bed and return to my chambers."

"I should," she said, brushing his hair back from his brow. "I'm leaving in two weeks, Your Grace. This folly, precious though it may be, changes nothing."

This was not folly. This was the beginning of a course they would chart together, one that would end at the altar.

"You shall not leave me," Hardcastle said, getting off the bed, lest he disgrace himself in his haste. "I did not come here intending to seduce you."

Not consciously, at least. A small fig leaf for his pride.

Ellen tied her dressing gown closed, then scooted back to rest against the headboard. She was oblivious to her braid coming unraveled, while Hardcastle could notice little else.

"You cannot tell me what to do, Hardcastle. I'm leaving your employ, and that is my final word. You are welcome to stay with me or quit the room as long as we're clear on my plans."

Less and less was becoming clear, except that Hardcastle was in the presence of his future duchess.

He began a circuit of the room, blowing out candles as he went. "You'd allow me the privileges of a lover, Ellen?"

God help him if she sought to become his mistress. Other women had offered to take his coin in exchange for enduring his intimate attentions. He'd set up such arrangements three times after coming down from university, and all three times he'd been disappointed—nigh disgusted—with the results.

"I am offering to be your lover," Ellen said, drawing her feet up and linking her arms around her knees. "Though the notion shocks me. In two weeks, I'll return to Derbyshire and resume a life with my parents and my sister. Our means are limited, and spinsterhood will be my lot."

The hell it would.

"And if I were to propose?" Hardcastle asked, blowing out the last of the candles on the escritoire. Thank God for the sophistication of the English language and the delicate possibilities of conditional phrasing.

"I'd refuse you, Hardcastle," Ellen said, without an instant's hesitation. "You are discommoded by the ladies here at the house party, and you see decades of such house parties before you. Rather than entrust your future to the first debutante who can get herself compromised with you, you're turning to a known quantity who's already a member of your household. Your thinking is practical, but I could not accept such an offer."

Good God. Her stubbornness would be admirable if it weren't so baffling. "What could possibly motivate you to refuse a tiara, madam?" He knew why a sensible woman would reject his suit—he was ill-tempered, as she'd said, much consumed with estate business, and completely lacking in... *charm.*

Ellen gazed at her toes, whose acquaintance Hardcastle was very pleased to make. Rather than take a seat at the escritoire, as any sensible duke might have done, he slid onto the bed and took the place beside her, resting against the headboard.

"I will not be your duchess of convenience, Hardcastle. You're simply having a bad moment. We all have them. I'll get you through this house party, and you can tell your grandmama you're considering possibilities. She'll leave you alone for the next two years, at least."

Hardcastle did not want to be alone. He took Ellen's hand in both of his. "I'm to content myself with some shared pleasure where you're concerned? A casual affair such as house parties are notorious for?"

She blinked at her toes. "Yes, and I will do likewise. I'll have my pleasure of you and retire to Derbyshire with some lovely memories."

What a foul abuse of a tender pair of hearts that would be. Something else was afoot here, but two things prevented Hardcastle from further interrogating the woman so resolutely rejecting his marriage proposal. First, he needed to think, to consider angles and possibilities, and this he could not do while reclining on a bed in full sight of Ellen MacHugh's exposed toes.

Second, she'd accepted his offer to become her lover. Not even a ducal paragon could give strategy his attention when faced with that distraction.

So he kissed her.

THREE YEARS of living with Hardcastle had convinced Ellen of two things. First, the duke would not be rushed. Not at table, not when exchanging pleasantries in the churchyard, not when reviewing Ellen's written reports regarding Christopher's progress.

Second, when in pursuit of an objective, Hardcastle could not be stopped either.

This second attribute was a great comfort as His Grace situated himself on all fours over Ellen, kissed her, then pressed his cheek to hers, like a cat trying to inspire caresses. She should stop him, and she should order him from the room, but Derbyshire loomed in Ellen's nightmares.

Beautiful scenery, the loving arms of family, and endless loneliness. As Hardcastle's duchess of convenience, she'd be lonelier still, and yet, Ellen could not deny herself a night in the duke's arms.

She'd have decades to regret this folly, but only *now* to indulge in it.

"Shouldn't you take your boots off, sir?"

Hardcastle sat back on his heels and shot a disapproving look at her. "If you can think of boots at a moment like this, my kisses are clearly wanting in some material particular."

"You're overdressed for a *moment like this*, Hardcastle."

His gaze went to the knot of her dressing gown's belt.

Oh no you don't. "Boots off, Hardcastle. Now." Ellen used the same tone she'd apply when Christopher aimed longing glances at the main stairway's banister railing.

"Your servant, madam," the duke replied, bouncing to the edge of the bed.

"Was it so difficult to follow an order for once, Hardcastle?"

"In this bed, Ellen MacHugh," he said, yanking off first one boot then the other, "I will follow any orders you give, even the ones you can't bear to put into words."

Those were legion. He should choose a duchess he could love, one who loved him, not merely settle for a convenient woman to whom he was attracted. He should make time for amusement, play the color game in all its silly pointlessness. Laugh, smile, flirt with the dowagers, and be late for meetings. Sleep in on rainy mornings and stay up half the night reading lurid novels.

"You grow silent," he said, draping his waistcoat over the chair at the desk. "Silence is not permitted if it means you're changing your mind. That's an order you must follow, madam. You've given me leave to be your lover, and lovers talk to each other."

"You've had so many?" She hoped he'd had a few. Lovers, women whose company he enjoyed, not merely sexual passing fancies.

He pulled his shirt off, and moonlight slipped through a crack in the drawn curtains to gild shoulders heavy with muscle. Hardcastle was an avid equestrian, and often went for long tramps with his stewards to call upon the yeomanry.

He was fit and beautiful, and that was before he shed his stockings and breeches.

"I've had enough experience to know what I'm about, Ellen. You must not be nervous. Whatever encounters you've had, including the great scandalous ones that sent you into service, they don't signify."

Hardcastle stood beside the bed, as confident in his nudity as he was in all his Bond Street finery, but what was he trying to tell her?

"Are you forgiving me for having a past?" Ellen had paid dearly for that past and could not expect him to ignore it.

The duke climbed onto the bed and kept coming, a predator on the scent, until he was once again crouched over Ellen, though this time, he wore not a stitch.

"I'm asking you," he said, "humbly suggesting, in fact, that you set aside your preconceived notions, about what happens next, about yourself, about *me*, and allow me to pleasure you as a lady deserves to be pleasured."

Ellen hardly knew what happened next, though she was very sure she wanted Hardcastle to be the one to show her.

The tone of his words was imperious, while the tone of his kiss was beseeching. Hardcastle's mouth was all delicate patience and tactful entreaty as he pressed his lips to Ellen's. His explorations were the gentlest invitations, and his presence became one of sheltering warmth rather than masculine demand.

When Ellen cradled his jaw with her palm, he moved into her touch. "Tell me," he whispered. "Say what you long for."

Ellen longed for time to absorb this beguilement, for years to explore Hardcastle's unexpected capacity for tenderness. Even more tempting, she sensed he longed to lay still greater treasures at her feet.

"I long for you," she said, the most honest summary of her dreams. "Only you, all of you."

He rested his forehead against hers, and she took the moment to savor the silky texture of his hair as she slipped her fingers through his dark locks. He bore the lemony scent of a hard-milled French soap, and his back and shoulders were hot beneath her touch. In winter, sleeping next to him would be...

Some other woman's privilege.

"If you're to have me," he said, rising from the bed and turning down the counterpane, "and I dearly hope you shall, then I'd best get under the covers."

A more prudent woman would use the moment to extract a promise from him that he'd support any children resulting from this encounter. Ellen didn't bother to ask, for of course he would. The greater question was, would she even let him know she'd conceived, when his child might be all she ever had of him?

"Shall I take off my night robe?"

Beneath her night robe, Ellen wore only a summer-length chemise. The fabric had worn thin over the past five years, but Emily had helped with the white work on the hem. Sentiment thus kept near what practicality would have surrendered long ago.

"Do you want to take off your night robe, Ellen?"

Of course she didn't. She was not young, her breasts were modest when men supposedly liked an ample bosom. Her hips were generous, and she—

"My dear?" the duke asked, unknotting the sash of her robe, but making no move to take it off of her. "To be next to you, right next to you, skin to skin, heartbeat to heartbeat, would be a rare and privileged pleasure, but your wishes must come before all else."

He'd wait all night, while Ellen dithered away another three years. She wiggled out of the night robe and handed it to him, then drew the chemise over her head and scooted under the covers.

"You may hide your treasures, *for now*," Hardcastle said. Ellen expected him to toss her chemise aside, but he instead remained by the bed, running his fingers over the hem. "Part of your trousseau, I'd guess based on this embroidery. The work is very fine."

"I enjoy needlework," Ellen said. "Though it's hard on the eyes."

His Grace was the opposite of hard on the eyes. Hardcastle's belly was divided into small, rectangular fields of muscle, arranged on either side of a trail of dark hair. The trail first narrowed before widening as it went south, and then....

Then Ellen had to look away. The sight of Hardcastle's bodily anticipation of their pleasures would stay with her for the rest of her life.

He bunched the fabric of Ellen's nightgown beneath his nose. "Lavender. Lilacs. *You*."

The nightgown went sailing to the foot of the bed as the mattress dipped. In the next instant, Hardcastle was under the covers, four-teen stone of hot, naked, unstoppable duke.

"You peeked," he said, sliding an arm under Ellen's neck and drawing her against his side. "I'm quite flattered that you peeked, and you a woman of such iron self-discipline."

"I could hardly avoid the sight of your wares right before my eyes. You gawked," Ellen countered, finding the perfect place to rest her cheek against his chest. "I wasn't flaunting anything, sir."

"You needn't flaunt your delights," he replied. "I can learn all I need to know about your various attributes by tactile exploration. You may make similar forays upon my person, and I will adore you for them."

Adoration wasn't love, but Ellen hugged the admission close to her heart anyway. "I didn't expect you to be so warm to the touch," she said, tracing a single finger down the midline of his belly—halfway down.

His reply was to take her hand and wrap her fingers around a hot, smooth shaft of male flesh.

"You didn't expect me to be so beastly aroused, but a duke is simply a man, Ellen. He's a man with more responsibilities than most, but no less human."

More human, maybe? Hardcastle's hand fell away, leaving Ellen holding... the ducal succession, as it were.

"What does one do...?" she asked, running a finger around the tip.

"One indulges one's curiosity, or—this is your only warning—two indulge their curiosity about each other."

Ellen could not have said how long Hardcastle endured her explorations, how many ways she touched and teased and tasted him, how varied were the kisses they shared. She let go of the entire burden of propriety, let go of all the tomorrows and next years, and reveled in intimacy with the only lover she'd ever have.

Hardcastle was relentless when it came to her breasts. He kissed, he fondled, he applied nuanced, maddening pressure, he put his mouth on her and drew forth groans such as no governess uttered in the company of her employer.

Ellen would have let him arouse her thus all night, except she gradually grasped that he was waiting for her permission to become her lover in the fullest sense.

She tugged on his hair, which he seemed to like. "Hardcastle?"

"My name is Gerard," he muttered, Ellen's earlobe between his teeth. "You even taste like lavender. When I put my mouth between your legs, will you taste of lavender there?"

Gracious heavens. "You would not dare."

He would, though. The reserved, sophisticated duke was nowhere in the bed. In his place was a lusty, lovely fellow who dared much and teased more.

"I can feel you blushing." Hardcastle sounded thoroughly pleased with himself as he shifted over her. "You have the most delectable ears, madam.

"Hard—Gerard, you've humored my maidenly vapors long enough. If I can't have you now, I will think you've had a change of heart."

His palm cradled the back of Ellen's head, and she pressed her heated cheek to his shoulder.

"Are you sure, Ellen?"

Now he asked that? Now, when she was so overwrought she was ready to bite him? But in this, he would be not the duke, but the gentleman, and the last piece of Ellen's heart not in his keeping slipped from her grasp.

"Now, please, Gerard."

Hardcastle braced himself on his elbows, a blanket of warmth and attentiveness. "I'll do this part, while you luxuriate in my desire and consideration, else I shall disgrace myself."

He was serious, also waiting for Ellen's acknowledgment of his pronouncement.

"I'm luxuriating, Hardcastle. You have my word on that."

"God knows, I'm desiring."

Despite that desire, he joined them slowly, with many lazy kisses, a detour here to draw on a nipple, a frolic there to nuzzle at Ellen's temple. She caught his rhythm, learned the tempo and phrasing of his passion, and of her own. Of discomfort, there was none, but along with a growing wonder, Ellen also suffered a yawning sense of loss.

Hardcastle's duchess would share this with him a thousand times, would hold him as passion crested higher and higher, would gather up the endearments lurking in his lectures and proclamations.

How could making love with him feel so blessedly, absolutely right, a long-awaited union of unlikely souls, a pleasure beyond description, and yet, all they would have was this short, drenching season of bliss, and then—

Hardcastle shifted, so he was more over Ellen, and that lined them up at a new angle, on a trajectory of sheer, mindless ecstasy. Ellen undulated into his thrusts, locked her ankles at the small of his back, and let desire pour into all the bleak questions and empty years ahead, let bliss have its long, lovely moment.

When Ellen could bear to ease her grip on him, Hardcastle was barely breathing hard, while she was panting in a near swoon.

"Now would also be an appropriate moment to luxuriate," he whispered, "for I assuredly am."

"If you move, Hardcastle, I will not answer for the consequences." Ellen would surely start crying, just as soon as she wrung herself out in his arms again.

"You move," he said, giving Ellen a lazy thrust that made her ears hum. "Play the color game. Close your eyes and see hues of passion, satisfaction, desire, and pleasure."

"I'd lose every round," Ellen whispered, smoothing a hand down Hardcastle's back to grab a muscular fundament. "For I cannot think, cannot form sentences."

"Splendid."

Splendid, indeed. Hardcastle drove her through the maelstrom again, and then once more, the last loving sweet and lazy and all the more wrenching for the deliberation with which he pleasured her.

When Ellen could bear no more, he gently withdrew, stroked himself a few times, and spent his seed on her belly.

This consideration, this proof that Hardcastle would make no claim on Ellen's future, brought all the misery and loss to the fore, worse than ever because now, she knew what she'd be missing.

"I'll be back," he said, shifting off of her and tenting the covers over her middle. Water splashed against porcelain, shadows moved beyond the slivers of moonlight. Ellen bestirred herself to find her handkerchief on the night table and deal with Hardcastle's spent seed.

Already, practical reality intruded, though the temptation to cry would not leave her.

"Shall I fetch you a flannel?" Hardcastle asked from across the room.

"I used my handkerchief."

Then he was beside the bed, a looming presence. "This is clean." He put a damp cloth in her hand, then he waited by the bed, clearly expecting her to use the cloth and pass it back to him.

Intimacy upon intimacy, but Ellen liked that Hardcastle wasn't pulling on his breeches and preparing to leave her.

"Move over," he said, when the ablutions had been tended to all around. "Now comes the part where you talk to me, in which activity you have been woefully deficient thus far, Miss MacHugh."

Ellen shifted to the side, unsure if she was being scolded or teased. Hardcastle's embrace left no doubt that she was being held though. He cuddled himself around her from the back, his arm at her waist, his fingers linked with hers.

"What shall I talk about?" Ellen asked, despite the lump in her throat.

If he wanted to gossip about the house party guests, she'd muster some string of insightful observations. If he wanted to talk about Christopher, she'd manage that. They'd likely have to face each other over breakfast, after all. Small talk would be required then too.

"Tell me about home," he said, "about Derbyshire, for that's where you'll go in two weeks. It must be lovely, to call to you so strongly even after five years."

Ellen had been back in those five years. A governess was given leave, while a duke was not.

"Derbyshire is home, Hardcastle. My only sibling is there, my parents, my girlhood memories. I was happy there."

Also lonely, bewildered, and frequently invisible when Emily was in the room.

"Tell me your earliest memory. Mine was of my cat, Henry, bringing a mouse into the nursery. I thought it was capital of him to decimate the wildlife. The nursery maid climbed on a table and shrieked down the rafters."

Ellen couldn't tell Hardcastle her earliest memory, of Mama explaining that sisters always looked out for each other. She instead told him of the day she'd got her first book, a storybook with woodcuts of giants, dragons, unicorns, and princesses.

Every decent fairy tale had at least one princess. Governesses did not feature prominently in fairy tales, however.

Hardcastle excelled at cuddling, and the dratted man also had a way with a backrub, kneading Ellen's shoulders, then her hip, with a slow, confident touch that made her eyes heavy and her words difficult to find.

"Go to sleep, love," he murmured, kissing her shoulder. "You've had a long day, and we've many days yet ahead of us."

No, they didn't. They were down to twelve days now, and most of that time would be spent in polite company. Ellen closed her eyes, despite wanting to argue with her lover, and lost a final round of the color game.

She appointed herself the task of describing this encounter with Hardcastle, the tenderness and surprise of it, the pleasure and heartache. Colors would not come to her, descriptions eluded her, for no matter which way she viewed the past hour, or what aspect she focused on, all that Ellen could see was a single deep, abiding shade of love.

CHAPTER FOUR

Hardcastle woke early, his body imbued with a sense of well-being in which his heart did not join. He'd left Ellen's bedroom deep in the night, unwilling to trouble her slumbers with more passion. He'd dreamed of East Anglia, a bleak and cheerless place the few times he'd visited, and he'd dreamed of Christopher.

Being a swain did not come to Hardcastle naturally, but as the morning wore on, he found that a capacity for stealth learned as small boy was yet his. The household mail was apparently collected on a sideboard in the library, so—after sending a footman to inspect for unchaperoned females—to the library, Hardcastle did go.

"What the hell are you doing, going through my mail, Hardcastle?"

Sedgemere's question was friendly, for Sedgemere.

"Looking for a letter I might frank for Miss MacHugh," Hardcastle replied, seizing on the missive in question. Save for the direction, the epistle had no writing on the outside, much less crossed writing, and was addressed to Miss Emily MacHugh, Hollowell Grange, Swaddledale, Derbyshire.

"I frank all my guests' correspondence, as do you, Hardcastle,"

Sedgemere said, stalking closer. "Miss MacHugh isn't writing to a beau, is she?"

"To her sister." Even the address was printed in large letters, which made no sense.

Sedgemere snatched the epistle away. "I won't let you read her letter, Hardcastle. Not under any circumstances."

"I've already read enough of it," Hardcastle replied. *Very dear, in his way,* indeed. "Why would a woman pass up a tiara for a life of spinsterhood in Swaddledale? Where is Swaddledale, for that matter?"

Sedgemere put the letter back on top of the correspondence piled on the sideboard. "Not far south of Chesterfield. You could be there and back in less than a day, particularly if you changed horses."

"Oh, Your Graces!" Miss Pendleton stood at the library door, upon which she had not knocked. "I do beg your pardon. I thought to borrow a book until the kite flying begins. Perhaps His Grace of Hardcastle would assist me to find something to help a young lady while away a pretty morning?"

Assist her to find a fiancé, perhaps? Ellen had told Hardcastle exactly what to say in this very circumstance.

"I confess," Hardcastle replied, "I am not sufficiently familiar with His Grace's collection to be of any aid, and I have taken enough of Sedgemere's time. I wish you good day and successful kite flying."

He strode past Miss Pendleton, enjoying the consternation his comment caused.

The entire day followed the same pattern, with Hardcastle barely dodging enemy fire but for Ellen's company or guidance, until he was taken captive in the late afternoon by Miss Pendleton and her familiar, Miss Frobisher. They asked his aid choosing a suitable mount for the next day's outing to admire the lake at the Duke of Stoke Teversault's nearby estate.

By the time Hardcastle stole into Ellen's room that night, he was so hungry for her company he nearly dove straight onto the bed.

"Madam, good evening." Hardcastle had let himself into her

bedroom and stood for a moment inside the door, beholding his beloved as she stared at a book before the fire. "What are you reading?"

She brushed a glance over him, and Hardcastle knew without a word being spoken, that something was amiss.

"Wordsworth," she said. "My sister Emily likes all the poems about lambs and daffodils, so I'm brushing up. You were very busy today."

Hardcastle locked the door and took the second chair facing the hearth. "I have renewed respect for those fellows who gathered intelligence for Wellington. A precarious existence lies behind enemy lines. Shall I kill Greenover for you?"

"Somebody ought to," she said, setting old Wordsworth aside. "He's a menace to the maids. The duchess now has them working in pairs to avoid his attentions."

Hardcastle nudged Ellen's slipper with the toe of his boot. "Were you avoiding my attentions this afternoon, Ellen? You were not gone from my side five minutes before the marital press gang descended."

She stared at the fire, which threw out some warmth without being a great blaze. "I cannot avoid you. You are in my every thought. I move to accept a plate from a footman, and my body reminds me of you in places a lady doesn't have names for. I brush my hair, and I feel your hands on my person. You have become an affliction for which I fear there is no cure."

"An affliction." Well, damn. He was apparently getting this swaining business all wrong.

Ellen swiped at her cheek with the backs of her fingers. "You are like the scent of roses on my favorite shawl, a sweet taste in my mouth. I did not anticipate—" She sighed mightily and tucked her foot under her. "Perhaps you'd better go, Your Grace. I seem to be in a lachrymose and difficult mood."

"You're always in a difficult mood. So am I. We like that about each other, but you're not usually irrational. Last night you called me Gerard, tonight I'm *dux non grata*?"

"Your Latin doesn't strike me—"

Hardcastle took her hand. "Talk to me, Ellen. Tell me about life as a girl in Upper Swaddlehog. Tell me about your parents, your sister, your first pony, your favorite book."

She rose, taking her hand from his grasp. "I am indisposed, *Gerard*. You needn't coax and charm me into bed, for it won't serve. I bid you good night."

Indisposed. Hardcastle knew what that meant. He'd been to university, he'd made the acquaintance of the women whose business was the education of the scholars in topics other than Latin or Greek.

"No charming or coaxing, then," he said, standing and scooping Ellen off her feet in one lithe move. "I'll simply deposit you on the bed and join you therein without further bumbling."

"Hardcastle! What are you—? Gerard!"

He was careful with her, settling her gently on the bed though the moment called for a hearty toss.

"A little insanity in my duchess will enliven the line considerably," he said, tugging off his boots. "And you have quite taken leave of your senses, madam, if you think my attentions are solely the result of animal spirits. Move over."

"Hardcastle, I cannot entertain you tonight," she groused, scooting an entire three inches toward the far side of the bed.

"You're entertaining me quite nicely, also ensuring that I get my exercise," he said, lifting her into his arms—mostly for the pleasure of holding her—then settling her two-thirds of the way across the bed. "If you need to use the privacy screen, I assure you, my delicate sensibilities won't be offended."

Well, this was amusing. Miss Ellen MacHugh, queen of the Hardcastle schoolroom and terror of twenty footmen, was gaping at him as he undressed. She'd propped herself on her elbows to have a better look, in fact, and hadn't even mentioned dousing the candles.

"Hardcastle, you are not paying attention."

No, but *she* was. "As if I could tear my attention from you, Miss MacHugh, when the livelong day I've been beset and beleaguered by your inferiors. Hounded from breakfast to brandy. Curls bouncing here, giggles twittering from over there, bosoms jiggling on all sides. Then they come at me in pairs."

"Bosoms generally do, Your Grace."

"My dear, do not mock a man clinging to reason by the slenderest thread. Get your night robe off, please."

Hardcastle pulled his shirt over his head and peeled out of his trousers. In the morning, his valet would cast martyred glances upon the resulting wrinkles, and Hardcastle *would not care.*

"Tell me about your indisposition," he said, taking the proffered night robe and hanging it on a bedpost.

"Tell me about the jiggling bosoms."

Ellen had stopped ordering him from the room, which was progress. Maybe he had potential as a swain after all. Hardcastle climbed naked under the covers.

"Nobody has used the bed warmer on these sheets," he observed. "How invigorating, as if present company were not stimulating enough. The bosoms were very pale and tended to quiver at me, like eager puppies straining to escape the bodices imprisoning them. We're not having daughters. I can assure you of this right now, my dear. My nerves will not endure such a trial."

"Hardcastle, calm yourself. We're having a liaison, or we were— we're not any longer—and children don't come into it."

Now Miss Ellen MacHugh was ordering matters on behalf of the Almighty, which even a duke knew was tempting fate.

Hardcastle rolled her to her side and wrapped himself around her. "Do you typically allow men with whom you're not having a liaison into your bed, madam?"

"I don't typically allow men anything, ever. But here you are."

Exactly where he wanted to be. "Why the tears, Ellen? Is it your indisposition? Her Grace, my grandmother, has offered a few choice sentiments regarding this indisposition. She doesn't approve of it."

"No woman does. What are you *doing* here, Hardcastle?"

"Settling my overwrought nerves, for one thing. A debutante who finishes her first Season without an offer of marriage is a ruthless, resourceful creature. Tomorrow you will do a better job of protecting me from them." He was settling Ellen's nerves too, he hoped. Stroking the tension from her neck and shoulders, easing anxiety from her fingers.

She shifted to her back. "We forgot to blow out the candles. Beeswax is very dear."

"So are you." Hardcastle got off the bed and did the honors, plunging the room into cozy shadows cast by the fire in the hearth. When he climbed back under the covers, he situated himself beside his intended, his cheek pillowed on her breast.

"What am I to do with you, Hardcastle? I cannot frolic with you, not tonight."

He'd mistaken Ellen's mood for stubborn, but a simpler explanation begged for his notice: She believed he had no use for her beyond the physical.

"You are to tell me stories, about Miss Ellen MacHugh, soon to be former governess. I'm sure the tales of Greater Goatswaddle are boring enough to put even an overwrought duke to sleep."

His arrogance must have been the reassurance she needed, for she launched into a story about picnics in the back garden, and Papa teasing Mama over breakfast, services on Sunday, and longing for a pony of her own.

Eventually, Ellen fell asleep, and Hardcastle stole from her room, intent on sticking to her side like a well-dressed cocklebur on the morrow. He had returned his clothing to the wardrobe and clothes press, and wedged a chair under his bedroom door when he figured out what about Ellen's recitation had bothered him.

Of puppies and kittens there had been numerous mentions, of Mama and Papa and the vicar and Mrs. Trimble, the housekeeper.

But she hadn't brought her sister's name up once.

～

FOR SEVEN NIGHTS, Hardcastle had come to Ellen's room, and he and she had developed a routine. She waited up for him, staring at poetry and wondering how on earth she'd manage when the house party ended.

He'd arrive, bristling with indignation at the latest attempt by some scheming young lady to compromise him, and Ellen would get him out of his clothes. As he shed waistcoat, cravat, shirt, and stockings, his mood would improve as well.

The prospect of losing one's liberty was terrifying. Ellen did not belittle the duke's worries in that regard at all.

She, however, had lost her heart, and at the worst possible time.

"Walk with me, Miss MacHugh," Hardcastle said, taking her elbow as she cut through the conservatory at midmorning. "Don't look over your shoulder. Hang on my every word, and I wouldn't mind if you put a bit of bosom into the conversation too."

"I have only a bit of bosom," Ellen retorted, keeping her attributes to herself. Hardcastle did this to her, made her bold and irritable. He could manage such a demeanor all in a day's duke-ing. On a governess quitting her post, the same mood came off as simply testy.

"Your treasures are abundant enough to drive me mad," Hardcastle said. "Though I'm already half insane. Sedgemere has decided we must go on a ducal progress, and sprinkle duke dust on all the local titles. In truth, Her Grace wants Sedgemere out of her hair for a day or two before the Dukeries Cup. I must oblige Sedgemere, or Anne will kill me. Consider yourself warned: Courtesy among ducal households can be a violent undertaking."

"You're leaving?" Ellen asked as they emerged onto the side terrace.

Hardcastle glanced around, and apparently heedless of who might be looking out of windows or lurking in the garden, kissed her cheek.

"Terrible timing for this outing, I know, my dear. You're no longer indisposed?"

Ellen shook her head. She was permanently disabled with

longing for Hardcastle's company. Her indisposition had departed, however.

"Death is too good for Sedgemere," Hardcastle said. "I'll be back by tomorrow, the day after at the latest, and you will please be here when I return."

He'd be back the day before the house party ended. One day—most of that taken up with some silly boat race—followed by one night, after that and then... Derbyshire.

"I will be here," Ellen said. "You will lend me the ducal traveling coach for my journey to Derbyshire."

"Shall I? I've not been accused of generosity by many, Miss MacHugh."

Hardcastle was very generous, spending night after night with her, reading her poetry, regaling her with stories from public school and university. His passion was breathtaking, but this other—this simple, friendly intimacy—was devastatingly dear.

"You're generous, Hardcastle. Witness, you will not send Sedgemere calling without an ally at his side, so nobody will grasp that his duchess has banished him from his own house party."

He peered down at her. "You have the most peculiar notions. We'll take an earl or two with us, any viscounts sober enough to sit a horse or barons who've lost too much at the whist tables. The ladies will get some peace and quiet before the final ball, and the fellows who need to brush up their rowing skills can do that."

"I don't want peace and quiet," Ellen muttered as Hardcastle escorted her down the steps into the garden. "I want another week, at least, and you here, and—"

He wrapped her in his embrace, as if she were *allowed* to resent this parting, as if a part of him already belonged to her.

"Ellen, why won't you marry me?"

The question had cost him. Ellen was bundled in close, holding on to Hardcastle for dear life, and she could feel the pride and bewilderment in him.

"My family needs me," she said, which was true. "My parents

are getting on, Christopher is ready for more rigorous instruction, and it's time. You must simply learn to avoid house parties, Your Grace."

His chin rested on her crown, so perfectly did they fit together.

"How would I have managed these past days without you, Ellen? You stayed with the Pendleton creature when she claimed to have turned her ankle. You put Greenover up to dancing with that forward redhead when she forged my name on her dance card. You sat next to me in every parlor where I might have found myself with a lapful of swooning debutante but for your vigilance."

This was the problem, right here. Hardcastle needed a duchess, any duchess, if he was to be spared more weeks of dodging and ducking his fate. Gratitude was not love, though, and passion was not love.

"You will enjoy this tour of the ducal neighbors," Ellen said. "Christopher will miss you."

"I ordered him to keep a close eye on you in my absence. He's having entirely too much fun with Sedgemere's ruffians, though."

All the more proof that Ellen was no longer needed in the ducal household. "I'll walk you to the stables, Your Grace."

He accepted that decision with ominous quiet and resumed their progress across the gardens.

"You will be here when I return, Ellen? No disappearing into the wilds of the Peak District, never to be seen again?"

"Not yet. That part comes at the end of the week, sir."

"The duchess in you allows you this calm. I wouldn't mind if you fell weeping on my neck, you know."

"You're welcome to fall weeping on mine, sir. I don't recommend it, though. Composure, like a reputation, is not easily regained once lost."

"More duchess-ing. Don't abandon me, Ellen. Be here when I return."

His Grace was, in his imperious and dear way, pleading.

They reached the stables, where the duke's horse stood patiently by a groom at the mounting block, and abruptly Ellen did want to fall weeping on Hardcastle's neck.

On his boots, even.

"I'll take the horse," the duke said to the groom, giving the girth a stout tug. When Ellen expected Hardcastle to swing into the saddle, he instead took Ellen by the hand and led the gelding off toward an enormous oak across the lane from the stable yard. "Madam, a moment of your time."

Ellen would never be able to refuse him anything, and grief made her reckless. "Hardcastle, perhaps it would be better if you didn't return before I leave."

"I see."

"What do you think you see?"

"I see that you are as stubborn as a duchess too. How many times must I propose to you? Your physical affection for my person has been evidenced convincingly, though on damnably few occasions. I don't think you object to my morals or even to my station. What deficiency must I address to win your hand?"

"You are not deficient, Hardcastle. You are in no way deficient, but my family needs me, and I've ignored them for too long. They love me, and they have no one else. You are fighting off prospective duchesses at every turn, but my family has only me."

Sedgemere came strutting down the garden path, his duchess twirling her parasol at his side. Before they could notice the couple in the shade of the oak, Ellen kissed Hardcastle as passionately as she dared when he was looking so thunderous.

Then she stepped back. "Safe journey, Your Grace."

"She makes no promises," the duke said to his gelding. "You will note, horse, that I am sent toddling on my way with no further reassurances of anything substantive, no real explanations, no apologies. I am a duke, though, so I shan't have a tantrum right here in the stable yard, such as *any governess* would know meant a fellow had finally been pushed too far."

"Your Grace, we have company."

Sedgemere was kissing his duchess farewell, rather shamelessly, or perhaps that was how a duke and duchess allowed a distraught guest a moment to gather her composure.

"We have company, and we are out of time," Hardcastle said. "Not even a duke can defy the dictates of time."

"I cannot deny the importuning of my family," Ellen said. "You understand duty, Hardcastle, and they are mine."

"I understand duty," he said, tapping his hat onto his head. "I do not understand you. If I'm not back in time for the Dukeries Cup, bet your pin money on Linton's boat."

He led his horse to the mounting block, swung up, and waited for Sedgemere to turn the duchess loose. Her Grace came to stand beside Ellen beneath the oak as Sedgemere's horse was brought out.

"They're a very handsome pair," Her Grace said.

"I prefer Hardcastle's darker coloring," Ellen said. "No offense to your husband."

"I meant the horses," the duchess replied. "Shall we sit by the duck pond for a moment, Miss MacHugh? I am not equal to dealing with the downcast expressions on the young ladies collectively grieving in my parlor."

There would be grieving by the duck pond, did the duchess but know it. "I am at your disposal, ma'am."

"Hardcastle has quite defied the efforts of the ladies to wrest a marriage proposal from him," the duchess observed. "You were instrumental in foiling their mischief."

"His Grace asked that of me, and I was happy to oblige."

They found their bench, and as before, a half dozen placid ducks paddled around on the pond's surface.

"You don't appear very happy now, Miss MacHugh. I apologize for sending some of the men away, but Mr. Greenover had lost more than he could afford to lose, and I could not allow the problem with the maids to worsen if I wanted my guests to sleep on clean sheets. Then too, you were not getting enough rest."

"I have never slept better, Your Grace." Never felt more safe and cared for than when sharing a bed with Hardcastle, though late night visits and cozy chats were not love.

"Miss MacHugh... May I call you Ellen?"

Oh, dear. A scold or condolences was loaded into the duchess's cannon, and either would be awful.

"Of course, ma'am."

"I am Anne, and you will think me very forward for what I'm about to say, but at night I send Sedgemere to make a final patrol of the hallways in the guest wing, and to do that, he traverses the family wing. Twice he spotted Hardcastle at your door. If you ask it of me, I will compel Hardcastle to offer for you. Sedgemere says I shouldn't, but he knows better than to expect meek complicity from me."

The ducks erupted into an altercation, with flapping and squawking and much splashing about where all had been calm a moment earlier.

"His Grace has proposed," Ellen said. "But I am needed elsewhere. He needs a wife of impeccable lineage and great consequence, while I... The very last thing I want is an offer of marriage compelled by propriety, exigencies, and ducal honor."

The ducks settled their differences, though turbulence echoed on the surface of the pond.

The duchess remained silent a moment, then fired off a broadside. "Do you love him, Ellen?"

"Endlessly, and I could not bear for Hardcastle's interest to cool in a year or two, while I'm left to console myself with his excellent manners for the rest of my life. If I marry Hardcastle, I'll trade a year of anxious bliss with him for all the years I owe my family, and be doubly miserable."

The ducks waddled onto the grass, their progress up the bank ungainly compared to their gliding about on the water. The lead duck raised his wings and flapped madly directly before Ellen, sending a shower of droplets all over her hems.

"Rotten boy," the duchess said, opening and closing her parasol at the duck. "Shoo, and don't come back."

Her Grace set her parasol aside, and there seemed nothing more to say, but one didn't hare off from the company of a duchess without being excused.

"Men are dunderheads, sometimes. Women are too," the duchess said. "We're like those ducks, taking odd notions for no apparent reason, our thoughts churning furiously while all appears serene above the surface. I cannot fault you for wanting to be loved for yourself. I put the same challenge to Sedgemere, and he figured out how to convince me of his regard. Hardcastle is no less determined and no less intelligent."

He was also no less a duke. Hardcastle wasn't the problem. "Shall we go in, Your Grace? I'm abruptly peckish, and I'd like to look in on Christopher."

"Oh, let's do repair to the nursery. We'll get up a cricket match with the infantry, and that will cheer the young ladies wonderfully."

No, it would not. Nothing would cheer the young ladies short of a decree from the Regent that dukes were allowed eleven wives apiece. Ellen soon found herself amid the noise and merriment of a cricket match anyway, though in Hardcastle's absence, all she wanted was to go up to her bedroom, lock the door, and start packing for the looming journey home.

"I SAW you twice on my evening patrols, Hardcastle, and I wasn't even looking for you," Sedgemere announced as they brought their horses down to the walk. "Anne is ready to turn you over her knee, but I've counseled against such violence."

"Your duchess has a stout right arm, does she?"

"I presented her with three boys upon her marriage to me, Hardcastle. Everything about my Anne is made of stern stuff. Why haven't you secured Miss MacHugh's hand in marriage?"

The countryside was summer-ripe, the rise toward the Peak District visible off to the west, and yet every mile traveled was a greater distance from the woman Hardcastle needed by his side. Ellen wasn't being entirely honest with him, and the urge to turn his horse around and gallop back to her became a greater torment with each passing moment.

"Hardcastle, I asked you a direct question using simple words. Your reply is to gaze off at the horizon looking noble and infatuated. Have you lost your wits?"

"Yes." And his heart.

Sedgemere let out a sigh of significantly longsuffering proportions. "Miss MacHugh turned you down?"

They were a good half mile ahead of the rest of the party, and privacy would be in short supply once they reached their destination.

"Ellen has refused my suit at least a half dozen times."

"Dear me, old boy. Appears you're bungling this rather badly."

Hardcastle mentally set aside the problem that was Ellen's stubbornness and focused instead on the problem that was the Duke of Sedgemere in a gleeful mood.

"Bungling should be easy for you to spot, Sedgemere, since you've done so much of it yourself," Hardcastle shot back. "I, however, am an utter tyro at the sport. Ellen says her family *needs* her, but I merely *want* a duchess, any duchess. I do believe my dearest love is trying to protect me."

This conviction grew the longer Hardcastle puzzled on the entire situation. Ellen's regard for him was genuine, of that he was certain. He cast back over three years of sidelong glances. Three years when his slightest sneeze or headache was met with an attentiveness from the staff he was sure she'd inspired.

Her regard for him had been right under his nose for years, and he'd failed to grasp that. He was similarly failing to grasp the obvious now.

"She's protecting you from *herself?*" Sedgemere said. "That makes no sense. Miss MacHugh is far better than you deserve."

And to think Sedgemere owed his present marital happiness to the patient good offices of a devoted friend and fellow duke.

"You're not helping, Sedgemere. A round of fisticuffs might restore my usual good cheer."

"Promises, promises. You have no good cheer, Hardcastle. Have you gone down on bended knee, done the pretty, delivered the maudlin speech?"

This was not good news. "A maudlin speech is required?"

Sedgemere tugged on his cravat and adjusted his hat. "You say the words, man. Ladies long to hear the words."

"I've asked Ellen to marry me in the King's English. No beating about the bush, no prevaricating—not after the first time—no dodging the issue. I've asked her as plainly as a man—if you are laughing, I will make you regret it, Sedgemere. I'm on quite good terms with your boys, one of whom is my god-son, and your estate is home to more toads than you can imagine."

"Anne is toad-proof. Put as many in our bed as you please."

"She has you in her bed. That's trial enough for any woman."

Sedgemere's smile faded to his characteristic glower. "Anne rather likes having me in her bed, I'll have you know. *Have you told Miss MacHugh that you love her?* That she is the only woman in the world for you? That no matter how little she brings to the union, no matter how much talk will result, your love is greater than any obstacle?"

"Sedgemere, have you been keeping company with Greenover?"

"As little as possible, why?"

"You have lost your wits. One doesn't make dramatic speeches to a woman of sense, as if one were any lack-wit viscount. One *shows* such a woman that she's loved. One cossets and cuddles, one reads poetry and rubs her feet. One spends time with the lady and opens his heart and his past to her. One doesn't..."

Maybe one did. Sedgemere was obnoxiously happy with his duchess, though she'd led him a dance all the way to the altar.

"Poetry, Hardcastle? You can recite Byron, but you can't say three little words?"

"Go to hell. That's three words."

"I suggest you try those with Miss MacHugh. That will enliven the house party considerably."

The words were easy—Hardcastle loved Ellen with all his heart— though his failure to give those words to her had been a dreadful oversight. She'd said her family loved her, told him that repeatedly, and he'd missed his cue every time.

Unease joined Hardcastle in the saddle. "Sedgemere, what do you know of Miss MacHugh's family?"

"She's granddaughter of the Earl of Dalton. Her aunt and Anne have a passing acquaintance. There's another daughter, but no sons."

"That's all?" Sedgemere was one of those troublesome people who never forgot anything. Not a horse's bloodline, not an article in the newspaper, not a speech in the Lords. "These people own land less than a day's ride from your family seat, and you know nothing more than that about them?"

"Does seem odd, doesn't it?" Sedgemere said. "Even if they can't afford to entertain, we'd see them at the occasional hunt ball or Christmas musicale."

A hunch blossomed into a suspicion in Hardcastle's mind. "You will make my excuses to whichever duke we're imposing on for the night. I have pressing business elsewhere." He wheeled his horse around and headed at a gallop back toward the last crossroads.

CHAPTER FIVE

"Those who were off visiting or enjoying the Dukeries Cup will be back in good time for tonight's gathering," the duchess assured Ellen. "Sedgemere has sent me no less than three notes confirming this scheduling, and I would sorely regret it if my duke's word were no longer trustworthy."

Ellen paced the length of the duchess's private sitting room, until she was at the window overlooking the drive.

"Sedgemere said nothing about Hardcastle needing the ducal traveling coach?" This vehicle had not been in the mews when Ellen had visited the stables with Christopher earlier in the day.

"Sedgemere did not mention the coach," Her Grace replied, sticking a finger into a bowl of white roses on the mantel. "Perhaps somebody was concerned about the possibility of rain, or a horse came up lame. Please do sit down, Ellen. You're making me dizzy with your peregrinations."

Her Grace shook droplets of water from her finger, and gave the bowl a quarter turn.

Ellen perched on the very edge of a pink velvet sofa, for one did not ignore a duchess's requests. Had Hardcastle been injured, that he'd sent for the coach? Had he decided to leave for Kent from one of the ducal residences he'd visited? How was Christopher to get home, and how was Ellen to return to her family?

"You are beyond hope," the duchess said, crossing her arms. "If you simply pressed your nose to the window glass and occasionally thumped a hopeful tail on my carpets, your sentiments could not be more transparent. I do not understand why you refused Hardcastle, if he's so very dear to you."

Ellen didn't bother pouring herself a cup of tea she'd neither taste nor enjoy. "I refused His Grace for two reasons. First, he deserves a wife whom he loves, deeply, madly, passionately, not simply a woman who's familiar to him, attractive, and useful for fending off debutantes."

This reasoning sounded tired to Ellen's own ears. This excuse. Hardcastle hadn't been much impressed with it either.

The duchess took a seat across from Ellen, her expression disgruntled. "A duke is not in the habit of yielding to mad passion, Ellen. He's a creature of duty and restraint."

No, he wasn't. Not under all circumstances. At times, he could be a creature of mindless pleasures and endless desire, a creature of genial good company and generous affection.

"A duke is but a man," Ellen quoted. "Sedgemere has told you he loves you, I'd guess. Told you he can't live without you, and no other woman could possibly be his duchess. Sedgemere's highest compliment is not that you've saved him from the clutches of the jiggling horde."

Her Grace gazed at the roses, one of which had dropped a few pale petals on the mantel. "Sedgemere has a surprisingly effusive streak," she said, rising to gather up the dropped petals and toss them into the unlit hearth. "Did Hardcastle use that term? Jiggling horde?"

"Several times, Your Grace." Ellen rose as well, because sitting still and staring down the maddeningly empty drive was impossible.

"This house party opened his eyes to his own marriageability, and he panicked, in as much as Hardcastle can panic."

"Or he was brought to his senses," the duchess said. "He's besotted with you. I saw that parting kiss, Ellen MacHugh, and that was not the kiss of an indifferent man."

"That was not the kiss of an indifferent woman, Your Grace." Ellen had already established that Hardcastle had not gone directly to the boat race, as several other gentlemen had. "The more compelling reason I cannot marry Hardcastle is that I am needed elsewhere. My family needs me, and His Grace simply wants me. I want him too—desperately—but one has a duty."

"Oh, duty," the duchess said, taking a place beside Ellen at the window. "Yes, duty is a great comfort, when one is old and sore in the joints and can't find one's spectacles. A fine liniment for the conscience, is duty. What of joy? What of love, Miss MacHugh? You accuse Hardcastle of caring too little for you, but do you care for duty too much?"

The duchess's tone was nearly bitter, as if somebody might have presented her with the same choice, between her heart's desire and inevitable obligation.

"There's your duke now," the duchess said, as a rider on a dark horse came into view. "I recognize his gelding. You'll want to take tea with him in his sitting room, though a proper duchess could never endorse such impropriety. The tray will be in his room in five minutes. A woman who loved him would be there in six."

His Grace galloped up the drive, man and horse a single flowing unit of grace and power that left Ellen's heart pounding in rhythm with the tattoo of hoof beats.

"The other young ladies are in the conservatory resting after the day's earlier festivities," the duchess said. "They won't know he's back. Upstairs with you, and if you'll take a word of advice, Miss MacHugh?"

Ellen was half way to the door, but paused when everything in her wanted to race up the stairs to the duke's rooms.

"You might have given Hardcastle your heart and your intimate favors, but you must also give him your trust. That last can be harder than the other two put together, but without trust, a marriage is doomed. Now, away with you, and I'll be sure the young ladies remain occupied until Hardcastle can join you."

Ellen fairly flew from the parlor, though in the past two weeks, she hadn't set foot in Hardcastle's rooms. She knew where they were though, a mere four doors down from her own and across the corridor.

She was waiting by the hearth, the silver tea service gleaming on the sideboard, when Hardcastle came through the door, his jacket already off and his riding gloves bunched in his hand.

The door swung shut behind him. "Miss MacHugh."

Ellen slammed into him and wrapped her arms around him. "I thought you'd gone home to Kent."

"You are my home."

Then Ellen found herself in the ducal bedroom, Hardcastle's nimble fingers undoing her hooks between passionate kisses and her own efforts to divest him of his clothes.

"I missed you," she said. "Missed you awfully." She had to let Hardcastle go while he tugged his boots off, and she allowed him to remove his shirt, then she pushed him back onto the bed and attacked his falls.

Hardcastle's palm cradled her cheek. "My dear, your enthusiasm flatters me no end, but there are matters we must discuss."

"Discuss later, Hardcastle," she said, drawing his aroused length from his clothes.

"I've prepared a speech for this moment, madam. Short but impressively maudlin. I thought I'd blush to deliver it, but now I find I want to give you these words."

Ellen swung a leg over his hips and tossed her chemise onto the nearest chair. "Give me the deeds, Hardcastle. The words can wait." Especially maudlin words that likely dripped with parting sentiments, tender regrets, and swain-ly blather. "I have words for you too, words of explanation, because I owe you that much."

"I'll listen. I will always listen to you, Ellen."

So with her hands, with her kisses, with her body, Ellen told Hardcastle she loved him, and she did not want to leave him, ever. She told him how very much he meant to her, how dear her memories of him would be, how much she longed to choose pleasure over duty.

Hardcastle's response was tenderness itself as he joined them.

"You thought I could leave you?" he whispered as he gently pushed his way inside her. "You thought I could saddle up my ducal consequence, turn my back on you, trot out smartly for Kent, without a word of farewell?"

"I can't think," Ellen replied, undulating into the sheer bliss of their union. "I thought I could leave you, but—"

He surged forward, obliterating words, thoughts, logic, resistance of any type. Ellen met him, measure for measure, until she realized Hardcastle was waiting for her to surrender to their joining, waiting for her to capitulate to desire.

"I love you," she whispered, as satisfaction dragged her under. "I will always love you."

"And I love you."

Hardcastle's words struck Ellen's heart like hammer blows, bringing both pain and freedom, as a smith's hammer strikes shackles from a pardoned convict.

The pleasure was terrible in its depth and duration, a whirling black torrent that left Ellen dizzy and panting in Hardcastle's arms. His breath came hot against her neck, her heartbeat thundered against her ribs.

And then... quiet. A breeze stirred the curtain. Laughter drifted up from the lawn. A plain, brown wren lit on the windowsill, then darted away.

Hardcastle was a heavy comfort over Ellen, and sleep tugged at her awareness.

"Wore you out, b'gad," he muttered, lifting up enough to let cool air wash over Ellen's belly. "Maybe you did miss me."

"Terribly. Horribly. Wonderfully."

"Addled your wits too, apparently," he said, crouching up and nuzzling at Ellen's breasts. "I like you muddled and rosy. Addled and drowsy. You'd best get used to it."

"Hardcastle, we must talk."

He sighed a great, bodily testament to male patience. "If you insist, but you will cease reminding me of your plans to abandon me and Christopher, the two fellows who love you most in the world."

"You have learned a new word," Ellen said, running her fingers through his hair. "You'll use it indiscriminately, like a fashionable French phrase making the rounds of the ballrooms."

He glowered at her, than glanced at the clock on the mantel. "Ballrooms, bah. This evening will be interminable. You will save all your waltzes for me."

"Of course, Your Grace."

He slipped from her body, kissed her forehead, then prowled across the room to the privacy screen. In broad daylight, Hardcastle was a sumptuous argument against clothing, against allowing the sun to ever drop below the horizon.

Except he was breathtaking by candlelight too.

"Shall I tend to you?" he asked, sauntering over to the bed with a damp flannel in his hand.

Ellen snatched the cloth from him and only then realized he had spent his seed without withdrawing. Her Grace's lecture about trust popped into Ellen's mind as she got off the bed and made use of the privacy screen. Let Hardcastle look at her in the afternoon sunlight, let him memorize the sight of her as God made her.

And Ellen would trust her duke with even more than that.

"Is the door locked?" she asked.

"Holy jiggling debutantes," His Grace muttered, marching into the sitting room and locking that door, then returning to lock the bedroom door. "The drawbridge has been raised, the arrow slits manned. Now into bed with you."

"With you too, sir."

With his hair sticking up wildly, not a stitch of finery upon him, the duke of Hardcastle bowed and gestured to the rumpled bed.

"Your servant, madam."

Ellen snatched a green paisley silk dressing gown off the bedpost and shrugged into it. The fabric was cool and redolent of Hardcastle's scent—also roughly the dimensions of Her Grace's back terrace. Climbing onto the bed was an undignified undertaking, and that was before Hardcastle wrestled Ellen to his side.

"You mentioned talking," he said, kissing her shoulder. "Talking is not your greatest strength, Miss MacHugh, but I will marshal my patience and endure your conversation nonetheless."

"Much obliged, Your Grace. I have a family."

That put an end to Hardcastle's kissing and nuzzling and petting. "Go on."

"A small family," Ellen said. "My parents, my sister, and me. We're rural gentry, and when the harvest is bad, we're impoverished rural gentry. I've sent my wages home, where they've been put to good use."

"One would expect no less selflessness of a future duchess."

Ellen hit him with a pillow, then settled back against his side. "I can't be your duchess. I must be my sister's governess. My parents have had that job too long as it is."

"This would be your twin sister, Emily?"

The caution in his voice cut deeply, but Ellen had decided to trust him. Not to marry him—he'd realize that soon enough—but to trust him.

"Emily, yes. My younger twin sister. I took too long to be born, and Emily wasn't breathing when she emerged from the womb. The midwife was able to revive her, but before we were a year old, it became apparent that Emily was not entirely thriving."

"You did not take too long to be born, and I'll thrash anybody who says otherwise. Your sister is physically impaired?"

Impaired. Such a tactful word for a condition that was not of Emily's making, but created endless burdens for her and the people around her.

"Physically, Emily is quite robust. Intellectually, she is... limited. She can read some, she can play the piano a very, very little. Her embroidery is excellent, but her reasoning powers are those of a permanent innocent. She needs me."

Hardcastle flopped about, and Ellen prepared herself to be left alone in the bed. Instead, he gently shoved her to her side and wrapped himself around her.

"The rest isn't difficult to figure out," he said. "Emily is very pretty and perilously friendly. All the reserve and self-restraint you've known from childhood is foreign to her nature. She is charming, despite or perhaps because of, her lack of accomplishments."

Hardcastle grasped the situation more quickly than most did. To appearances, Emily was simply a pretty young woman, one well blessed with health and looks. She could manage pleasantries, she could behave appropriately at church services, but then in the churchyard...

"She likes to climb trees," Ellen said. "In broad daylight. She'll have her bonnet off and her skirts hiked before you can stop her. She laughs too loudly, and she—"

"Kisses boys," Hardcastle said. "Or men. You slipped, Ellen. You claimed to have fled into service because you were caught kissing a fellow, then you informed me I was the first man to kiss you. Emily was the one sharing her favors, wasn't she?"

He'd caught Ellen in the lie that others, her own neighbors, her own pastor, hadn't questioned. "Emily was very fond of this fellow, and I think he was honestly fond of her."

"The road to hell is paved with fondness. I also saw that you printed your letters to her."

Ellen could detect no tensing in Hardcastle, no withdrawing. "I lied to you, Hardcastle."

"You gave me your first kiss, Miss MacHugh. You've given me all your kisses, in fact."

His smugness was like another species of kiss, a soft, comforting warmth pressed to Ellen's heart. Dissembling in the interests of protecting family was expected behavior from his perspective.

How like a duke. How like this duke.

"The fellow who tempted Emily so badly before has moved back to Swaddledale," Ellen said, "and my parents need me at home. They're aging, and my years in service have been an embarrassment to them."

A ducal toe ran up the back of Ellen's calf. "They consider your status in *my* household an embarrassment?"

Hardcastle would get along with Papa very well, were they ever to meet. "My parents are proud, Your Grace. Emily's situation has been a trial since her birth, though they love her fiercely."

"I'm of the belief that daughters are a trial to any parents. Sons too, most likely. So I'm to send you back to Derbyshire, allow you to ensure the domestic tranquility in Mideast Hogwash, and protect your sister from the attentions of the dashing swains?"

Ellen drove her elbow back into Hardcastle's belly as she rearranged herself on her back. "Don't ridicule my family, Your Grace. Emily has apologized for her behavior and she tries very hard to be good. She was passionately attracted to Mr. Trentwich though."

"Passion must run in the family." Hardcastle shifted over Ellen, and abruptly, she was gazing into his eyes, where not a hint of levity shone. "Do you trust me, Ellen?"

"I've just told you my every deepest, darkest secret Hardcastle. You see why I must return home now? You need a duchess, not a squire's daughter with an addled sister. Let the gossips get hold of that, and the talk would never cease."

Hardcastle kissed Ellen for a while, as if he needed time to choose his words and sort options. Ellen kissed him back because she loved him, and loved kissing him.

"If you trust me, madam, then all will come right. I promise you this. Hadn't you better scamper along now and start primping for the evening gathering?"

Ellen would rather kiss Hardcastle some more. The entertainments would go on until all hours, and this might be the last private moment she had with him.

"I do not primp, Hardcastle. Come tomorrow morning, you'll send me home in the ducal coach, and there's an end to it."

"You'll make a very fine duchess," he said, settling closer. "Giving orders, making pronouncements, telling a duke how matters in his own life will unfold. Your imperious demeanor makes me amorous."

Ellen lifted her hips and met... evidence of the duke's veracity. "Simply being around you makes me amorous. I will miss you terribly."

That was the last thing she said before joining the duke in shared amorous activities, but that evening, as Ellen donned a lovely green ball gown lent to her by the duchess, a thought intruded:

Hardcastle had mentioned a prepared speech, a maudlin prepared speech, and he'd not delivered that speech. Whatever the sentiments—of parting, true love, regret?—they apparently no longer signified.

Now that Ellen had confided her situation to him, perhaps they never would.

"IF YOU LOOK any more fierce, even the intrepid Miss Pendleton will banish you from her dance card," Sedgemere muttered beneath the trilling of the violins.

"If I look any less fierce," Hardcastle replied, "she'll knock me over the head and drag me to her room. This house party has not gone as the mamas and debutantes planned."

"The house party has gone as Anne planned," Sedgemere said, beaming a smile across the dance floor at his duchess. "The Dukeries Cup made for some excitement today, and now we'll round out the gathering with a nice, boring ball. My duchess is very much in charity with her duke."

"For God's sake, Sedgemere. Have some dignity." The receiving line had disbanded, and yet, not all the guests had arrived. Hardcastle's own dignity was imperiled by that fact alone.

A footman sidled up to Sedgemere. "Late arrivals, Your Grace of Sedgemere. They asked that His Grace of Hardcastle be notified."

Relief coursed through Hardcastle. "I'll tend to the new arrivals. Sedgemere, keep an eye on Miss MacHugh, and do not allow Greenover within twenty paces of her."

Sedgemere offered an ironic formal bow, and Hardcastle followed the footman up the stairs to the entrance hall.

"We're here!" Miss Emily MacHugh said, bouncing on her toes. "You told us to come, and we're here!"

In her pale green ball gown, she was charm personified, not an ounce of guile in her, and thus Hardcastle deviated from protocol and bowed over her hand before greeting her parents.

"I am exceedingly glad to see you," he said, "and I know your sister will be too. The first waltz will start in a very few minutes. Do you recall what we talked about, Miss Emily?"

Emily was taller than Ellen, but she had Ellen's perfect complexion, also the *joie de vivre* Ellen kept hidden under most circumstances.

"I recall, sir. I've been practicing with Papa." She winked at Hardcastle, a slow, solemn undertaking that boded well for the rest of the evening. "Come along, Duke. I'll show you."

Sedgemere had positioned himself at Ellen's elbow, and when the orchestra had brought its delicate minuet to a final cadence, the herald thumped his staff to announce the latest arrivals.

From the top of the stairs, Hardcastle watched Ellen start forward, only to be checked by Sedgemere's hand on her arm. She was delectably attired in dark green velvet, and Hardcastle had reason to know the décolletage, though quite flattering, would reveal not a single additional freckle.

Perhaps that might change in future.

Emily tugged at his arm. "There's Ellen! There's my Ellen!" She waved enthusiastically, and Ellen waved back, more slowly.

Hardcastle waved at Ellen too, then Sedgemere returned the gesture, as did the Duchess of Sedgemere from her corner of the ball-room, and all around the ballroom, curious glances were exchanged.

"Shall we dance, Miss Emily?" Hardcastle asked. "I've been looking forward to this waltz since we parted earlier today."

"So have I! Will Ellen dance? Is that your duke friend who looks like Wotan? I have a storybook about Wotan and Thor and their friends. They weren't always nice. Loki was a rotter sometimes, but I like him too."

Emily MacHugh was exhausting in her chatter, in her mental nimbleness, in her artless observations, and she was very, very dear.

"Do you hear the orchestra, Miss Emily?"

She stopped dead at the foot of the steps and cocked her head, her parents pausing three steps up.

"Yes. I can't wait! I've waltzed before, at the assemblies, with the vicar or Papa. You are handsomer than they are, but I should not have said that."

"We'll let that be our secret," Hardcastle said. "May I have the honor of this dance, Miss Emily?"

She composed herself, though Hardcastle could feel the effort that required as she sank into a lovely curtsey.

"Sir, I would be honored." Then she bounced up and grabbed his hand. "Did I do that right? When can I talk to Ellen? I will hug her so hard she'll burst, and we'll laugh, and then she'll cry, and I'll hug her all over again."

"She'll hug you back, I'm sure," Hardcastle said. "As soon as this dance is over, you must hug her as hard as ever you can."

Emily let him lead her to the dance floor, while Sedgemere

appropriated the same honor from Ellen. She shot Hardcastle incredulous, wondering glances, which he hoped meant he'd guessed correctly.

The music started, and within sixteen bars, Emily was trying to lead, laughing, stepping on Hardcastle's toes, then laughing some more. The hours he'd spent twirling her around her mother's music room had been a pointless undertaking, for no amount of patient instruction could have curbed her exuberance.

"The music will soon end," Hardcastle murmured, several athletic minutes later. "Do you recall what comes next?"

"You bow, I curtsey, and *then* we get some punch, which I must not spill on *anybody*, and I must only sip, *delicately*, like a bird at the fountain in the garden. I want to talk to Ellen first. She'll think I'm vexed with her, but I'm not. I never could be."

"Neither could I. What say we meet her at the punchbowl?"

"I like that idea. I like you. No wonder Ellen has let you be her friend. You're very sweet."

Hardcastle bowed. "As are you, Miss Emily."

She sank into another curtsey, though this time Hardcastle was ready for her when she shot to her feet and grabbed his arm.

"Ellen!" she shouted. "Meet us at the punchbowl! Bring your duke, and I'll bring mine!"

The ballroom grew momentarily quiet, until the Duchess of Sedgemere called out, "Save a glass for me!"

"For me as well!" the Duchess of Oxthorpe called, only to be echoed by the Duchess of Linton.

A hundred conversations broke out as Emily dragged Hardcastle to the punchbowl, then flew from his side into Ellen's arms.

"Oh, Ellie, I have missed you so. I have missed and missed and missed you!"

"I've missed you too, Em," Ellen said, blinking madly and hugging her sister back. "You look very pretty."

"I look all grown up," Emily said, stepping back and holding her skirts out as she twirled. "I know how to waltz. Did you see me?

Hardcastle taught me this morning. He's very serious, but I like him."

"You like everybody," Ellen said, snatching another brief, tight hug. "I like Hardcastle too."

"Perhaps you'd introduce us, Miss MacHugh," the Duchess of Sedgemere said. "Miss Emily is our guest, after all."

At Hardcastle's request, Sedgemere and his duchess personally took Emily around and introduced her to half the Midlands nobility.

"I don't know whether to hug you, or smack you," Ellen said. "What could you be about, Hardcastle? Emily will think she's making friends, and instead, she'll be a laughingstock."

"No, she will not," Hardcastle said. "I've enlisted the aid of the duchesses, and they are very pleased to ensure Emily will have an enjoyable evening. She will be an original, you see, and you will be my duchess."

Emily made a lovely bow before the Dowager Duchess of Alnwitter, who then laughed heartily at something Emily said.

"You sent the coach for my family, didn't you?" Ellen asked. "You invited them in person and then made sure Emily would have a partner for the waltz."

"Are you listing my transgressions, Ellen, or reconstructing my day? If the latter, you've stopped short of the best part."

The first violinist of the little orchestra had resumed his seat and was tapping his bow on his music stand.

"The part where I welcomed you back," Ellen said, while across the ballroom Mr. Greenover, sober for once, bowed over Emily's hand.

"That was lovely too, but rather than refer to an aspect of my schedule best left private, I allude instead to what follows now. Come with me, if you please."

Hardcastle left Ellen no choice, tugging her out onto the dance floor.

"Your Grace, I'd rather keep an eye on Emily."

"I'd rather you let your sister enjoy herself, and let the duchesses enjoy themselves. Now pay heed, my dear, for you won't often see the spectacle you're about to behold. And mind you, I've already spoken with your parents, and matters regarding any settlements are quite well in hand."

"Settlements?"

Hardcastle untangled their arms and went down on one knee. He waited, because Ellen deserved for everybody to hear what he'd say to her. Within moments, a circle had formed around them, and quiet descended.

"Ellen MacHugh, dearest lady of my heart, will you make me the happiest duke in the realm—even happier than that strutting jackanapes, mine host, His Grace of Sedgemere—the happiest of all men, and accept my proposal of marriage? I will have no other but you, for you are the home my heart has longed for, the mother I would have for my children, and the wife I would have ever at my side. I love you, I need you. Please marry me, Ellen."

"Say yes, Ellie!" Emily bellowed, and the chant was taken up by the duchesses, and then by the entire crowd.

"Hardcastle, you'd best get up," Ellen muttered. "I assume you've already hired a companion for Emily?"

He sprang to his feet. "Not yet, because she'll live with us, though I expect your parents will want to visit frequently, and you and Emily will interview appropriate candidates. I'll warn the footmen about her propensity for kissing handsome men, but I don't expect them to be saints. The MacHugh women are formidable creatures."

The shouting and clapping were dying down, but Hardcastle's heart was thumping as hard if he'd just rowed to victory in the Dukeries Cup.

"You don't look happy," he said. "I have overstepped, I know, but you were determined to leave me, and I cannot very well be the Duke of Lesser Swaddlepie, now can I? Will you be my wife, Ellen, not simply my duchess—for you're right, prospective duchesses are thick on the ground—but my wife, my love, the mother of my children, and the only lady for me?"

Damnation. He'd made her cry. That couldn't be a good thing.

"Of course, I'll be your wife," Ellen said, pitching herself against him. "And you will be my husband, and my love, and the father of my children, and if you absolutely must, you shall be my duke too."

She kissed him, right in the middle of the ballroom, kissed him resoundingly and for such a protracted period that even the debutantes and drunken viscounts would realize the Duke and Duchess of Hardcastle were a love match.

When Ellen let Hardcastle up for air, Sedgemere called for a toast to the newly engaged couple and a betrothal waltz. In the minstrel's gallery, from among Sedgemere's three ruffians, Christopher sent a thumbs up, while Emily, laughing hugely, dragged a dazed Mr. Greenover onto the dance floor.

"I do love you," Ellen said, as Hardcastle offered his hand. "You didn't have to do this. A simple 'Will you marry me? I promise to provide for your sister' would have done."

Hardcastle bowed, Ellen curtseyed. A commotion at the other end of the ballroom suggested Emily was explaining to Mr. Greenover who would lead whom for the duration of the dance, or perhaps simply for the duration.

"I tried asking you to marry me, tried ordering you to marry me," Hardcastle said as he drew his prospective duchess into a cozy version of waltz position. "That left only begging, but a fellow likes to ensure the odds are in his favor if he's to make a spectacle of himself; hence, I paid a small call on your family. I did not want you to worry."

"I think we should be worried about Mr. Greenover."

The music started, Mr. Greenover yelped, Hardcastle leaned closer to his beloved. "I think we should be worried about sneaking out of the ballroom at the end of this set and repairing above stairs to celebrate our betrothal."

Ellen appeared to consider that suggestion as Hardcastle turned her down the room. She looked every inch a duchess tonight, regal, lovely, and *all his*.

"I have a better idea," she said. "Sneak me out of the ballroom *now*, Hardcastle."

"In this, as in all things, I will be pleased to heed my duchess's guidance."

Hardcastle twirled her down to the French doors, danced her out into the cool night air, and happily ever after, Ellen danced in the arms of her beloved duke.

And they lived happily ever after!

Read on for excerpts from Grace's upcoming releases...

TO MY DEAR READERS

Greetings, Dear Reader!

As soon as I'd written Hardcastle's story (Dancing in the Duke's Arms, April 2015), Sedgemere's (Once Upon a Dream, May 2016) was a foregone conclusion. The two friends ended up in different anthologies and both of those anthos are no longer available. It's a pleasure to reunite these fellows in one book.

And there are more dukes on the horizon! **A Duke by Any Other Name**, my fourth **Rogues to Riches** story, comes out April 24, 2020. Lady Althea Wentworth seizes upon the notion of recruiting the neighborhood's reclusive, testy peer to aid her in her battle to gain entré into the local society. Nathaniel, Duke of Rotthaven has worked long and hard to be ignored by his neighbors, but the notion of being *seized upon* is ever so tempting... Nathaniel has withdrawn from society for reasons, Althea is determined to take her place in society for other reasons. Thank heavens true love can sort these two out! Order your copy of **A Duke by Any Other Name**. Excerpt below.

But you don't have to wait until April for our next happily ever after. February 2020 will see the release of **A Woman of True**

Honor, my eighth **True Gentlemen** tale. Valerian Dorning is not a duke, not a lord, not much of anything but decent man who's good at navigating complicated social situations. Emily Pepper is an heiress. Valerian refuses to pursue her for her fortune, she refuses to let him go merely because he lacks one.

And then the real trouble begins... Order your copy of **A Woman of True Honor**. Excerpt below.

Oak Dorning's tale should be on the shelves by June. If you'd like to get a quick alert when that title become available, please do follow me on **Bookbub**. In addition to sending new release alerts, Bookbub will also notify you of deals, discounts, and pre-orders. You might want to keep an eye on my website **Deals** page too. Every month, I put a different title on discounted download, and occasionally, I release new titles early on my webstore or put up a freebie. (**A Woman of True Honor**, for example, will be available **on the webstore** Feb. 8, and on the **major retailers** Feb. 18.)

If you'd like to see a particular title or bundle discounted, please let me know. I love to hear from my readers!

Happy reading!

Grace Burrowes

Read on for an excerpt from **A Duke by Any Other Name***!*

EXCERPT — A DUKE BY ANY OTHER NAME

From **A Duke by Any Other Name** (April 2020)

Lady Althea Wentworth's prize sows have gone a-waltzing into the walled orchard of her ladyship's notoriously reclusive neighbor, Nathaniel, Duke of Rothhaven. His Grace is not happy, and thank heavens he's left his ancestral pile to tell Althea so in person... exactly as she'd hoped he would.

Althea heard her guest before she saw him. Rothhaven's arrival was presaged by a rapid beat of hooves coming not up her drive, but rather, directly across the park that surrounded Lynley Vale manor.

A large horse created that kind of thunder, one disdaining the genteel canter for a hellbent gallop. From her parlor window, Althea could see the beast approaching, and her first thought was that only a terrified animal traveled at such speed.

But no. Horse and rider cleared the wall beside the drive in perfect rhythm, swerved onto the verge, and continued right up— good God, they aimed straight for the fountain. Althea could not look away as the black horse drew closer and closer to unforgiving marble and splashing water.

"Mary, Mother of God."

Another smooth leap—the fountain was five feet high if it was an inch—then a foot-perfect landing, followed by an immediate check of the horse's speed. The gelding came down to a frisking, capering trot, clearly proud of himself and ready for even greater challenges.

The rider stroked the horse's neck, and the beast calmed and hung his head, sides heaving. A treat was offered and another pat, before one of Althea's grooms bestirred himself to take the horse. Rothhaven—for that could only be the dread duke himself—paused on the front steps long enough to remove his spurs, whip off his hat, and run a black-gloved hand through hair as dark as hell's tarpit.

"The rumors are true," Althea murmured. Rothhaven was built on the proportions of the Vikings of old, but their fair coloring and blue eyes had been denied him. He glanced up, as if he knew Althea would be spying, and she drew back.

His gaze was colder than a Yorkshire night in January, which fit exactly with what Althea had heard of him.

She moved from the window and took the wing chair by the hearth, opening a book chosen for this singular occasion. She had dressed carefully—elegantly but without too much fuss—and styled her hair with similar consideration. Rothhaven gave very few people the chance to make even a first impression on him, a feat Althea admired.

Voices drifted up from the foyer, followed by the tread of boots on the stair. Rothhaven moved lightly for such a grand specimen, and his voice rumbled like distant cannon. A soft tap on the door, then Strensall was announcing Nathaniel, His Grace of Rothhaven. The duke did not have to duck to come through the doorway, but it was a near thing.

Althea set aside her book, rose, and curtsied to a precisely deferential depth and not one inch lower. "Welcome to Lynley Vale, Your Grace. A pleasure to meet you. Strensall, the tea, and don't spare the trimmings."

Strensall bolted for the door.

"I do not break bread with mine enemy." Rothhaven stalked over to Althea and swept her with a glower. "No damned tea."

His eyes were a startling green, set against swooping dark brows and features as angular as the crags and tors of Yorkshire's moors. He brought with him the scents of heather and horse, a lovely combination. His cravat remained neatly pinned with a single bar of gleaming gold despite his mad dash across the countryside.

"I will attribute Your Grace's lack of manners to the peckishness that can follow exertion. A tray, Strensall."

The duke leaned nearer. "Shall I threaten to curse poor Strensall with nightmares, should he bring a tray?"

"That would be unsporting." Althea sent her goggling butler a glance, and he scampered off. "You are reputed to have a temper, but then, if folk claimed that my mere passing caused milk to curdle and babies to colic, I'd be a tad testy myself. No one has ever accused you of dishonorable behavior."

"Nor will they, while you, my lady, have stooped so low as to unleash the hogs of war upon my hapless estate." He backed away not one inch, and this close Althea caught a more subtle fragrance. Lily of the valley or jasmine. Very faint, elegant, and unexpected, like the moss-green of his eyes.

"You cannot read, perhaps," he went on, "else you'd grasp that 'we will not be entertaining for the foreseeable future' means neither you nor your livestock are welcome at Rothhaven Hall."

"Hosting a short call from your nearest neighbor would hardly be entertaining," Althea countered. "Shall we be seated?"

"I will not be seated," he retorted. "Retrieve your damned pigs from my orchard, madam, or I will send them to slaughter before the week is out."

"Is that where my naughty ladies got off to?" Althea sank into her wing chair. "They haven't been on an outing in ages. I suppose the spring air inspired them to seeing the sights. Last autumn they took a notion to inspect the market, and in summer they decided to attend Sunday services. Most of our neighbors find my herd's social inclinations amusing."

"I might be amused, were your herd not at the moment rooting through my orchard uninvited. To allow stock of those dimensions to wander is irresponsible, and why a duke's sister is raising hogs entirely defeats my powers of imagination."

Because Rothhaven had never been poor and never would be. "Do have a seat, Your Grace. I'm told only the ill-mannered pace the parlor like a house tabby who needs to visit the garden."

He turned his back to Althea—very rude of him—though he appeared to require a moment to marshal his composure. She counted that a small victory, for she had needed many such moments since acquiring a title, and her composure yet remained as unruly as her sows on a pretty spring day.

Though truth be told, the lady swine had had some *encouragement* regarding the direction of their latest outing.

Rothhaven faced Althea, the fire in his gaze banked to burning disdain. "Will you or will you not retrieve your wayward pigs from my land?"

"I refuse to discuss this with a man who cannot observe the simplest conversational courtesy." She waved a hand at the opposite wing chair, and when that provoked a drawing up of the magnificent ducal height, she feared His Grace would stalk from the room.

Instead he took the chair, whipping out the tails of his riding jacket like Lucifer arranging his coronation robes.

"Thank you," Althea said. "When you march about like that, you give a lady a crick in her neck. Your orchard is at least a mile from my home farm."

"And downwind, more's the pity. Perhaps you raise pigs to perfume the neighborhood with their scent?"

"No more than you keep horses, sheep, or cows for the same purpose, Your Grace. Or maybe your livestock hides the pervasive odor of brimstone hanging about Rothhaven Hall?"

A muscle twitched in the duke's jaw.

The tea tray arrived, and in keeping with standing instructions, the kitchen had exerted its skills to the utmost. Strensall placed an enormous silver tray before Althea—the good silver, not the fancy silver—bowed, and withdrew.

"How do you take your tea, Your Grace?"

"Plain, except I won't be staying for tea. Assure me that you'll send your swineherd over to collect your sows in the next twenty-four hours and I will take my leave of you."

Not so fast. Having coaxed Rothhaven into making a call, Althea wasn't about to let him win free so easily.

"I cannot give you those assurances, Your Grace, much as I'd like to. I'm very fond of those ladies and they are quite valuable. They are also particular."

Rothhaven straightened a crease in his breeches. They fit him exquisitely, though Althea had never before seen black riding attire.

"The whims of your livestock are no affair of mine, Lady Althea." His tone said that Althea's whims were a matter of equal indifference to him. "You either retrieve them or the entire shire will be redolent of smoking bacon."

He was bluffing, albeit convincingly. Nobody butchered hogs in early spring absent dire exigencies. "Do you know what my sows are worth?"

He quoted a price per pound for pork on the hoof that was accurate to the penny.

"Wrong," Althea said, pouring him a cup of tea and holding it out to him. "Those are my best breeders. I chose their grandmamas and mamas for hardiness and the ability to produce sizable, healthy litters. A pig in the garden can be the difference between a family making it through winter or starving, if that pig can also produce large, thriving litters. She can live on scraps, she needs very little care, and she will see a dozen piglets raised to weaning twice a year without putting any additional strain on the family budget."

The duke looked at the steaming cup of tea, then at Althea, then back at the cup. This was the best China black she could offer, served on the good porcelain in her personal parlor. If he disdained her hospitality now, she might...cry?

He would not be swayed by tears, but he apparently could be tempted by a perfect cup of tea.

"You raise hogs as a charitable undertaking?" he asked.

"I raise them for all sorts of reasons, and I donate many to the poor of the parish."

"Why not donate money?" He took a cautious sip of his tea. "One can spend coin on what's most necessary, and many of the poor have no gardens."

"If they lack a garden, they can send the children into the countryside to gather rocks and build drystone walls, can't they? After a season or two, the pig will have rendered the soil of its enclosure very fertile indeed, and the enclosure can be moved. Coin, by contrast, can be stolen."

Another sip. "From the poor box?"

"Of course from the poor box. Or that money can be wasted on Bibles while children go hungry."

This was the wrong conversational direction, too close to Althea's heart, too far from her dreams.

"My neighbor is a radical," Rothhaven mused. "And she conquers poverty and ducal privacy alike with an army of sows. Nonetheless, those hogs are where they don't belong, and possession is nine-tenths of the law. Move them or I will do as I see fit with them."

"If you harm my pigs or disperse that herd for sale, I will sue you for conversion. You gained control of my property legally—pigs will wander—but if you waste those pigs or convert my herd for your own gain, I will take you to court."

Althea put three sandwiches on a plate and offered it to him. She'd lose her suit for conversion, not because she was wrong on the law—she was correct—but because he was a duke, and not just any duke. He was the much-treasured dread duke of Rothhaven Hall, a local fixture of pride. The squires in the area were more protective of Rothhaven's consequence than they were of their own.

Lawsuits were scandalous, however, especially between neighbors or family members. They were also messy, involving appearances in court and meetings with solicitors and barristers. A man who seldom left his property and refused to receive callers would avoid those tribulations at all costs.

Rothhaven set down the plate. "What must I do to inspire you to retrieve your *valuable* sows? I have my own swineherd, you know. A capable old fellow who has been wrangling hogs for more than half a century. He can move your livestock to the king's highway."

Althea hadn't considered this possibility, but she dared not blow retreat. "My sows are partial to their own swineherd. They'll follow him anywhere, though after rioting about the neighborhood on their own, they will require time to recover. They've been out dancing all night, so to speak, and must have a lie-in."

Althea could not fathom why any sensible female would comport herself thus, but every spring she dragged herself south, and subjected herself to the same inanity for the duration of the London Season.

This year would be different.

"So send your swineherd to fetch them tomorrow," Rothhaven said, taking a bite of a beef sandwich. "My swineherd will assist, and I need never darken your door again—nor you, mine." He sent her a pointed look, one that scolded without saying a word.

Althea's brother Quinn had learned to deliver such looks, and his duchess had honed the raised eyebrow to a delicate art.

While I am a laughingstock.

"I cannot oblige you, Your Grace," Althea said. "My swineherd is visiting his sister in York and won't be back until week's end. I do apologize for the delay, though if turning my pigs loose in your orchard has occasioned this introduction, then I'm glad for it. I value my privacy too, but I am at my wit's end and must consult you on a matter of some delicacy."

He gestured with half a sandwich. "All the way at your wit's end? What has caused you to travel that long and arduous trail?"

Polite Society. Wealth. Standing. All the great boons Althea had once envied and had so little ability to manage.

"I want a baby," she said, not at all how she'd planned to state her situation.

Rothhaven put down his plate slowly, as if a wild creature had come snorting and snapping into the parlor. "Are you utterly demented? One doesn't announce such a thing, and I am in no position to..." He stood, his height once again creating an impression of towering disdain. "I will see myself out."

Althea rose as well, and though Rothhaven could toss her behind the sofa one-handed, she made her words count.

"Do not flatter yourself, Your Grace. Only a fool would seek to procreate with a petulant, moody, withdrawn, arrogant specimen such as you. I want a family, exactly the goal every girl is raised to treasure. There's nothing shameful or inappropriate about that. Until I learn to comport myself as the sister of a duke ought, I have no hope of making an acceptable match. You are a duke. If anybody understands the challenge I face, you do. You have five hundred years of breeding and family history to call upon, while I..."

Oh, this was not the eloquent explanation she'd rehearsed, and Rothhaven's expression had become unreadable.

He gestured with a large hand. "While you...?"

Althea had tried inviting him to tea, then to dinner. She'd tried calling upon him. She'd ridden the bridle paths for hours in hopes of meeting him by chance, only to see him galloping over the moors, heedless of anything so tame as a bridle path.

She'd called on him twice, only to be turned away at the door and chided by letter twice for presuming even that much. Althea had only a single weapon left in her arsenal, a lone arrow in her quiver of strategies, the one least likely to yield the desired result.

She had the truth. "I need your help," she said, subsiding into her chair. "I haven't anywhere else to turn. If I'm not to spend the rest of my life as a laughingstock, if I'm to have a prayer of finding a suitable match, I need your help."

Order your copy of **A Duke by Any Other Name**, and read on for an excerpt from **A Woman of True Honor** (Feb. 2020)

EXCERPT — A WOMAN OF TRUE HONOR

Valerian Dorning has fallen in love, but he's doomed to worship Emily Pepper from afar until his means are sufficient to support a wife—and not just any wife. Emily is an heiress, and Valerian refuses to play the role of fortune hunter. Emily doesn't care if Valerian's poor, but she minds very much that the scandal drawing ever closer to her could also destroy the prospects Valerian has worked so hard to earn.

Chapter One

A man raised with six brothers should have been impossible to ambush. Valerian Dorning's excuse was that the typical sibling skirmish involved a pair of fists, and those, he'd become adept at dodging.

Miss Emily Pepper's weapon of choice was a pair of lips—hers—and luscious, soft lips they were too. Valerian's body had no inclination whatsoever to escape her fire, and had surrender been honorable, he would have gone gratefully into captivity after at least fifteen minutes of heroic struggle.

His honor, alas for him, was yet in evidence. "Miss Pepper..." he murmured as she tucked in closer. "Emily..."

She was a well formed young woman, which Valerian noted in

less genteel terms every time he clapped eyes upon her. Now, purely in defense of his sanity, he laid his hands on her person. Her biceps seemed a safe enough place to grasp her, except that she twined her arms around Valerian's neck, and his hands landed on the sides of her ribs.

Her breasts—more luscious softness—were mere inches from his touch, while his gentlemanly restraint was threatening to gallop off into the next county.

"Miss Pepper, we must not."

Though *he did.* For one, glorious, demented moment Valerian kissed her back, reveling in her blatant desire and the sheer perfection of her body pressed to his. He dreamed of Emily Pepper, he cursed her in the darkness, and he subjected himself to long, cold swims in the millpond trying to exorcise her from his imagination.

This utter folly masquerading as a kiss would make Valerian's nights only more tormented. Miss Pepper's hands roaming his back conveyed equal parts eagerness and determination, and when a fellow had never been particularly sought out by anybody, much less by a comely female with a lively mind, a wonderful sense of humor, and a fiercely kind heart, he was easily felled.

Her questing hands wandered south, giving Valerian's bum a luscious squeeze.

"Miss Pepper." Do that again. "We must not forget ourselves."

She did it again, and Valerian forgot whose royal arse sat upon the British throne. When she clutched at his backside, she brought her womanly abundance into greater proximity to Valerian's chest, and the battle to deny arousal became an utter rout.

He stepped back lest he have to depart from the picnic with his hat held over his falls.

Miss Pepper kept her arms around his neck, her breath coming in soft pants that sent Valerian's wayward imagination in all the wrong directions. What she lacked in subtlety she made up for in delectability.

"I have bungled even this," she said, gaze fixed on his cravat. "You are trying not to laugh, aren't you?"

If anything could drag Valerian's attention from the rise and fall of Miss Pepper's charms, it was the note of misery in her voice.

"I beg your pardon?" Why must her hair be such a soft, caressable brown? Why must her fingers stroking his nape bring poetry to mind?

"I cannot even manage a stolen kiss with a gentleman bachelor. My dancing is a horror, my laughter too boisterous. I will never be accepted even in *Dorsetshire*."

Valerian took her hands in his and managed another half-step back. "You make Dorset sound like a province of Lower Canada. I assure you, your neighbors all hold you in very high regard." They held her father's money in high regard. From what Valerian could tell, the local gentry weren't quite sure *what* to make of Miss Pepper herself.

Fools.

"I will not attend the summer assembly." She dropped his hands and turned, so she faced the woods that backed up to the garden of the Summerton estate. "I refuse to be made a laughingstock.

Shall we take a stroll to the stream, Mr. Dorning?"

Wandering the woods together was not quite proper, except that other guests were also enjoying the shady paths winding beneath the trees. The occasion was meant to feature the out of doors, and the estate where Valerian's brother dwelled with his new wife was beautiful in any season.

Valerian offered his arm, Miss Pepper curled her hand into the crook of his elbow, and they set off at a sedate meander.

"I will miss you if you don't attend the assembly." A partial truth. Valerian would not miss watching every bachelor, widower, and squire stand up with her. Would not miss seeing her smile at all the babies and children. Would not miss hearing her laugh at some lout's attempt at humor.

Miss Pepper had a genuine laugh, one that conveyed warm-heartedness and a convivial spirit. She also had a temper, and Valerian liked that almost as much as he liked her sense of humor. Too many women pretended they never had grounds for offense, and too many men were content to believe the ladies' fictions.

"You are being gallant," she said. "If I'm not at the assembly, the general opinion will be that I think I'm too good for my neighbor's company. I am getting off on the wrong foot with them and I don't know what to do about it."

Earlier in the year, Emily's father, Jacob Pepper, had purchased a local estate sunk in debt. She was overseeing refurbishment of the manor house, one of many properties she would inherit upon her father's death.

"The local folk don't know what do about you either." The uproar in Valerian's breeches was subsiding to a familiar ache, and turning his mind to Miss Pepper's social situation helped reduce the ache to a pointless yearning. "Country life comes at a slower pace than what you're used to in Town. Your fortunes here won't be decided in the space of a few Wednesday night gatherings at Almack's. You have time to ease into the community."

"You're saying if I don't attend the summer assembly, I can simply show up at the autumn gathering?"

"Or winter, or next spring... Though the summer gathering is in some ways the best."

"Why?"

"Because the engagements are announced at the spring assembly, typically, and summer is when the courting couples preen and prance about. The weather is usually pleasant enough that most people walk both to and from the gathering, and the whole business has a more relaxed, congenial air. I do hope you'll come."

Every bachelor in the shire hoped she'd come.

They reached the stream, which today ran a placid course between grassy banks. "Why did you kiss me, Miss Pepper?"

She took the bench which some obliging soul had placed by the water a century or two ago. "Why did I *try* to kiss you?"

"I'd say the venture was a success. May I join you?" The bench sat in shade, and the view across the steam was a sunny pasture on Dorning property. Mares cropped grass, tails whisking at the occasional fly. The foals napped at their mama's feet or frisked about with each other like enormous milk-drunk kittens.

"A kiss is not a success when the gentleman's primary reaction is dismay," Miss Pepper said, arranging her skirts. "I should apologize."

"Please don't. I'm simply out of practice in the kissing department. My dancing is much more reliable."

He'd made her smile, and that was... that was worth all the thwarted yearning in Dorset.

"I don't know how to kiss, and I don't know the country dances," she said. "Papa's finishing schools and governesses made sure I learned the ballroom dances, just as I have passable French and can mince about in a fancy riding habit without tripping over my skirts. That education is inadequate for the challenges I face now."

Miss Pepper wasn't much of a horsewoman. Valerian had seen that for himself and her ballroom dancing qualified as passable at best.

"Dances can be learned," he said, "as can the equestrian arts which figure so prominently in rural life. You picked up French; you can learn a few more dances."

"I did not *pick up* French, Mr. Dorning. I gathered it, one word at a time, over years of hard labor at the hands of experts. Most of my governesses concluded that the daughter of a cit could not be very bright, and I came to agree with them, at least as regards languages."

Why did you kiss me? He could not ask her that again, though neither could he explain the sheer nonsense that came out of his mouth.

"I hold dance classes every Wednesday evening for the four weeks before any assembly. The young people like an excuse to stand up with one another, and few of us want to attempt our first waltz on a crowded dancefloor." He did not dare inform her that he charged for those classes on a donation basis.

Nobody need pay anything, but those who could afford to did put a few coppers in the box. He needed the money, though not desperately enough to insist on payment when many of his neighbors were one bad harvest away from needing it more.

"You suggest I make a limited spectacle of myself."

"I suggest you have some fun with our younger neighbors, who tend to be less hidebound and serious. Come a bit early and I'll get you started. One can practice the waltz with only a single partner, and other dances require only four couples. The country dances, though, often form lines, and that means learning them in company."

"You won't let me fall on my backside?"

Her question was endearingly in earnest. "No guarantees, Miss Pepper. Anybody can take a tumble—I have myself—but I do promise to help you up."

"*You* have fallen on the dance floor?"

"Went sprawling before the entire company. My brother Hawthorne gave me a hand up"—Hawthorne's boot might have precipitated Valerian's fall, purely by accident, of course—"swatted at me a few times, and gave me a shove in the direction of my partner, who like the rest of the group, was laughing uproariously. I made it a point to conquer the dancefloor thereafter." And the drawing room, and any battlefield where a man could be felled by manners or deportment.

"Very well," she said, rising. "I will join you for these tutorials, and we shall see what progress can be made, if any."

They ambled back to the garden where the buffet had been set out, and still Valerian had no answer to his question—why had she kissed him?

Order your copy of **A Woman of True Honor!**

CPSIA information can be obtained
at www.ICGtesting.com
Printed in the USA
LVHW092100140820
663150LV00003B/303